M.C. Higgins, the Great

VIRGINIA HAMILTON

M.C. Higgins, the Great

Aladdin Paperbacks

Aladdin Paperbacks
An imprint of Simon & Schuster
Children's Publishing Division
1230 Avenue of the Americas
New York, NY 10020
First Aladdin Paperbacks edition, 1993
First paperback edition, 1987
Also available in a hardcover edition from
Simon & Schuster Books for Young Readers

Printed in the United States of America
10 9 8 7 6 5 4 3 2 1

Library of Congress Cataloging-in-Publication Data
Hamilton, Virginia.
M.C. Higgins, the great / Virginia Hamilton. —
1st Aladdin Books ed.
p.   cm.
Summary: As a slag heap, the result of strip mining, creeps closer
to his house in the Ohio hills, fifteen-year-old M.C. is torn between
trying to get his family away and fighting for the home they love.
ISBN 0-689-71694-X
[1. Family life—Fiction.   2. Afro-Americans—Fiction.]
I. Title.
PZ7.HI828Mac   1993
[Fic]—dc20   92-27919
ISBN 0-689-86228-8

for
Susan Hirschman

M.C. Higgins,
the Great

1

MAYO Cornelius Higgins raised his arms high to the sky and spread them wide. He glanced furtively around. It was all right. There was no one to see his greeting to the coming sunrise. But the motion of his arms caused a flutter of lettuce leaves he had bound to his wrists with rubber bands. Like bracelets of green feathers, the leaves commenced to wave.

M.C., as he was called, felt warm, moist air surround him. Humidity trapped in the hills clung to the mountainside as the night passed on. In seconds, his skin grew clammy. But he paid no attention to the oppressive heat with its odors of summer growth and decay. For he was staring out over a grand sweep of hills, whose rolling outlines grew clearer by the minute. As he stood on the gallery of his home, the outcropping on which he lived on the mountainside seemed to fade out from under him.

I'm standing in midair, he thought.

He saw dim light touch clouds clustered behind the eastern hills.

Bounce the sun beside me if I want.

All others of his family were still asleep in the house. To be by himself in the perfect quiet was reason enough for him to wake up way early. Alone for half an hour, he could believe he had been chosen to remain forever suspended, facing the hills. He could pretend there was nothing terrible behind him, above his head. Arms outstretched, picture-framed by pine uprights supporting the gallery roof, he was M.C. Higgins, higher than everything.

M.C. smiled. Going to be my best day, he told himself. He let his arms fall, and sniffed a bracelet of cold, fresh vegetable. He bit gently into a lettuce stem, pulling at it until he had an entire leaf to chew.

Will it really be mine—this mountain? Daddy says it will one day.

He loved the mountain, its long, lingering dawns. But he frowned, squinting off at the hills with night still huddled in their folds.

Now it won't ever be mine.

He shivered as with a sudden chill, and stepped off the gallery.

Pay no mind to what Daddy says.

"We have to leave it," he said softly, "and that's a shame."

M.C. walked quickly to the edge of the outcropping

where tangled undergrowth made deep shadows. He avoided looking at the side yard with its burial ground covered with car junk, and his prize like no other.

See it later, he told himself, thinking of the prize. See it when the sun is making it shine.

Slipping through the undergrowth, he took one of the paths down the mountainside Soon he was striding swiftly through piney woods. The leaf bracelets wafted on air as though in flight, as he plunged and wove among the trees.

M.C. was barefoot, wearing carefully ironed blue jeans and a brown, faded T-shirt. The shirt was the color and fit of a second skin over his broad shoulders. Already he was perspiring. But his motions remained lithe and natural, as he moved easily among trees and shade. Pushing through pine boughs, he continued on his errand.

Bet I haven't caught a single rabbit, just like on Thursday and Saturday, too.

He had to check all three of his rabbit traps and then get home to wait for this new dude to arrive.

They were saying in the hills that some new kind of black fellow had come in with a little box of a tape recorder. All slicked down and dressed to kill, they were saying he was looking to put voices on the tape in his box.

And now M.C. knew how he could get around his daddy and get his mama and his brothers and sister off the dangerous mountain. The idea had come to him after he heard about the dude. Two days ago, greeting the sunrise, there it began in his mind, growing and growing with each new ray of light.

Dude going to make Mama a star singer like Sister Baby

on the radio, M.C. thought. We'll have to travel with her—won't that be something? But Mama is better than Sister Baby. He'll make her the best anybody ever heard.

The dude had already been told about M.C.'s mother and the kind of voice she had.

What if he gets to home when I'm gone? No, too early for him. He'll have to walk it, M.C. thought. Probably lose himself about twice before he makes it up the mountain.

M.C. lived three miles inland from the Ohio River. His rabbit traps were strung out at the edge of a plateau between Sarah's Mountain, where he lived on the outcropping, and a low hill called Kill's Mound. On the Mound lived the Killburn people, whose youngest son was the same age as M.C.

M.C. smiled to himself as he moved like shadow through the damp stillness. Ben Killburn was just his age but only half his size. M.C. was tall, with oak-brown skin, like his mother; yet he was muscular and athletic, like his father. He had a hard strength and grace that helped make him the best swimmer ever to come out of the hills. The first time he had tried to swim the Ohio River, a year and a half ago, he almost drowned.

His father, finding him exhausted, vomiting on the river bank: "You think that river is some mud puddle you can wade right into without a thought?"

And then, his father beating him with his belt: "A boat wouldn't go into that water not knowing how the currents run. (*Whack!*) I'm not saying you can't swim it (*Whack!*), as good a swimmer as you are. (*Whack!*) But you have to

4

study it, you have to practice. You have to *know* you're ready. (*Whack-whack-whack!*) I'll even give you a prize, anything that won't cost me to spend some money. (*Wham!*)"

M.C. left the path and plunged into weeds of ginseng and wild daisy in a clearing. Standing still a moment, he searched until he spied the first trap half-hidden. Cautiously he picked his way toward it, for he had placed the trap at the edge of a long, narrow ravine. Across the ravine was Kill's Mound but he could hardly see it. An abundance of trees grew up from the bottom of the ravine, blocking his view. He couldn't glimpse the Killburn land, or houses and barns at all.

M.C. stopped again. He gave off a soft call. Cupping his hands tightly around his lips, he pitched the call high enough to make it sound like a young turkey gobbling. He remembered that when he was a child out with his father, they often came upon a whole flock of wild turkeys. Now all such birds were rarely seen.

M.C. listened.

Deep in the ravine, there came a soft answering sound, a yelp of a hound puppy nipped on the ear by his mama.

Ben Killburn was there waiting, as M.C. figured he would be. And after M.C. checked his traps, he would have time to spend with Ben.

Calling like birds and animals wasn't just a game they played. It was the way M.C. announced he was there without Ben's daddy and his uncles finding out. M.C. wouldn't have wanted to run into the Killburn men any more than he would want his own father to know he was playing with Ben. Folks called the Killburns witchy people. Some said that the Killburn women could put themselves in trances and cast out the devil. Killburn men and women both could heal a bad wound by touching, although M.C. had never seen them do it. Boys scattered around the hills never would play with Ben. They said it was because he was so little and nervous. But M.C. had played with Ben from the time he was a child and didn't know better. When he was older, he had been told. Now he guessed Ben was like a bad habit he couldn't break and had to keep secret.

The traps M.C. made were a yard long, a foot high and a little more than a foot wide. He had put them together from scraps of wood and chicken wire.

Better soon take them apart, he thought. Stack them, so when we move . . . .

He checked them. Not a one of them is sprung, he said to himself.

Peering through the chicken wire, he saw that his lure of lettuce was still in place and rotting from two days of heat. The animal trails took the rabbits through the weeds into the ravine where they drank at a stream, and on to Mrs. Killburn's large vegetable gardens.

Maybe her greens have gone sour, M.C. thought. Not one rabbit come even close.

Disgusted, he held the raised trapdoor in place. He reached inside and tore lettuce loose from the first trap. He threw the rotting lure as far as he could into the ravine. Cleaning out the other two traps, he took fresh lure from his wrist bands.

6

Just a waste of time, he thought, shoving lettuce into the traps. But I'd sure like to taste some wild meat.

Finishing the chore, M.C. fluffed up weeds where he had trampled them down, making the traps less obvious. Then he started down into the ravine, grabbing hold of a wood post of a vine bridge. The bridge hung across the ravine to a landing on Kill's Mound.

My bridge, M.C. thought.

One time he had kept on thinking about how often Ben's mother had to climb up the side of the ravine to go anyplace. Usually she carried one of her babies on her hip. Slowly it had come to him what could be done.

"Vines are thick," he had told Ben. "You get your daddy and your uncles to cut them and make a weave."

He told Ben that wood posts had to go in solid ground on each side of the ravine. He told how to soak the vines, then loop them at the top and bottom of each post, and how to weave the vines so they'd stay tight. How to tie them.

I figured it, M.C. thought, admiring the simple lattice weave of the bridge.

Only one trouble.

Ben was so used to living the same, he hadn't trusted a new way of doing. It had taken Ben forever to make up his mind that M.C. knew what he was talking about. When he had finally told his father, Mr. Killburn dropped everything and set to work making the bridge.

Stretching himself out, M.C. held onto the post for as long as he could. Then he let go and plunged, running, sliding and falling down into the ravine. He had to keep watch for patches of seepage, which dried up in one place only to form again in another. The patches could be soft and muddy, or bottomless like sink holes. Growth covering them was yellow-green or black with rot.

Either way, M.C. thought, each is trouble.

He made it down the ravine without any danger to himself and into the midst of it, where the stream gurgled along.

Something swooshed over his head. M.C. ducked in a crouch. He smiled and turkey-gobbled softly. Staying down, he craned his head up and around to see.

Ben Killburn had come swinging out of the trees on the opposite side of the ravine, his hands and legs spidery tight around a strong, old vine. He swung back, swooshing through the air some four feet above M.C.'s head.

"Hurry up." Ben silently mouthed the words as he glided, rising into the trees on the Kill's Mound side.

The ravine was an ancient place, with trees taller than most others over the hills. Once there had been a river through it. Ben's grandmother remembered all about it. She'd put on her bonnet and ride that river meander to the town of Harenton near the Ohio River.

Now there was only the stream and seeping wetness. Because the trees grew so huge, M.C. suspected that the river still flowed underground. Not only were they massive but they were entwined with vines as thick as a man's arm. Maybe the vines were poison ivy grown monstrous from Killburn magic.

M.C. liked the idea of witchy vines.

Funny they never cause me to itch, or Ben, either.

The vines tangled up and up to the very tops of trees.

They connected with other vines and other branches, forming a network that shut out hard sunlight. Dampness became trapped with heat, causing fog to hang eerily just above the ground.

Wouldn't want to be caught down here in the night, M.C. told himself. He shuddered, picturing vines reaching for him and looping themselves around his neck.

M.C. jumped over the stream and headed for Ben waiting on a high branch. Ben's unsmiling face was pale yellow and always looked slightly peaked. He had shocking red hair, thick and long. All of the Killburn children had the same hair, in varying shades of red.

As M.C. came nearer, Ben's gray eyes lit up. He grinned, showing small, pointed teeth. He straightened his knees, then bent them, as if he would jump for joy.

M.C. always felt bigger and strong around Ben, like he wasn't just anybody passing by. He was M.C., and he made a show of examining the vine he would use, which hung down the side of the tree trunk. He grabbed it above his head and braced his feet against the trunk. Leaning far back, he tugged hard on the vine. Positive it would hold his weight, he walked up the tree and climbed onto the branch next to Ben.

The branch twisted horizontally from the tree, searching for sunlight. To balance themselves, the boys had to stand still and hold tight to their vines. For a moment they stared at one another in a silent regard. M.C. liked Ben and felt sorry for his being small and alone when he didn't want to be either. He admired Ben because Ben was a witchy. And he knew that Ben thought a lot of him, since he was like no other boy and would play with Ben. Tall and powerful, M.C. didn't mind being by himself, could do anything well.

Between them was an unspoken agreement. Ben was never to touch M.C. with his hands and risk losing his only friend.

The problem for both of them was that they couldn't walk a path together for fear M.C.'s father or others might see them. M.C. would walk the paths and Ben would stalk him, hidden in the trees. That way they could be together and have no trouble.

"I go first," M.C. suddenly said. He shoved off the branch, swinging out through the ravine. He was carried in a long sweep through the ground fog. In an instant, he appeared shadowy, like a ghost riding lazily on thin air.

Vines are fine, he thought lightly. He felt the coolness of mist on his bare arms. But they aren't the best ride.

M.C. reached the far side. Then Ben swung off the branch and rode low through the fog. Just above the stream, he passed M.C. on the way back.

"I got a ticket to ride," M.C. sang softly as he passed.

Ben grinned with pleasure.

M.C. landed on the branch and pushed off at once. Again he and Ben reached the stream at the same time, from opposite directions.

"Hi, you bro'," M.C. whispered.

"Hi, you M.C.," Ben whispered back, holding tight to his vine.

In slow, ponderous sweeps, they rode back and forth.

Their old vines creaked with the strain. The boys swung slowly, and finally they slowed completely.

M.C. caught up his vine with his feet. When he could reach it with one hand, he twisted it up and around his legs and wrapped it around his waist. He let himself hang there above the stream, with his feet dragging in the cool water. Ben did the same.

They swayed gently around in the stillness. Ben looked just as happy as he could be. M.C. was feeling pretty good himself, just listening and feeling the depth of silence. He even glanced at Ben's hands. They were small and appeared almost ordinary, except each hand had six fingers. Ben had six toes on each foot. Folks said all the Killburn men had toes and hands the same.

Eying Ben's witchy hands, M.C. assured himself that the sixth fingers weren't wildly waving and making magic. They were the same as the other ten holding onto the vine. Only they were extra.

M.C. let the sound of the stream become distant. He could hear voices from the Killburn land nearby—snatches of words, their meaning lost on the mist. Dishes made their scraping noise. Chickens, clucking and fussing for food. Farther off, he thought he heard the deep cough and hum of machines.

Bulldozers, working so early?

Sound again from the house—a fretful cry of a child.

"Where's your daddy now?" M.C. said softly to Ben.

"He's at home," Ben said. "And Uncle Lee and Uncle Joe. No work until tomorrow but they fill up the icehouse by eveningtime."

11

"Are they going to cross that swinging bridge any time soon?" M.C. didn't like running into Killburn men.

"Not likely before afternoon," Ben said. "Then I have to help them."

If M.C. ran into the Killburn men, his father had warned him never to let them cross his path.

"And your mama?" M.C. said. "Haven't seen her in a while."

"She at home," Ben said. "She was gone most of last night."

"Getting out the devil?" M.C. said, respectfully. He tried to be polite when speaking of Mrs. Killburn's power.

"Deliverin' a baby," Ben said.

"Oh," M.C. said, and then: "Are her greens any good this year?"

"Nothing's any good this year," Ben replied. "My daddy says it will get worse with mining going on everywhere."

"What does mining have to do with your mama's vegetables?" M.C. asked.

Ben was silent a moment, as if he didn't want to talk about it. Reluctantly, he said, "Well, Daddy and Uncle Joe went for miles north and east following the coal seam, looking for mining cuts. They didn't go to Sarah's Mountain because of what your daddy might do. But wherever else, they lay hands on the cuts. . . ."

"You mean they thought to work magic on the hills?" M.C. stared at Ben in disbelief.

"I'm just telling you what they had to do," Ben said. "Daddy says it didn't work straight off but that maybe it will slow the ruin down."

"Naturally it didn't work," M.C. said. "That's why folks stay clear of your father, for doing things like that."

"He just can't find a way to heal a mountain is all," Ben said. Looking at M.C., his eyes were anxious, innocent.

"Shoot," M.C. said and fell silent. He pictured Ben's father pressing his hands on giant gashes made by strip mining. And it just about irritated him to death, he didn't know why. Two years ago bulldozers had come to make a cut at the top of Sarah's Mountain. They began uprooting trees and pushing subsoil in a huge pile to get at the coal. As the pile grew enormous, so had M.C.'s fear of it. He had nightmares in which the heap came tumbling down. Over and over again, it buried his family on the side of the mountain.

But his dreams hadn't come true. The spoil heap didn't fall. Slowly his nightmares had ceased and his fear faded within. But then something would remind him, like the chance to get off the mountainside with the dude's coming. Like Ben's father acting the fool. M.C. would get edgy in a second.

"Tell me about the dude again," M.C. said, to hide his irritation.

"Is it time for him to be coming?" Ben asked.

"Soon time," M.C. said. "And I have to be heading back, too, so tell me about him."

"I already told you," Ben said.

"I know that," M.C. said, "but I want to hear it one more time before he gets here. Tell me again."

Ben sighed. "Well, I did just like you said. I asked everybody if they seen him, from here to Harenton. Just on the outskirts, on this side of town, folks had seen him. He appear to be heading east toward the river. He's staying close to town, afraid of the hills, I guess. Anyway, I head for the river and I ask everybody: 'You seen a dude come by here with a tape recorder?' And they say, 'Yea!' And laugh their heads off. They been putting him on just to hear how they sound on the tapes. Say, 'This song been in my family for a hunnerd and fifty year.' Dude believe them, too, and tape them up good."

"Tell about how he looked," M.C. said eagerly.

"I haven't even got to him yet."

"Well, hurry up, you taking too long!" M.C. said.

"He was all right," Ben began. "I find him sitting on the dock with some men fishing. You could tell right away he was the dude."

"Tell it," M.C. said.

"Well, he was eating his lunch real careful and slow, like he wasn't that hungry. He looked more tired than hungry and more blue than tired. I guess he finally figured out that folks had been putting him on—'a hunnerd and fifty year' made up last week. He didn't look like he was very happy about that. Wonder why a one made last week ain't no good?"

"Maybe that wasn't it at all," M.C. said. "Maybe what he got wasn't any good."

"Maybe," Ben said. "Anyhow, here's the part you're waiting for: He had on some of the prettiest boots I ever did see. A real baby-soft leather, man, and shining like two black stars."

"And the hat was leather, too?" M.C. asked.

"The hat was *suede*," Ben said. "And the jacket was suede, too. And the pants must of cost more than thirty dollars."

They sat above the stream in awed silence, with great, still trees leaning near.

Finally Ben broke the quiet: "I told him all about your mama. I didn't lie one bit. He'll come over, as excited as he was—what will you say to him?"

"Not much, at first," M.C. said. "Seems like I been waiting forever for him to come. So I might as well wait to see what he'll offer." He grinned. "And if he's really going to do something for Mama, I'll ask for some money. You know, just enough for us to pack up with some new clothes so we can travel on out of here."

"You really believe he's going to make your mama a star?" Ben asked. He saw M.C. stiffen. Quickly Ben added: "Sure will hate to see you leave." Uncomfortably, he looked away from M.C.

"I'll come back, maybe," M.C. said kindly. "See if you be still swinging." He laughed softly.

"Is your daddy going to want to leave the mountain?" Ben asked him.

M.C. went tight as a drum inside. "What you want us to do—let Mama go off all by herself, huh? With some dude we don't even know?"

"I was just asking," Ben said. "Shh, don't talk so loud. I know you have to get out from under the spoil heap. I just can't see why you think some—" Abruptly he left off, afraid of upsetting M.C. again.

"I'm wasting my time," M.C. said. "Have to get on out

15

of here." He loosened the vine around him. Pumping his body slightly, he slid to the ground next to the stream.

"Why can't you stay?" Ben said.

M.C. sighed. "You know why." Ben never wanted him to leave. "Because the dude might already be at home."

"Well, I'll walk you part way," Ben offered.

"Suit yourself," M.C. said, "but we'd better say so long here, in case we run into somebody."

Although they were only a few feet apart, M.C. raised his hand in a wave.

" 'Bye," Ben said.

"You keep yourself cool, you hear?" M.C. told him.

Ben sat dangling above the stream, odd-looking and shriveled, festering on the vine.

"Ben? I'll be back maybe on Wednesday."

"Maybe I'll see you before then, on the paths," Ben said. "Okay."

M.C. turned from the ancient place of vines and of mist. He scrambled up the steep side of the ravine as fast as he could go. At the top, he stopped to look down. There was Ben coming toward the side, ready to climb. M.C. pushed through the weeds into the woods. In less than five minutes, Ben was somewhere off the path, stalking M.C. from behind.

The thought that Ben was near but unseen was all right with M.C. Although M.C. was still edgy, he felt his senses become heightened with minute sight and sound. Where he moved and saw, Ben was moving and seeing the same. The fact was a comfort.

He's my spirit, M.C. thought. He can see me and everything around me and the path, too. Good old spirit.

Only a few miles from the Ohio River, they were in country where once—no more than ten years ago—there had been elk and deer. It was still deep country where people liked nothing better than the quiet of staying close to home. Boys M.C.'s age endured school in the steel town of Harenton. Awkward, with twitching hands and no pine needles to touch or branches to hang from. In class, tongue-tied, they thought themselves stupid. Their teachers thought them slow. They endured it all. Until time to go home, to live again, ingenious in the woods.

Hills were crisscrossed with footpaths and animal trails. Only a hunter like M.C. could distinguish the telltale signs of trails. Anyone could follow the footpaths. Some had names from long ago, such as Wee Woman Path, Mighty High and Mighty Low. There were still some old, rutted wagon roads, which deadended at blinds and began anew up steep hill slopes. A few of the roads near coal seams had been broadened and flattened smooth by heavy machines. No one M.C. knew walked the roads.

As always, M.C. kept to Sarah's High Path. It ran the length of the plateau shouldered by hills, with Kill's Mound at one end of it and Sarah's Mountain at the other. Where the woods angled up and then down sharp inclines, M.C. had no sweeping view in any direction. He could see the path ahead of him and he could sometimes see miles of blue sky above. There were houses scattered throughout the plateau, but the path veered away from them. To reach a house, hidden, M.C. would have had to take lesser paths branching off from Sarah's High.

He could hear birds singing, some doves and quail. When bobwhites sang in the morning, it meant rain to come in the night. He heard the drone of catydids rising and falling. His own breathing was loud in his head. In his ears, gnats whined thinly and he could feel close, damp heat.

"*M.C.*" Ben's voice light on the air, as if he had spoken within M.C.'s mind. "*There's somebody.*" So near him off the path, M.C. was startled.

Someone was ahead of M.C. on Sarah's High. Probably some woman going into town. He knew everybody within a square mile of Sarah's Mountain. He knew them by sight, if not to say more than good morning.

M.C. studied the figure, but she didn't move with any kind of ease.

It's not any woman. It's a girl.

He bent his knees slightly so he could move silently on his toes. He knew Ben would be doing the same.

Think it's Mary.

Willis people lived in the south plateau quite near Sarah's Mountain. Mary was one of the daughters and not much older than M.C. She was as strong as any boy and she would slap you for looking at her. Mary had thick, coarse hair that was black-shiny and almost straight.

"Some Indian blood," M.C.'s mother had told him. "That long hair hold all of her strength. You just see how weak she is if you twist her hand around."

M.C. grinned again. Mary Willis was as strong as a horse. He knew because, thinking she had no strength, he had caught her once on the path. Coming up noiselessly behind her the way he knew how to stalk, he had grabbed her arms and tried to pin them. He had whispered that he thought she was just so nice.

"*M.C., you let me go!*"

He had tried to steal a kiss right from her cheek. Leaning around her pretty hair, he'd almost made it. Mary Willis broke his grasp and hit him with her fist.

Made my nose bleed a minute, too, M.C. remembered.

He was now within ten feet of the figure ahead of him.

Catch her again!

But it wasn't Mary, he knew in a moment. The one ahead of him didn't look like anyone from the hills. She carried a bundle. It was a round kind of green cloth sack on rope fixed with slipknots on her back. She moved warily, glancing to either side of the path.

A stranger.

M.C. stalked expertly, tense with a hunter's joy of discovery. Strangers didn't often come into these hills alone. When they did come, they took pictures of hills and houses, even of weeds and rocks. To M.C.'s amazement, they'd pick anything that bloomed, even when it was poison. And usually they ended up by getting themselves lost. Once some of them had come up Sarah's Mountain to get a view. They'd asked for water, but seeing Jones, M.C.'s father, they had backed off.

I got them some water, M.C. thought. So what did they do?

They had watched Jones. They came near, to smooth water over their necks and faces, but they wouldn't drink.

Smiling and nodding at M.C., quickly they had gone down the mountainside. M.C. never did figure out whether they feared well water or his father.

The girl on the path ahead of him now wasn't one of them. He could see her dark skin showing beneath a light blue shirt. M.C. stalked nearer, close enough for her to hear him. Right on her heels, he gave her a low whistle, knowing he was wrong to scare her. He had a loud, screaming whistle through his teeth, just as if he was older and whistled at girls every day.

She kept on walking. He couldn't tell if he had frightened her. She reached back to adjust the bundle on her back. Turning sideways but not missing a stride, she gave M.C. a look that slowed him down. She wouldn't bother to yell at him, the look seemed to say, let alone hit him. He had time to notice she wore a clump of bracelets, when suddenly she walked off the path into the trees. M.C. listened. By the quickening swish-swish of pine boughs, he knew the moment she discovered Ben and broke into a run.

Ben must have been standing as still as some light-colored tree trunk, with eyes. M.C. had to smile.

"Wouldn't've hurt you!" he called.

When he could no longer hear any sound of her running, he continued on, trying to picture what the girl had looked like. She wasn't tall, that he could remember. But he was left with no general impression.

Just her eyes, M.C. thought. Dark and slanty. Looking old.

He felt more than a momentary interest in her, but not much of an image of her on which to play his curiosity.

In his rush to get home, he let her slip away out of his thoughts.

Just some stranger.

It was probably eight o'clock by now. The dude would have to be on his way.

The path dipped off the plateau and ended at what had once been a wagon roadbed reaching all the way around the base of Sarah's Mountain to its far side. Where M.C. came off the plateau, it was a gully formed in years past by rainwater running off the mountain into wagon ruts. It was a bone-dry, barren place edged with trees.

M.C. stood, feeling heat rise from the bald earth of the gully. He looked in back of him up to the plateau. He knew Ben had stopped there, and was turning around now, ready to trot home.

See you, Ben, he said to himself.

Ben answered in his thoughts, *See you*.

M.C. turned back to the gully again and walked a third of the way into it. To his right was Sarah's Mountain, a great swell of earth rising to outline the sky. Her growth of trees was washed light green by morning sun and mist. Halfway up was the ledge of rock, the outcropping, on which M.C. lived with the rest of his family. The whole outcropping was partially hidden by trees. Only one who knew where to look would see a house at all.

Near the house, something was shining. M.C. caught a blinding gleam right in the eye. He smiled, clambering over the lip of the gully and onto a path that rose steeply up the face of the mountain. Holding onto tree trunks and branches when he had to, he picked and sometimes nearly clawed his way. There was an easier path beginning farther along the lip of the gully, but M.C. was in too much of a hurry to take it. He panted and grunted with the effort of his climb. He paused to look up and was rewarded by a sharp flash of light.

"I got a ticket to ride," he gasped. "I . . . got-a-ticket-to . . . ri-i-ide."

The path veered closer to the outcropping where there was undergrowth of sweetbrier. It cut through the tangled, prickly mass of the brier and brought M.C. out onto the outcropping. The ledge he stood on was like a huge half-circle of rock sticking out of the mountain. Behind it, the mountain rose another three hundred feet to the summit. Up there, just below the summit, was a gash like a road all the way across. It had a seventy-foot vertical wall made by bulldozers hauling out tons of soil to get at the coal seam. And up there was something like an enormous black boil of uprooted trees and earth plastered together by rain, by all kinds of weather. Some internal balance kept the thing hanging suspended on the mountainside, far above the outcropping, in a half-congealed spoil heap bigger than M.C.'s house.

At home, finally, he saw that the house was shut tight. His mother, his father, both gone to work. The kids, on their way to swim. One side of the house to the rear was smack up against the mountain where the ledge curved around it. On the other side of the house was a grape arbor, the expanse of yard and M.C.'s prize like no other.

It was always his shining beacon.

Pretty thing, you.

He had won it, practicing on the Ohio River, testing his strength against strong currents every day for weeks. He had known when he was ready.

I wasn't scared. I did it and I never want to do it again. I won't ever have to.

Jones said, name what you want, real quick. And I saw it just as clear. All over town in Harenton. Front of the post office. The police station.

His prize was a pole. It was forty feet of glistening, cold steel, the best kind of ride.

M.C. gazed up at its sparkling height. There was a bicycle seat fixed at the top. He had put it there himself and had attached pedals and two tricycle wheels below it on either side.

He didn't know how his father had got the pole without money. Jones had let him deep-foot the pole in the midst of the piles of junk in their yard. There were automobile tires, fenders, car bodies, that Jones had dragged up the mountain over the years. But Jones had long since forgotten about putting together a working car.

Wonder why he won't ever throw away that junk, M.C. thought. How'd he get the pole? Probably the same way he got the junk. Maybe he just took it.

Maybe it had been abandoned, like the cars, or perhaps it had been given to Jones out of the rolling mill in the steelyard at Harenton. Ten feet too tall, it could have a flaw somewhere, a weak structure from uneven firing.

Looks just fine from here, M.C. thought. He stood there

studying his pole, admiring its black and blue tint in the sun. It was the one thing that could make him feel peaceful inside every time he saw it.

Gingerly, M.C. climbed up on the car junk. He leaned over and gripped the pole.

"Let's go for a ride."

He dried his sweating palms on his shirt. Then he jumped off the pile. And twisting his legs around, he climbed the slippery, smooth steel the way only he knew how.

2

E VER so gently, M.C. leaned
his body forward on the steel pole. He pushed his feet
on the pedals. The wheels spun around. The pole swung
forward in a slow, sweeping arc. Beyond the hills, he
caught glimpses of the Ohio River. Its sheet-metal brightness rushed to meet him and he had the sensation he was
falling free.

Into the river. Bounce off the hills into the silver water.

When the pole reached the outer limit of its arc, it swung
back. Blue sky rolled over M.C.'s vision as if someone had
pulled down a bright window blind. Back and forth the
pole swept until his head felt as light as a floating ball. The
sensation was pleasant until he began to feel sick.

Going to lose my balance up here.

He stopped pedaling. The wheels stopped spinning. He

held himself utterly still until the pole shuddered and did not move again.

Forty feet up, he was truly higher than everything on the outcropping. Higher than the house and higher than the trees. Straight out from Sarah's Mountain, he could see everything in a spectacular view. He occasionally saw people clearly walking the hill paths nine miles away. Thinking they were absolutely alone, they had no inkling his eyes were upon them.

I'm all alone, M.C. thought.

The house was shut tight. In the morning sun, the whole place appeared to have been abandoned. And for a fleeting moment he pretended: Mama and Daddy in the ground, he told himself. Dead a long time. That's not so bad. They lived to be each a hundred. The kids, grown old, too, and died. I lived longer than each of them. I'm old now but I can still get around. Never did leave the mountain. None of the others did, either. But buried here. Ghosts. Just like Great-grandmother Sarah and the other old ones who really did pass away long ago.

M.C. shuddered at the thought of all the dead on the mountain, under the junk around his pole.

Effortlessly his mind brought Sarah back to life. There she was, hurrying over the last hill facing the mountain. She always glanced behind her, never trusting the empty trail as she raced ahead, carrying something.

M.C. knew the story by heart. He knew she ran for freedom. She carried a baby.

Concealed by the hill haze, she had been hiding for two

days before she knew what lay ahead of her. What it was hadn't revealed itself until the third day. On that dawning, sunshine broke through veiled mist. Cautiously Miss Sarah crept from her hiding place.

Looking around, M.C. thought. Real hungry. Hold the baby tight to search for food. She start out again, northward.

It was then she saw it. It climbed the sky. Up and up. Swelling green and gorgeous. Huge. Mountain.

As if in a trance, M.C. gazed out over the rolling hills. He sensed Sarah moving through undergrowth up the mountainside. As if past were present. As if he were a ghost, waiting, and she, the living.

The sensation startled him out of his trance. Fearfully he willed Sarah back to her grave. At once his father and mother, brothers and sister sprang to life in his mind.

Whew! M.C. blinked rapidly. Almost scared myself in the daylight.

But the idea nagged at him, worrying him, that a hundred years of the past seeped out of the hills to surround him.

Suddenly he was aware of the deep whine of machines in the hills behind Sarah's to the north. He raised his arm so that his hand seemed to slide over the perfect roll and curve of the hill range before him to the south. He fluffed the trees out there and smoothed out the sky. All was still and ordered, the way he liked to pretend he arranged it every day.

The steel town of Harenton looked close enough to touch. He reached for it and pushed and shoved pieces of the town together until he had it just right. He smoothed out the stacks of the steel mill, sweeping them clean of dust and run-off gases. He placed boats in the river.

"Now," he said softly, "you're looking good."

Something out there caught his eye. He focused on the hill across from Sarah's Mountain. Somebody was moving in and out of trees.

M.C.'s palms began to itch with premonition. Absently he scratched one hand with the other. His mother always said itching hands meant a visitor.

Bet it's the dude, M.C. thought, but he's going the wrong way. "Hey!" he yelled.

The figure went up and over the hilltop, away from Sarah's Mountain.

"Shoot," M.C. said, under his breath. Must have been somebody . . . .

At once he thought of the girl he had seen on the path.

What does she mean, roaming around all by her lone-some?

He had to smile. He made a muscle in his arm and felt it jump up hard.

Should I go out there, scare her again?

It wouldn't have taken much for him to climb down his pole and hunt for the girl. Already the sun had started to burn him from his scalp down the side of his body to his bare feet. He gritted his teeth, about to slide down, when a clear sound of laughter drifted out of the hills. He turned quickly to the right, where low mountains and more foot-hills curved gently toward Sarah's. Over there was a lake nestled in a cirque, a natural amphitheater between foot-

28

hills. Laughter was coming from there. His brothers and his sister had just reached the lake.

Almost forgot about them, M.C. thought.

The kids, Lennie Pool, Harper and Macie Pearl, always swam in the lake on a hot morning. The lake water could be cold as ice; it had blue holes and grottoes emerging into pools a short distance from it.

Squinting, M.C. saw the children wade gingerly in the water and then swim out. They were like fish, gliding and diving. After a while a few town kids drifted over the hills and down to the lake. Half afraid of water, they splashed in the shallows along the shore.

M.C. let his pole sway gently. He caught a sudden gust of breeze. He continued to sit more comfortably now, for he did have to watch out for the kids over in the lake. He had to wait for the dude. And he let the thought of a lone stranger, a girl in the woods, slip out of his mind again.

Macie Pearl and M.C.'s brothers could swim well enough to care for themselves in the water. But if one of them did commence to drown . . . .

Don't think about it.

M.C. frowned.

They don't know how lucky they are. Swimming. Playing. Without a worry for food or nothing.

His mother, Banina, was off cleaning houses. Jones, his father, worked as a laborer in the steelyard at Harenton when somebody was sick, like today. A whole month could go by and often did before someone became ill. Whenever work was scarce and food was low, M.C. didn't count on his rabbit traps.

Depend on them, we'd starve.

He hunted with a burlap sack, a rock or two and a paring knife. He had no dog, and so he had taught himself how to be the hunter. He would read animal signs around trees or in wetlands and along streams where they came to drink. Hunting was hours and hours of stalking, of blind trails, of studying the ground and listening. It could be bloody, too. But he could hunt well when he had to, using the paring knife to skin and gut the animal.

When M.C. couldn't be around sitting on his pole to watch the kids, he made them stay inside the house, sometimes for hours. He had taught Macie Pearl to sit in the parlor for as long as it took him. She wouldn't even move her hands.

"I can't hunt so good," he told her, "if I'm not positive you are safe here. I can't catch me a shameful thing if you be running the hills or swimming the lake without me to watch."

Whatever Macie Pearl thought about during the long, half-hungry hours when she had to sit, she could do it because M.C. had told her to.

They stay safe. They listen to me.

Now M.C. kept watch over the lake, straining his eyes so, that they began to ache. He shifted his gaze back to the hill range. Hills rolled eastward and became faded with haze.

Across from Sarah's, he again saw somebody moving. His pulse quickened as he saw it was a man moving slowly in and out of trees. The man slid a ways on the hill slope, and then he rested.

He think he's lost? It's the dude for sure!

M.C. made his pole move in its graceful sweep forward and back. If the dude would just look up the mountain, he might see the shiniest needle in the world. M.C. made the pole move more quickly. But the figure still rested on the hillside.

M.C. stopped the pole in the middle of its arc, causing it to shudder violently along its length. He was pitched forward on the bicycle seat but managed to twist his legs around the steel and hold on.

"Hey!" M.C. yelled as loud as he could. "Up here! Up here! Hey, over here!"

His voice echoed off the hills. The dude was standing. He started moving down toward the gully stretched along the foot of Sarah's.

"Hey!" M.C. called again. The dude stopped still, trying to locate the echoing voice. "Don't go down, go along it—where it narrows. There's a path!"

The dude looked up and up. Seeing something, he was moving again and he went straight into the gully.

"Fool," M.C. whispered. He lost the dude at once, his view blocked by trees along the gully lip.

There was a fairly easy path up the mountain continuing off the hill from town. The dude had gone beyond it along the gully. M.C. waited, but the dude didn't come out of the undergrowth onto the ledge outcropping.

He's gone too far to the left, M.C. thought. "Hey!" he yelled. *"Hey-hey-hey,"* the hills echoed.

M.C. twisted around on his pole. Minutes passed. Staring

31

up and up behind him, he searched the summit of Sarah's Mountain but saw nothing. Again he waited.

After some time a figure appeared up there. Stick-like, it was etched against the outline of mountain. It walked along the summit to a point directly above the deep gash made by mining. It was the dude, waving both hands above his head.

M.C. waved back as hard as he could. "Here!" he called. "Hi!"

"Hi-theeere!" the dude called down. His voice wasn't deep. It sounded kind of thin and scratchy, echoing.

He *acts* okay, M.C. thought. Impatiently, M.C. waited, but the dude made no move to come off the summit. He stood up there like a black scarecrow rooted to the spot.

Maybe he's height-sick. Do I have to go get him?

Since the mining, M.C. never went up there. And uncertain what to do, he sat a moment longer. He gazed off to the cirque and the lake where the children played, now skipping stones on the water's surface.

They'll be all right, sure, he told himself. He slid down his pole as fast as he could without burning his hands from the friction. And scrambling over the junk around the pole, he rushed to the edge of the outcropping.

Find the dude something to lean on.

He searched the undergrowth for fallen limbs of trees; presently he found a dry and sturdy piece of branch.

That ought to do him.

M.C. took the stick, hurried back to the rear of the outcropping and began picking his way up Sarah's final slope. He used the stick like a paddle, jabbing it into the mountain on his left side, and leaning heavily on it, he walked up the mountain.

He found the dude in the midst of what had been the summit of Sarah's Mountain. Now it was an empty place as large as a five-acre cornfield. Only there were no cornstalks. Where M.C. and his father had once hunted wild game, there was no longer a tree left standing. Trucks and mining cats had stripped and flattened the summit until it was bald, like the gully.

The dude was bent over. One hand was on his hip and the other braced his knee, as though he had a pain in his side. He wore a tan suede hat—the one Ben had told M.C. about. It had a wide brim turned down.

Carrying the stick, M.C. ran over to the dude. "Hi," he said, breathlessly, coming up to the man. Then he stood there staring.

The dude straightened with a look of pain that vanished as quickly as it had come. "How-do, son," he said finally. He extended his hand to M.C. "James K. Lewis, they call me," he said.

"Hi," M.C. said again. "I'm called M.C." Hesitantly, he reached for the dude's hand. It felt hot, full of minute tremors that seemed to flow up M.C.'s arm.

Limply, the dude let go. He was still breathing hard. He shook with the exertion of climbing the mountain and sweat rolled off him. Down his shoulder hung a black box on a strap.

The tape recorder, M.C. thought. He felt a sweet surge of excitement.

Take Mama's voice for sure!

James Lewis's gray trousers had got wet somewhere and were drying with mud to the knee. His black city boots were a disaster, dirt-caked and soggy clear through. M.C. watched his every move.

"Whew, Lord!" Lewis said. "That's some climb up here."

"You went wrong," M.C. said. "I try to warn you."

"Heard you, too," Lewis said, "but I couldn't tell a thing with all the echoing."

"You get used to figuring it out," M.C. said, and then shyly: "You come from far?"

The dude nodded, smiling feebly. "Come clear from the town of Harenton and I tell *you!*" he said.

M.C. couldn't help laughing. "That's not but a little over two mile," he said.

"You sure of that?" Lewis said. "It felt like a long kind of desert, and me without my camel."

M.C. laughed again. Right away he liked the dude.

With the heat still to get hotter, Lewis wore the suede jacket Ben spoke about, and a long-sleeved white shirt. He had on a black tie. Both tie and shirt looked wringing wet. Now he took a white handkerchief out of his shirt pocket. Though folded neatly, the handkerchief was smudged and soiled. Lewis wiped his face and neck with it. He removed his hat. There was a deep line around his forehead where the hat had been. He rubbed at it with his handkerchief before putting on his hat again.

M.C. studied his face. It was the color of barn-dried walnuts with deep creases, which M.C. guessed were lines of worry and maybe some laughter. His eyes were black but clouded with fatigue. His hair was graying all the way through.

"I sure got myself lost," Lewis said. "Least, I think I was lost. How do you know if you're lost when you don't know where you are to begin with? Anyhow, I walked right into some kind of bog clear to the knee. Sure thought I was a goner in some deathtrap of quicksand."

M.C. smiled nervously. He wasn't sure what he should do for a man who had come to take his mama's voice. So he waited and tried to look friendly and to speak as pleasantly as he could.

"What I mean," M.C. began, "where did you come from before you ever came to the town of Harenton?"

"Oh, well," the dude said, "I come from a far jump from here. Yes, indeed," he added vaguely. He was gazing out at the landscape behind Sarah's Mountain to the north. His hands rested on his hips as he stared. After a moment he spun around and looked south again toward the Ohio River.

"Now this here is called Sarah's Mountain, if I'm not mistaken," he said.

"Always has been," M.C. told him. He had softened his usually hard hill voice to fit the gentler, flatter tones of the dude. And he was quick to grasp the matter-of-fact rhythms of Lewis's speech and match them.

"I've heard of Airy Mountain," Lewis said, "and Baldy and Eagle, but I've never heard tell of Sarah's Mountain before."

"Yessir," M.C. said. "She was my Great-grandmother Sarah."

"Was she, now?" Lewis said "Well, it's some mountain, I'll say that for it. But they ought to rename it the Awful Divide, they surely should." Quickly, glancing at M.C.'s anxious face, he smiled engagingly. "Oh, I don't mean to say there's a thing wrong with naming it after your great-grandmother. That wasn't my point, no-sir. But just you look back there." He was squinting north, behind Sarah's.

"I come that way," Lewis continued. "I mean, I had to ride through there to get here. And I'm telling you, I've never seen anything so clear in my life. You look back there and then you look over here to the river and you have two lands about as danged different as right be to wrong. Two lands separated by this mountain. Can you see it, son?"

M.C. couldn't help feeling strange at finding himself standing on the mountaintop after so long a time. Everything was so hot and still. No sound of insects. No birds. He hadn't had to view the desolate landscape, either, in two years. For the configuration of Sarah's Mountain, the plateau and Kill's Mound successfully blocked his vision. Now he had to face the northern hills behind Sarah's.

He nodded in answer to James K. Lewis. He shrugged his shoulders.

To the north and east had been ranges of hills with farm-houses nestled in draws and lower valleys. But now the hills looked as if some gray-brown snake had curled itself along their ridges. The snake loops were mining cuts just like the one across Sarah's Mountain, only they were a continuous gash. They went on and on, following fifty miles of a coal seam. As far as M.C.'s eyes could see, the summits of hills had been shredded away into rock and ruin which spilled down into cropland at the base of the hills.

Glad I don't have to see it, M.C. thought. He turned away riverward, where the hills in front of Sarah's rolled and folded, green and perfect.

"Now that's beauty-*ful*, I'll tell you," the dude said, gazing after M.C. He breathed in deeply, as if he would swallow the sight of the rich river land. "It's like a picture-painting but ever so much better because it's so real. Hills, untouched. Not a thing like it where I come from."

M.C. felt suddenly better, proud of his hills. "Where do you come from?" he asked.

"Oh, I guess the edge of nowhere," Lewis said. He chuckled. "West of Chicago, the windy city—you ever been there?"

"No," M.C. said, studying his bare feet in the dust.

"It's where the prairie begins," the dude said. "The land is flat and flat and forever flat."

"I saw pictures in school," M.C. said, "but I haven't traveled much." He waited to see if the dude would mention that he intended taking his mother's voice away.

"My father before me was just the same as I am," Lewis said, "always moving. Way back when, hill people thought he had brought a plague of hunger with him."

Lewis shook his head with the memory of his father. "He sure could tell a story or two about that time. It was the Depression, you see, and folks were awful hungry. And here I come collecting again. There's not supposed to be any Depression but folks is still feeling the hunger."

M.C. listened and wondered about folks being hungry.

He thought of Kill's Mound, Ben, all the witchy folks with their lands full of crops. Sarah's Mountain wouldn't farm. But M.C. and his family had something to eat every day. It was true, though, they did have to work hard to get it.

"Did you come here to get my mama to sing?" M.C. finally blurted out. He hung his head, ashamed at having to ask.

Lewis didn't seem to mind. "Well, sure," he said. "I was heading down there to see you all but I couldn't figure an easy way to get down."

"There's not much of an easy way," M.C. told him, "but I brought this stick for you. Here."

"Well, thank you, son," Lewis said, taking the stick. "You're real thoughtful. Now you lead and I'll follow."

At once M.C. struck out along the top of Sarah's until he came to where a road began, twisting down into the mining cut. The walk along the road was not hard and soon they were standing in the cut, with seventy feet of a sheer wall to their backs.

"Son, doesn't that wall have an odor to it," Lewis said, "like a kind of rot?"

M.C. nodded. He began to walk again. "It always smells like that when we have some rains. Acids come out of the mountain and run down it."

"Was all of this wall a coal seam at one time?" Lewis asked him.

M.C. sighed inwardly. He didn't want to talk about it. He wanted to get down to home. But he found himself answering, his hands moving, scratching his neck and arms:

"Only about ten feet at the bottom of it was ever coal. The rest was just trees and rocks and soils."

"Lordy," the dude said, shaking his head. "Sixty feet of mountain gone for ten foot of coal. I tell you, there ought-a be a law."

"They take most of the dirt and rocks away in trucks," M.C. said. "But a big pile they just push over the edge of the road with the trees. Then they blasted that coal."

"They didn't!" the dude said.

"Yessir," M.C. said. "We were just playing down around the house when there was a bursting noise. Some rock and coal hit the back of the house real hard. It fell all around my sister on her tricycle. Knock holes in her spokes, too. It fell all around her and she never was touched."

"That surely was a blessing," the dude said.

"Yessir," M.C. said, and continued: "Daddy was running around and yelling up there. And then he came down with a fist full of dollar bills for damage, right in his hand."

"They paid off real quick, did they?" Lewis said.

M.C. grinned and nodded. "Then a bunch of the machine men came on down. They fix the back of the house right off. They say they want no trouble. But they never did fix my sister's tricycle."

M.C. walked off the road and down the mountainside. Carefully he skirted the huge and silent spoil heap in his path. He knew it was a rotten, terrible thing. But it didn't turn him cold; it didn't paralyze him with fear the way it once had in his nightmares. It had no plunge and roar of menace.

Just big, M.C. thought. And dangerous. But we'll get out of its way.

The dude stopped to look at the heap. M.C. was some feet below him at the base of it. He sighed again, watching the dude waste his time walking around the heap.

"Near good-sized, isn't it?" Lewis said, making a joke.

M.C. smiled at him but said nothing.

To balance himself on the mountainside Lewis cautiously held on to trees jutting out of the spoil. M.C. climbed back up over to him to wait. For the first time, he noticed that James Lewis had a leather case—full of his lunch, probably—strapped to his back. He also had a canteen, empty, with the top dangling down on a short, metal chain.

Wish he'd come on, M.C. thought. M.C. had his arms around a tree trunk sticking out of the spoil. He swung on it, lifting his feet off the ground, just to see if it would hold him. There was a thin, cracking sound somewhere deep within the heap.

"Son!" the dude yelled, his eyes wide with terror.

Instantly M.C. let go of the tree. He backed away from it.

"That's nothing to play with," the dude said, more calmly.

M.C. felt cold fear spread inside him. "I have to get on home," he managed to say. Fleetingly, he thought of the kids at the lake. He glanced over there, where all seemed calm.

"I was just seeing how this thing works," Lewis said. He

was at the top of the spoil and motioned for M.C. to come up. Reluctantly, M.C. climbed back.

"See, right there," the dude said, when M.C. was at his side.

M.C. looked and saw. The heap was plastered to the mountainside. There was a crack all along its base where it met the mountain. There were two inches of black, oily slime left on the mountain behind the crack. Still M.C. did not comprehend. He gave Lewis a nod and turned to leave.

"It's moving, all right," Lewis said. "It's growing, too, and sliding about a quarter-inch at a time. I suppose your daddy is prepared."

M.C. stood stock still. Rooted to the mountain, his back to the dude, he swiveled his head around as far as it would go. "What?" he said, in the faintest voice.

"Why, it's absorbing rain like a sponge," the dude went on, "and then seepage reaches the mountainside and acts like an oil. This whole thing is just sliding along on the oil, getting a free ride."

"You mean, it's moving?" M.C. said.

"Been moving," the dude said. "Lucky it takes off the pressure by moving a little. But give it the right angle of steepness and that pressure is going to build up until it crashes down."

Waves of fear swept over M.C., as if they had been holding back, waiting for the time they could let loose all at once. It was his nightmare come to life. Having somebody like the dude say what he had often dreamed made him sick with dread.

41

M.C. started down the mountainside again. His legs felt rubbery. He sat down hard, twice, when they buckled under him.

It won't give any sound of warning.

M.C. could hear the dude coming on from behind, grunting and stumbling. He could see his pole gleaming down in the yard. He felt drained, weakened. The heavy stillness of the whole outcropping drenched in sunlight was like a scream. The house, shut tight against impact. The trees, wilted and dusty, waiting to be swallowed whole.

Next to the well pump they no longer used was a sunflower. His mother loved the flower, the single one that ever would grow and come back each year. Loved the way it turned its dark roundness always to the sun.

Spoil will just fill up the backyard.

M.C. struggled over car bodies and dragged himself up his pole. His arms flexed too tight. He could feel them hurting as they trembled and jumped. Finally he pulled himself up on the bicycle seat. In a moment he swept the pole out in its long, delicate arc.

Bend my pole so it won't ever straighten out again.

The hills rushed to meet him. A sudden gust of wind made the trees moan before it died. The pole swayed and bowed in an arc of light.

It'll hit the house. But we'll be long gone—will we?

His stomach turned over as the sky rolled down.

We don't want to go, we have to.

With the thought, his strength returned as mysteriously as it had left him. His arms didn't shake as he held them straight out from his sides. He pedaled with all his might as James Lewis made his way with agonizing slowness down to the outcropping.

M.C. tested his strength with a pole trick. He let his feet dangle off the pedals. Gingerly he grabbed hold of the bicycle seat, one hand in front and one in back. He lifted his body up with the strength of his arms and extended his legs out on either side of the pole. It was a difficult and awkward position. He would have liked to pull his legs back in a shaky handstand.

Fall, and snap my neck in two.

He held the position for about five seconds. Then he sat again.

The dude came into the yard behind M.C.

"You're some kind of acrobat," he yelled up at M.C. "And that sure is some kind of pole." He made his way over the junk cars, to crumple finally at the foot of the steel pole.

James Lewis sat, breathing hard for a time, as if he would never get enough air. Again he shouted up to M.C.: "I've seen poles like it before, on a beach down in Florida. But I never have seen a one that could move by pedaling it." His breath broke again and he had to rest.

M.C. slid down the pole. "Sound rises with the heat," M.C. told him. "Don't need to shout."

Pulse beats jumped in Lewis's neck. His mouth was set in a grim line. Worn out, he looked older than he had seemed up on the mountaintop.

"Where'd you ever find a pole like that?" Lewis asked,

finally, mopping his brow with the wet handkerchief.

"Never even found it," M.C. said. "My daddy gave it me for swimming the river."

"The Ohio River?" Lewis asked.

"Yessir," M.C. said.

"You're a swimmer then," Lewis said.

"I'm a hunter, too," M.C. told him.

"A hunter and a swimmer and a pole-setter. What else can you do?" Lewis asked.

"I can do about anything," M.C. said simply. "But what I need," he added, "is someone to carry the other end of my pole."

"Where you planning to take it?" Lewis said. He folded the handkerchief and stuffed it into his shirt pocket.

"Well," M.C. said. He glanced significantly at the tape recorder on the dude's shoulder. "Like to take it with me in case we have to move." He waited for Lewis to tell him they would travel once Lewis had taken his mother's voice.

Lewis looked up the mountain toward the spoil heap. Grimly, he smiled and nodded. "You won't be able to take that pole, son, it'd be too heavy. And anyway, you might have to move real quick."

"I can't leave it." M.C. spoke eagerly, now that he knew that the dude intended them to leave.

Lewis frowned, staring up Sarah's final slope. "To leave a place," he said gently, "you'd best leave everything behind; all your possessions, including memory. Traveling's not as easy as it's made out to be. See, look at my poor old boots." He laughed and held up his trouser leg so M.C. could take a good look at the ruin caused by travel. "But

44

for me, it's worth it all to discover voices like the kind your mother is said to have. Would you call her out here, son, so I can speak to her?"

"Did you think she was home?" M.C. said. He blew out his breath, ashamed he hadn't thought to tell the dude before. "She works and won't be home until darkness."

The dude's face fell.

"All that walk for nothing," M.C. thought to say.

"Oh, now, it's not your fault," Lewis said. "I just took it for granted she'd be here and that was my mistake."

"She'll be here by darkness, you can stay and wait if you want."

"Think I'll go on around and see some others. Some Pitcairn people who group sing?"

"Sure," M.C. said, "in the west plateau."

"I do like to make first contact," Lewis said. "And then I can just come back here around evening time."

"Sure," M.C. said again, "Mama'll be here by dark."

"Can she really sing the way folks like to say?"

"She can sing," M.C. said, "like nobody else." He looked longingly at the tape recorder. Lewis followed his gaze.

"You want to see it?" he said.

"Sure," M.C. said.

"Well, here then." Lewis took it off his shoulder. "Just take it out of the case and lay it on your lap. I've got some banjo playing that I like to listen to and some group singing on it right now, I think. And you know where I got it?"

M.C. put the case on the ground and the recorder on his lap. He touched the machine lightly here and there but he said nothing.

"I got it in Cleveland. Cleveland, of all places," the dude said. "Some brier hop . . . some hill people just moved there. There are thousands of them have moved up from Kentucky. And you know what?"

"What?" M.C. said, the word barely out of his mouth when the dude went on anyway and without a pause.

"They don't only bring their instruments—the banjos and guitars. They bring all of their hounds, their kettles and boards from their barns. *Boards!*" The dude's eyes lit up suddenly through a film of fatigue.

"And every weekend, thousands of them just pile into these cars without windshield wipers or without hardly enough gas—

"—Oh, I don't mean to say some of them don't have new second-hand cars. But the majority, thousands of them, they get on the interstate in anything metal racked-up from Detroit—

"Am I boring you, son?" Lewis said to M.C.

"No." M.C. had time to shape the word before the dude plunged ahead.

"And they head for home over the border, right across there." Lewis gestured beyond the Ohio River where distant mountains loomed. "They kind of flow out on Interstate 60. We lose a few there in about sixteen spectacular highway deaths between Friday, 4:30 P.M., and seven minutes after midnight on Saturday. A portion of them never make it back to that dreamland they loved so much but had to leave—the one they can't wait to get back to when the plant or mill or factory closes on Friday—because they get caught up in the turn-offs every time," the dude said. He shrugged.

"I don't know where they end up. But maybe they roam the interstates forever, growing their gardens on the shoulders of the road."

He laughed uproariously at the picture. M.C. stared at him, awe-struck for a moment. He had one finger on a gray key of the recorder as his mind attempted to grasp the will of thousands to leave home and go back again and again. But he managed to press the key. Soon, music came, and singing. It sounded distant and muffled, not at all like he had thought.

After a time M.C. said, "I've seen smaller ones. Maybe a little heavier. The stores in Harenton have them."

Smiling, James Lewis watched him. Leaning forward, the dude clutched his soiled pant legs at the knees. His face was puffy now with tiredness. He swallowed often.

"You'll never get the way my mama sounds with this," M.C. told him.

"Just an idea of the voice is what I want," Lewis was quick to say. "I'll get that much, if she'll let me. When I have that, I'll have something to work with."

M.C. smiled from ear to ear.

Going to sell Mama to a record company, he thought.

He could see her in a long gown covered with sunflowers, and in a coat of white fur. He felt so good all of a sudden, he wanted to shout loud and long. And he joined in with the music by clapping his hands.

The dude wasn't smiling. He stared at M.C., his eyes unreadable. They flicked away from M.C. as his hand came up, shaking, to his throat. A frown spread over his face as he tried to swallow. Pain.

"Water," Lewis said, hoarsely. "Could I please have some water right away?"

M.C. jumped up. He set the tape recorder on the ground and climbed up on the car junk. Before he jumped down, he caught a glimpse of the river and then the cirque with the lake. The kids were all right. Squinting, he could see they were lying on the shore, drying darker and darker in the sun.

M.C. went inside the house. A moment later he was back with a pitcher of cold water out of the icebox. Lewis took up his canteen and M.C. filled it.

"Here," he said to the dude. "Now just a little. I had that pitcher right next to what little piece of ice is left. It's awful cold."

"All right," Lewis said, his voice a hoarse whisper. He turned up the canteen, pressing it on his parched lips. He took a small swig and then another.

"Lordy," he whispered. And then he drank. When he had finally finished, M.C. filled the canteen again and screwed the top on tight.

Lewis quickly opened the second leather case he carried and took out four sandwiches wrapped in cellophane. He lined them up on the ground. "I've got two egg-salad and two ham and cheese," he said quietly to M.C. "You are welcome to have either kind with me."

M.C. couldn't think when he'd had an egg-salad sandwich. He knew he wasn't to take food or anything else from strangers.

He's a friend, M.C. thought. "I'll have an egg-salad," he said. "You better have the other egg-salad or it will spoil.

48

Save the two ham and cheese. I don't have food to give you."

"I'll just do that," Lewis said.

M.C. had to hurry and eat the delicious egg-salad; then scoot back up the pole in order to watch the children. He told the dude this.

"You can't call it watching them, not from way here, can you?" Lewis asked.

"Watch them everyday," M.C. said.

"I mean, what if something was to happen to them?" Lewis said.

M.C. shook his head. He gobbled the food and drank water directly from the pitcher.

Shortly after, he returned the pitcher to the house. When he came back, he said, "I have to go up. You going to stay?"

"No," Lewis said. "Think I'll go on, see what I can find. But I'll be back this evening."

"Mama'll be here."

"You tell her I'm coming, will you, son?"

"I sure will tell her," M.C. said.

"You think she'll be too tired to sing?" Lewis asked.

"She sings every night," M.C. said.

Lewis smiled. "Then she knows she's good."

"No sense pretending she's not," M.C. said.

"Well then," Lewis said, "I'll see you later on."

M.C. shimmied up his pole, saying so long to James K. Lewis. At the top, he settled on the bicycle seat, staring out on the expanse of hills. Below him, Lewis still sat, munching on his sandwich. Across from Sarah's, something glinting caught M.C.'s eye. It sparkled in the sun and it was moving, half-hidden by foliage. He watched it, curious for a moment because he couldn't identify what was glinting and moving. Suddenly, it was gone.

"I thank you for the water," James Lewis called up to him. Squinting into the sun, he looked up at the dark form of M.C., forty feet above him. "Hope you don't mind if I just rest here a little while longer, get up all my energy."

"Sure," M.C. said mildly. "And thank you for the sandwich. Better be careful, though," M.C. told him. "Saw something I can't figure moving out there. . . ." He had only wanted to sound important, like the dude. But then he paused, remembering the morning and the nice kind of surprise he had discovered on the path to home. He had to smile.

"What kind of something?" Lewis called.

"There's some girl out there," M.C. said. "Saw her early, just walking along. Some new kind of a girl. And just now I saw something shining. But I don't see it now. Don't know if it's the girl for sure. You have any protection against girls?" He laughed.

The dude smiled up at M.C. "Is she a pretty little thing with a back pack?"

"Sure, a green pack," M.C. said. "You know her?"

"Why, yes," the dude said. "She's my ride."

"What?"

"My ride. My ride. She brought me into Harenton. She's got a little car. Picked me up on the road."

"Oh," M.C. said. He was both disappointed to hear that the dude had no automobile and that the girl was old enough to drive one.

"Nice kind of little girl," the dude said, "just moving around. Kind of moody, though, trying to figure things out, I guess. Now was she bothering you, son?"

M.C. could hear the amusement in Lewis's voice.

"If I see her, I'll tell her she's bothering you," Lewis said.

"Shoot," M.C. said, and snickered.

Lewis laughed. Later he gathered up his canteen, the tape recorder and the leather sandwich case. M.C. heard him scramble and strain his way up the slope of Sarah's Mountain. Why the dude felt he had to climb up in order to get down was beyond M.C.'s understanding.

Guess up is easier than down for him, M.C. thought.

He never did see the dude climb out over the gully at the foot of Sarah's.

"He'll make it all right," M.C. told himself, and then: "Hope that girl gets lost." He studied the hills, but could see no one, not even a glint. "Then I'll have to find her and lead her by the hand." Smugly he turned his face to the sky and swung his gleaming pole into the stifling air.

3

M.C. called an odd, impelling yodel over to the lake in the cirque about a minute before the steel mill whistle blew for lunch.

"Yad'dlo! Yo'dlay-dio! D'lay-dio!"

He gave it off with time enough for it to echo around the hills. He knew it was a peculiar sound and hoped the dude out there somewhere could hear. Get an idea of how his mama would sound. M.C. hurt his throat, too, pitching the yodel high and loud enough to outdistance the sounds drifting from the river and out from Harenton.

Other yodel cries echoed ordinary, as commonplace as horns of river boats. Mothers calling their children home and children yodeling sassy, answering back. Only M.C.'s yodel seemed to spread out over the hills with a rolling, yearning minor cadence. It caused his brothers and sisters to pause. From the cirque, they looked over to Sarah's Mountain.

M.C. swept his arm slowly out and back to his chest, motioning the children home. He wasn't certain they could see him in the midst of the trees. But he could see them. He saw his sister, Macie Pearl, stamp her feet and shake her legs like a young pony ready to break loose.

The mill whistle rose like a welt on the air as the three Higgins children moved away from the cirque and lake. M.C. kept them in sight until they disappeared through scrub trees of a pass through hills. He waited with arms folded over his chest. Sitting so still, he looked like a totem. But he held close the excitement of the dude's coming and going. He actually felt peaceful, knowing that Mr. James K. Lewis would come again.

I won't mind leaving, he said to himself.

Never seen a big city like Chicago. Never even seen any kind of big city. Get me a prairie dog for a pet.

It took M.C.'s brothers and sister nearly half an hour to break out of the scrub trees and come down over the hill across from Sarah's. In a ragged line, they disappeared in the gully and emerged again. They scrambled up the side of the mountain. M.C. watched them come. Macie Pearl was in the lead, not because she was fastest or in the most hurry, but because she was the smallest and liked to pretend she was the biggest.

They came out of the undergrowth of sweetbrier and raced across the yard to stand near M.C.'s pole. Macie Pearl leaped up on a car fender. Her knees were scabby and already scraped and bleeding again. It hurt M.C. to see her spindly legs always so full of scratches. And he didn't have not one piece of adhesive tape or bandage.

Leaning far out from the fender, she jumped and tried to climb M.C.'s pole. Scratchy, hungry bird, she couldn't get a firm grip on the smooth, gleaming steel.

"M.C., it's cold as ice!" she called. "How come your pole never will warm up with the sun?"

"It'll warm up by evening," M.C. said. "Stay warm almost 'til morning. Now leave it alone."

"Let me climb it when I'm big?" his brother Harper asked. "Let me sit up there and pedal and make the pole move?"

"When you're way big as me," M.C. said.

They all looked up at him, shielding their eyes from the sky full of burning light. They could see only the blackened figure of him against the blue, swaying with the strange and marvelous rhythms of the pole.

They believed the pole moved by pedaling. But the pedals and wheels were not of any use. It had been M.C.'s fancy to make the children cherish the pole even more than they would have, by putting shiny wheels and hard-looking pedals on it. He had never taken the time to figure out why he had needed them to cherish it. But he guessed he just wanted them to love it the way he loved it.

Only prize I ever won, he thought. Sure will hate leaving it.

"You all get inside," he yelled down. "Lennie, you set the table," he told his youngest brother. "Jones is coming."

M.C. called his father Jones to get himself in a mood for

play. And to get himself ready to soften up Jones in order to tell him about the dude. The children hurried inside.

The vague grind and hum of mining machines drifting out of the hills had ceased for the lunch hour. Most of the time, M.C. was conscious he had been hearing their noise only after it stopped. Now it was quiet behind Sarah's Mountain and all around, except for the sound of cars heard from Harenton. Somewhere in the flatter land to the west, there was a supershovel twenty stories high, and moving closer, some said. M.C. had never seen it.

Wonder if it's real?

Once, just before noontime, he thought he'd heard it, growling like a mountain coming to life.

M.C. listened, but heard nothing unusual. He sat, flexing the muscles in his left arm while gazing peacefully out toward town. Beneath his shirt, his arm was rock hard. The feel of its strength—all his own—made him smile.

"Hurry up, Jones," he said softly.

Jones Higgins always rode M.C.'s beat-up bicycle through the foothills. There had been a time when M.C. hadn't the strength yet to ride the bike on the hills. But now he could ride it better than Jones, two hundred feet up and then down. Lately it seemed to get harder and harder for Jones to make the trip from the steel mill to home.

His daddy: "*M.C., don't you never live in no steel town and work in no steel mill. Now me, I like steel but I don't have no union. No yard labor by the day has the union. But give me the union and I'll be the best in the open hearth.*

I'll be the best crane man they ever seen. I got the kind of hands for a crane machine if I just had the union."

M.C. grinned now as his father broke over the summit of a hill. He swung his pole in its graceful sweep as Jones speeded down the slope. Riding too fast to see where he was going, his father hit a hole. The bike lifted clear off the ground. It hit a bump and skidded sideways. Jones fell off on his side. He rolled over; in a wheeling motion, he got to his feet, grabbed the bike and rode again.

M.C.: *"So you can't have a crane and you can't have a union 'cause you are day labor."*

His daddy: *"That's right."*

M.C.: *"So why don't you get a strip-mining machine? They don't care if you are day labor or if you are union."*

His daddy: *"They ain't machines."*

M.C.: *"They machines just the same as a crane."*

His daddy: *"They don't handle steel. They ain't machines."*

M.C.: *"They handle the earth."*

His daddy: *"They ain't machines."*

M.C.: *"So what are they, Daddy?"*

His daddy: *"They a heathen. A destroyer. They ain't machines."*

Jones rode the bicycle twisted forward over the handlebars, like a hunchback. He appeared like a phantom only to disappear again in the trees. He came back into view, suddenly, speeding down the last foothill across from Sarah's. He narrowly missed rocks and clumps of trees as he hurtled down. At the base of the hill, he slid to a stop in a cloud

56

of dry earth dust. Then he walked the bike down into the gully and on up the side of Sarah's.

M.C. prepared to slide down his pole. First he stood with his feet balanced on the pedals. Then he squatted down until he had a firm hold on the pole below the wheels. He pushed his feet off the pedals one at a time and gingerly hung from the pole by the full strength of his hands and arms. When his back muscles tightened to the point of pain, he wrapped his legs around the pole and slid slowly, easily, down.

He went quickly to the grape arbor built on the near side of the house. The leaves concealed a water spigot connected to the house. The arbor was green now but skimpy. Grapes grew small and not at all sweet to the taste.

Used to be Mama could make quarts of jelly out of a yield, M.C. thought, but not now.

Reluctantly, he thought of the mining cut at the top of Sarah's, and the harsh acids that washed down when it rained.

Did they poison the grapes?

He felt a momentary dread. But he calmed down, thinking of the dude.

M.C. connected the hose to the water spigot. He opened cold and hot water valves on either side, mixing the water from the spigot to a warm flow. Both hot and cold water had the same source, the well with its pump at the rear of the house. No longer did they need to use the pump, for water came from the well through the spigot under pressure. There was a force pump in the crawl space under the house. M.C. and Jones had connected a hot-water tank to one pipeline from the well. They had been lucky to find the tank with just one busted seam. And they had taken it, rolling it the miles to the mill to have it soldered and seamed. For a month they had covered it with brush and pine boughs at nightfall so no one would steal it. Now M.C.'s family was one of the few in these hills who had both hot and cold running water.

Jones Higgins was about to die from exhaustion and from the searing midday heat. He threw down the bike with a loud clatter, as if he couldn't stand to touch it a second longer, as though its rusted, twisted metal was poker hot. The bicycle chain jumped off its track on impact. But Jones didn't stop. He peeled off his shirt and overalls once he was moving on the path through the sweetbrier. He glanced back at the stricken bike and cursed with all of the meanness he had in him after a morning at the mill.

"M.C.," he yelled, meaning for M.C. to come fetch the bike and fix the chain.

M.C. didn't move.

By the time Jones reached the grape arbor, he had stripped down to his undershirt and shorts. Panting and sweating, his brown skin glistening, he tore off his undershirt and handed the whole bundle of salt-stiff clothes to M.C.

"Whyn't you answer somebody when somebody calls?" he said. His eyes were shot through with bloodlines. They were fierce but with a hint of warmth, as though he waited for something.

"Hi," M.C. said softly. He expected no answer and got

none as he passed the clothes through the side window to his oldest brother. Harper snatched them up and disappeared.

M.C. took up the hose. Shielding the spigot with his body, he turned on only one faucet. He spun around, aiming the hose. He let Jones have all the force of cold well water full in the face.

Jones had his mouth open, ready to say something. He had just inhaled when icy water hit him. He doubled over, but M.C. kept the flow from the hose trained on his mouth.

Gleefully, M.C. moved in closer. He laughed and laughed as he sprayed his father's ears and neck and soaked his underwear.

One child and then another peeked out through the window. No sooner had they seen what was going on than they darted away and out of sight.

"Confound you . . . trying to drown me . . . you son of a gun . . . you . . . you're going to get it this time. . . ." Jones choked out the words and sat down on the wet ground, his body trembling with cold. He coughed and sputtered.

M.C. whooped and shouted. It was the first time in a long while that he had caught his daddy off guard. Swiftly he swung the hose around and sprayed Jones from head to foot.

Jones jerked with cold spasms. But suddenly he was on his feet again. He forced himself forward, heading right into the spray. In a crouch, his hands were in a position for sparring.

Instantly M.C. dropped the hose. He moved around Jones as Jones stalked him. His gaze never left his daddy's eyes with the lashes now soaked into points like star tips.

M.C. raised his hands in front of his chin and held them about a foot apart with palms facing each other. He knew his daddy would want to play the game, although they hadn't played it in many months. Years ago it had been the hardest kind of game for M.C. to take. Jones had tried to slap M.C.'s face hard, as he would attempt to do now. Only then M.C. never had been fast enough to chop his father's hands away. He always ended up crying.

M.C.: *"Stop it. Stop it, Daddy."*

His daddy: *"Going to make you so tough, anyone try to worry you will break his bones."*

Jones moved in with a lightning swat toward M.C.'s cheek. But M.C. broke its force with a powerful cut with the side of his hand.

"Ouch!" Jones yelled.

"Sure! Come on," M.C. said, "try to get in."

Jones leaned close to M.C., but try as he might, he couldn't get anywhere near M.C.'s face. His blows landed as fouls on M.C.'s hard arms or sharp elbows. Or they were broken by M.C.'s tough palms like scoop shovels.

Jones rubbed his hands. A frown of pain crossed his face. All at once he let his arms drop to his sides, signaling time out. M.C. continued to hold his own hands up in defense.

"You're getting good," Jones told him.

M.C. nodded, waiting.

"I wasn't trying too hard, though," Jones said.

M.C. had to smile. "Admit you can't get in," he said.

"Never," Jones said.

"Go on," M.C. said, grinning, "admit I'm too good for you."

Jones shook his head. "No sir." Dripping with cold, his arms and legs were covered with goose flesh. He eyed M.C. and then began backing away from him.

M.C. watched him a moment, not comprehending what his father was up to. When Jones reached the yard near the junk, M.C. caught on.

"Hey!" he yelled.

Jones was scrambling over car bodies.

"Get away from my pole!"

Jones leaned out and grabbed the pole above his head.

"Get away! It's mine, you can't climb it!"

"Dollar says I can." Jones twisted his legs around the pole. Pushing with his thigh muscles, he tried to scoot up it. He would shimmy up a foot or two only to slide slowly down to the bottom again.

"You gambled and lost! Hee!" M.C. shouted.

Frantically, Jones pumped and pushed, but try as he might, he couldn't get more than a few feet up the pole.

"Dollar-dollar!" M.C. said. "You see? There's a secret to it and only *I* know what it is."

"What's the secret?" Jones said.

"Never tell you," M.C. answered.

For a moment Jones rested. Then he let go of the pole and climbed back over the car junk looking sheepish. "I could have done it," he said, coming across to M.C., "but I been working all morning and I'm all wet, besides."

"You're getting too old," M.C. said, with mock sadness.

Jones hugged his shoulders, shivering. "Old, nothing," he said. "Just tired is all." There was a wistful tone in his voice before it was gone.

M.C. took up the hose again. "Dollar-dollar. You said so," he told his father.

"I know what I said. I'm good for it," Jones answered.

M.C. was surprised and pleased at the sudden windfall of money. He ended the game by opening the hot-water faucet and spraying his father with warm water.

The chalk color caused by caked salt from Jones's sweat washed off his skin. Soon he would be his own true black self again. He sat back down on the ground. Breathing deeply, he rubbed his chest contentedly.

But there was a glint in his eye when he looked up at M.C. "I'll have to get you one time," he said. "Any minute, before this day is done, I'm going to even the score."

"Bet you won't," M.C. said.

"You want to bet that dollar?" Jones asked him.

"No," M.C. said. "Easiest dollar I ever made."

Their playing had taken only a few minutes. Now he wouldn't come too close to his father, even though Jones looked worn out.

"Think I'll tell your mama on you, instead. Playing tricks on me," Jones said.

M.C. looked down at his feet. Even Jones suddenly looked uncomfortable. Both of them knew it wasn't fair to bring his mother, Banina, into fooling-around business, when she had to be gone the whole time, and they missing her.

"Take that pole of yours and wrap it around your head," Jones said, by way of getting his wife off his mind.

"Touch my pole again, and you won't ever stand up."

M.C. had barely got the words out when Jones was on

him, wrestling him to the ground. He had knocked M.C. down and had pinned him before M.C. realized he was lying with the hose running water under him. Jones took up the hose and put it down the back of M.C.'s pants. He smiled at his son. Planting his knees just above M.C.'s hips, he squeezed, too hard.

Pain took M.C.'s breath away. He tried to warn Jones with his eyes. Jones squeezed twice, and each time M.C.'s waist and shoulders jerked off the ground. Finally M.C. managed to scream.

Instantly Jones leaped away. "Did I hurt you? I didn't mean to hurt you," he said, anxiously.

Holding back tears, M.C. forced himself not to cry.

"I don't know my own strength," Jones said. He bent over to help M.C. up.

"Wasn't trying to hurt *you*," M.C. said. A moment ago they had been playing. Sure, they played rough, but he had got his father in a rare good mood. Now there was tension between them and he hated to admit that his father was still the stronger.

"I wasn't trying to hurt you, either," Jones was saying. "But sometimes you do take too much on yourself."

"I was just *playing*," M.C. said.

"Okay," Jones spoke calmly. "But you get to thinking because you can swim and because of that pole, you are some M.C. Higgins, the Great."

"I never thought it!" M.C. said.

"Just mind who was it taught you to swim and who was it gave you the pole," Jones said. "Now come on, hose me good. I have to get back to the mill business."

M.C. did as he was told. And yet he felt a sullen anger at his father and an abiding admiration at the same time, he didn't know why. The hard-edge pain at his waist was now a dull kind of throb. He hosed Jones from head to foot, aware that he and his father greatly resembled one another.

Jones was a powerfully built man. He wasn't tall, but he had a broad chest and lean but wide, muscular shoulders. He was narrow through the hips just as M.C. was, and his legs were long with muscles grown lengthwise. His toes were splayed with the bridge flattened wide, as were M.C.'s, the way a swimmer's feet will look. Jones was a swimmer. But somehow, his fine, physical equipment had never quite come together. As a man, he wasn't as good a swimmer as M.C. was right now.

What will I be, at his age? M.C. wondered.

Be on this mountain, his mind spoke for Jones.

No, M.C. thought.

His brother, Lennie Pool, thrust a clean towel and a dry pair of shorts out of the window. M.C. shut off the hose, took the clothes and towel and handed them to Jones. Automatically, he turned his back to his father so Jones could wipe dry, take off his wet underwear and put on the fresh pair.

M.C. went inside the house into the kitchen. There, Macie Pearl had pulled four chairs and a crate covered with blue linoleum up to the kitchen table. The children had taken from the icebox the greens with pork butt and cornbread which M.C. had prepared the night before. They had warmed all of it in the oven of the wood-burning cook stove. M.C. found that the food in the oven was hot and ready to eat. He dished it out onto plates Macie handed him. Then he poured milk into brown cups for Macie and Lennie Pool. Lennie got just half a cup even though he was bigger because he tended to spill a full cup. It was Macie Pearl who could have most of the milk. If she left it over, Lennie could have it. And if he didn't want it, the next in line to get it could have it.

The children stared at M.C. in his soaking wet clothes. He went by them, passing through his father and mother's bedroom into the place given to him for himself.

Jones had cut through the wall and clapboard of the house right on into Sarah's Mountain. M.C.'s room was a cave dug out of Sarah's side for him. The cave was always cool, no matter how the weather was outside. M.C. liked the space of it, with his bed made of oak jutting from the middle of a cave wall. He liked the way the walls were plastered and whitewashed, forever giving off a scent of lime.

Jones had braced the ceiling with oak beams so that the mountain would not come falling down on M.C. in the dark of dreams. There was one light bulb hanging down from a beam. There was a straw rug. There were objects M.C. had collected and arranged on a block of wood, and his few clothes on hooks by the bed. That was all. It would take him no more than ten minutes to pack his belongings.

There were no windows.

M.C. put on dry clothes. From the block of wood, he took up the kitchen paring knife he kept clean and sharpened in case he felt like hunting. He tested the blade and then wrapped it in a piece of rabbit fur. Carefully he pocketed the knife with the handle down.

All three rooms, the cave, his parents' bedroom and the kitchen, were in a straight line. Jones had come into his own bedroom to put on dry, fresh work clothes and had gone back out to eat. M.C. stood in the cave buttoning his shirt. He could see all the children and Jones seated at the kitchen table, quietly eating. He didn't feel hungry. He felt worn out.

As he watched the shadowy figures in the kitchen, his thoughts seemed to float away from him. He fell into a kind of reverie as he heard, deep in his mind, a wild creature's roar. He thought he must be out somewhere hunting in the hills when he was not quite old enough for the silence and the darkness. He must be tracking when he was not yet brave enough for the feel of tall, black trees behind his back. He saw something, a silhouette there in the forest waiting for him. Or was he the image, waiting for another part of himself to reach it? He tried to move toward it when a numbing cold rose around his ankles. It climbed to his knees and then his neck. His leg muscles jumped, but he could not run. He was rooted to the mountainside as the sour and bitter mud of the spoil oozed into his mouth and nostrils. At the last moment before he suffered and died, he knew he was not outside. He was still in his cave, his fingers on the buttons of his shirt.

Jones was turned around from the table. "M.C.?"

M.C. shook himself seemingly awake.

"What you standing there like that for?" Jones said. "Come on out here and get you something to eat."

In a moment M.C. had seated himself on the crate next to his father's chair. Jones looked at him narrowly and passed food to him, but said nothing. M.C. took a little to eat as Macie Pearl reached over and pressed her hand on his cheek. Her fingers came away wet with the sweat from his skin.

"You all were fighting outside the house," she said simply.

"Macie, you worry so much," Jones told her.

"She's not worrying," Harper said. "She has to nose."

"Stop it," Jones told him. "We weren't fighting," he said. "We were just playing." He glanced at M.C.

M.C. was silent, thinking about what he had seen in his mind just now in the cave.

Abruptly, he said, "The dude was here."

They all stared at him. "He was?" Harper said.

"A Mr. James K. Lewis," M.C. said, "looking for Mama . . ." He stopped, uncertain whether this was the moment to tell his father they would have to leave.

"Mama won't be home until darkness," Harper said. "I heard her say so even when I was still asleep."

At the mention of their mother, Macie suddenly began to cry. Tears fell to her cheeks like silver beads. Jones patted her a minute. "She'll be home by darkness, you stop it now," he said.

M.C. blurted it out: "He was just looking to get Mama's voice down. Say he's coming back tonight for sure.

Should've seen him, with the best clothes and everything. Boots all muddy—he let me listen to his tape recorder."

M.C. stared at all of them watching him. "He going to take Mama out of here. Make some records with her."

Macie sucked in her breath, her eyes glistening through tears. Lennie Pool began to bob up and down.

"Everybody says she's good," M.C. said eagerly. "Dude couldn't wait to hear her. She going to have to go."

"That's something," Jones said, clearly impressed. "You sure you got it right?"

"Sure, I'm sure," M.C. said.

"Well, if she's got to make records, she's got to make records," Jones said.

"She can't go off to Chicago by herself," M.C. said. He waited, afraid to breathe.

"Who said anything about Chicago?" Jones said.

"That's where the dude come from, he told me," M.C. said.

"But that's not where they make the records," Jones said. "All Banina has to do is catch the bus to Nashville. She'll be there in a few hours and be back in maybe two days. Nashville is where they make the records."

"Mama will be a star singer," Harper whispered.

"She's a stone singer right now," Jones said, "but it'll take a little time for her star to rise." Never doubting that it would rise, he laughed and began eating again.

Stunned, M.C. sat silent. His mother would go to Nashville and they would stay behind.

I had it too fast.

They would have to wait for her to become a star and they didn't have time to lose.

How am I going to get him to leave? Why come he can't see that spoil is going to fall, when even a dude out of nowhere can see it? When the kids can. They don't say nothing 'cause it scares them. But they can see it. He *must* see it. So what does he think he's doing?

M.C. felt alone, desolate. He stalked out of the house and stood on the porch, unable to fathom his father or to think what to do.

Soon the children came, grabbing at him. Swiftly he shook them off and roughly shoved them away. He raced for his pole and climbed it as Macie happily leaped up on the junk. She pulled out a chrome strip bent into a small stick. She commenced to beat the pole with it, causing piercing vibrations along its length.

Jones came out of the house and stood on the step, watching his children jumping around like crazy. Where they got their energy in the heat, he'd never know, his look seemed to say. They surely could be foolish one minute and with good sense the next.

He gazed up at M.C. on his pole with a look of pride for his difference, but with caution, too.

"You stay on the mountain, you hear?" he called to M.C. "Keep these kids to home until I come off from work." When M.C. paid him no attention, he added, "I'll be going in a minute."

Jones went inside. When he came out a few minutes later, M.C. still said not a word to him. He wouldn't even give a glance down at Jones's leaving. He wouldn't pay any mind to the kids, less interested in saying good-by to their father than they were in play-fighting one another to be first to climb M.C.'s pole.

Later, M.C. thought. Tell him just like the dude told me. It's sliding down. Makes no kind of sense to stay. We have to leave. He can't say no—can he?

4

M.C. sat up straight with his hands folded over his knees. Relaxed now, he was prepared for his mother's coming home. For the dude. But evening was still a long way off.

Jones had come home from work a little after 4:30. He had worked a full day. But the foreman at the mill had told him, no use for him to come back before next week since everybody in the yard felt strong and there probably would be no sickness before then. Jones would have no work for the rest of this week.

Now Jones scraped his feet on the floorboards as he eased down next to M.C. on the first step below the front porch. M.C. caught a whiff of Jones's freshly washed hair. It gave off an odor of Fels-Naphtha as did his skin.

They breathed the wind, gusting and dying; the trees, giving off a sweet, hot scent.

"Just about smell the fall coming," Jones said. "In another week or two, I will for sure."

Lennie Pool, Harper and Macie Pearl stood around the edge of the porch. They wanted to go into Harenton and waited, fidgeting, for either M.C. or Jones to release them. Most of the time, the children were in M.C.'s care. But when Jones was home, he usually took over. When he was too tired to bother with them, he would let M.C. be their judge.

M.C. didn't want them to go to Harenton. He'd had to stay on the mountain all day watching over them. Now make them stay home and make Jones watch them. Meanness, anger, welled up inside him.

"Something out there," he told Jones. He kept his voice low so the children wouldn't hear.

"Talking about the dude?" Jones said.

"No. Something else. And there's a girl, some kind," M.C. said. "She back-pack her way and she walking around quiet. Dude say she pick him up hitchhiking." Suddenly, he wished he could tell his father that the dude had a big, shiny automobile. "She just follow him in here, I guess," M.C. finished.

"You see her for sure?" Jones asked.

M.C. studied his knuckles. "I ran into her on Sarah's High." He tried to stifle a smile, but was unable to before Jones had seen it.

"When?" Jones asked.

"This morning."

72

"Funny you didn't mention her before now," Jones said. He fixed M.C. with a cool gaze. "Bet you said good morning to her real polite. And then you sidestepped her and went on your way."

M.C. hung his head, but he couldn't hold back the smile.

"Or you told her she could come up here and visit after I'd gone back to work," Jones said softly.

M.C. looked sharply at his father. It hadn't occurred to him to say anything to the girl.

"Better tell me," Jones said. "I can ask Macie and find out, anyway."

"I didn't ask her nothing," M.C. said. "I didn't say a word to her."

"That's about as wrong as being smart," Jones told him. "If you see somebody is a stranger, you act polite until you see what they're up to. That's how you show you have some manners and find out something besides."

He gave the children a bunch of pennies he had in his pockets. Shyly they took the money; then they raced down the side of Sarah's to reach the big five and dime in town before its six o'clock Monday closing.

Jones laughed harshly to see them run. "Nobody catch them kids, not when they have money to spend. Look at them go."

M.C. stayed quiet, thinking about being polite if he ever ran into the girl again.

Jones sighed deeply and in a ragged breath. His eyes were red-rimmed from tiredness. "Me, I'm too whipped," he said.

Shyly, M.C. turned to his father. "I know it, you," he

said. He could feel himself inside, reaching out for his father and taking him in.

It wasn't often that he and Jones could sit down together without Jones having to test him or think up a game to see if he could win it. He knew Jones only wanted to have him strong and to have him win. But he wished his father wouldn't always have to teach him.

Just have him listen to me, M.C. thought. Have him hear.

Maybe now he and Jones were sitting without a war between them. Maybe he could speak about what was on his mind.

"Daddy?" he said, "you taken a look up there, at the spoil heap behind us?"

"Way behind us," Jones said, easily and without a pause. He was looking off at the hills he loved and at the river holding light at the end of the day. He was thinking about his wife, his Banina, who would not have had time yet to concern herself with coming home. But in another hour or so, she would think about it. She would say to herself, *It's time!* No clock was needed to show her. From where she was across-river, she could look away to these hills. She might even be able to see M.C.'s needle of a pole. No, not likely. But maybe a sparkle, maybe a piercing flash in the corner of her eye. She would have to smile and come on home.

Jones sighed contentedly.

"Daddy," M.C. said, "it can cause a landslide. It can just cover this house and ground."

"That's what's bothering you?" Jones asked. "That's why you were standing tranced in the cave. You thought I didn't

74

know but I did. You worry about everything you don't need to worry from."

A shudder passed over M.C. like a heavy chill. Jones studied M.C.'s face. M.C. was so skilled at living free in the woods, at reading animal signs, at knowing when the weather would change even slightly. Jones could convince himself at odd moments that the boy had second sight. And now, half afraid to ask but worried for his children on their way to Harenton, his Banina, he said, "What is it you see?"

M.C.'s eyes reflected light bouncing green and brown from one hill to another. Deep within the light was something as thick as forest shadow.

"Just some rain coming from behind us," M.C. said. "You listen and you can maybe hear it come up Sarah's other side." There was more. It was a feeling M.C. hadn't known before. He kept it to himself.

Jones stepped off the porch and turned around in order to see behind him. Beyond the rim of the outcropping, he saw Sarah's final slope with shade slanting halfway across it, and trees, made more dense with late-day shadow. As the trees appeared heavier this time of day, Sarah's seemed to pierce the sky.

Jones gazed at the spoil and beyond it to the bare summit where he had spent so much time with M.C. when the boy was small. Looking, he remembered how he had taught M.C. all he knew about hunting bare-handed. He recalled Sarah's cut, trees falling.

Now he listened. He saw the sky grow heavy with mist as he watched. It turned gray and, finally, dark. He heard sound coming. Rain, like hundreds of mice running through corn. He watched it come over the mountain and down the slope in a straight line.

M.C. hadn't bothered to move from the step. He had already felt the rain, seen it without seeing.

Wind hit Jones first. It ran before the rain. Jones didn't want his clothes soaked, so he stepped onto the porch while rain came full of mist, but hard all the same.

They watched it. The rain marched down Sarah's and on across, turning hill after hill the same shade of silver mist clear to the river. Then it was gone from the mountain. As it had come, clawing through cornstalk, it vanished with the same familiar sound.

"Huh," Jones grunted. "That will cool it off maybe a minute. Wish it would rain hard enough to fill up that gully. Then I could take me a swim without sweating a mile to do it."

M.C. had his mind on the spoil heap. He couldn't see it but he could feel it, the way he felt Sarah's above him pressing in on him when he lay in his cave room.

"It holds the water," he told his daddy, "just hanging on up there. It'll rain again and it'll grow just like it's alive."

"Now why did you have to catch hold of that all of a sudden?" Jones asked him. "You get something in your head, I swear, you don't let it go. Glad when school gets going. Catch hold of your math work like that one time. Don't talk to me no more," he added and sat down again on the step.

The step was wet. So was M.C., who seemed not to

notice. The rain was just dripping now. The mist had grown intense with light.

"It already cover all the trees they root up," M.C. forced himself on. "It'll tear loose, maybe just a piece. But without a warning. Maybe a roar, and sliding into the yard and trying to climb my pole."

"Quit it," Jones said. "Just . . . don't talk to me."

M.C. couldn't tell if there was any worry in his father's face. He could see only an intensity of anger at being bothered.

Suddenly the sun came out. M.C. bowed his head until the light leveled off, softened and shaped by the green of hills.

Doesn't even hear me, M.C. thought. Fool, Daddy. All at once, he wanted to be back up on his pole.

Dude'll have to tell him. He'll have to listen.

Bright sunlight began to dry up the truth seen so easily in the rain.

"These old mountains," Jones said. He looked out over the side of Sarah's and beyond. "They are really something."

M.C. stayed quiet. Sullen.

"It's a *feeling*," Jones said. "Like, to think a solid piece of something big belongs to you. To your father, and his, too." Jones rubbed and twisted his hands, as if they ached him. "And you to it, for a long kind of time." He laughed softly. To M.C., it sounded full of sadness.

"Granddaddy came here in his mama's, Sarah's, arms," Jones said quietly. "She wasn't free yet. The war wasn't

77

started but it was coming. Only Sarah couldn't wait. I expect she ran until she found a place big enough to free her troubles. Just the clothes on her back, that half-dead child and the song she sang to him, my granddaddy. He grew up and sang it to my daddy. And he to me."

And then Jones began the weirdest chant: "*O bola*," he sang, "*Coo-pa-yani, Si na-ma-gamma, O deh-kah-no.*"

M.C. stared at his father. Jones looked embarrassed. "Don't know how I forgot it this long. Sing it always to the sons. One son to another, down the line."

"Daddy!" M.C. whispered, awed and excited by the sound of the words. "What does it mean?"

"Well, I had a *feeling* I knew, once," Jones said. "But I guess even Great-grandmother Sarah never knew. Just a piece of her language she remembered."

"Does it mean something pretty?" M.C. asked. They sat, close and still.

"It might just mean something too awful to forget," Jones said. "We'll never know."

M.C. felt awed by the past's enormous mystery.

"Is there more about Sarah?" he asked.

"Just only two more things," Jones said. "The one is that there's an old title I have to this mountain slope. Show it to you sometime. Says deeded fee simple from McKelroy lands to Sarah McHigan, 1854."

"McHigan?" M.C. said.

"He was the one she married, but he was sold away from her. That was maybe one reason she ran in the first place. McHigan, and then later in Granddaddy's time, changed to Higgins."

"Man, I sure don't remember hearing about that," M.C. said softly.

"I must of told you," Jones said, "but you were little."

"Man," M.C. said again, and then: "What's the other thing? You said there were two things."

He looked at Jones and Jones looked at him. "You can believe it," Jones began, "or you can misbelieve it. But I know and your mama knows. Times, in the heat of the day. When you not thinking much on nothing. When you are resting quiet. Trees, dusty-still. You can hear Sarah a-laboring up the mountain, the baby, whimpering. She say, 'Shhh! Shhh!' like a breeze. But no breeze, no movement. It's just only Sarah, as of old."

"I know," M.C. said, simply.

"You know?" Jones said.

"When I'm all alone," M.C. told him, "up on my pole, all of a sudden, I know she is coming."

"Yea, Lord," Jones said.

"It scare me so," M.C. said.

"Don't you be afraid," Jones said quietly. "For she not show you a vision of her. No ghost. She climbs eternal. Just to remind us that she hold claim to me and to you and each one of us on her mountain."

They fell silent. Between them now was the *feeling* Jones had spoken about. M.C. recognized its nameless certainty. Whatever happened would be the same for both of them. For a moment, he believed that. But truth had its way.

How the same, M.C. thought, if he won't leave the mountain?

Abruptly, he said, "Daddy, sing that song again."

Jones chanted it again, slapping his knee on the offbeat:

O bola
Coo-pa-yani,
Si na-ma-gama
O deh-kah-no.

When he had finished, Jones turned to M.C. "We've always lived here," he said. "The children can stay put forever if they want. Raise their families, whatever. But you are the one responsible."

"I know," M.C. said. He could feel the rope within that bound him to the mountain. It was always there, like a pressure on his mind.

"You figure you will want to leave someday?" Jones asked him.

Never had M.C. thought of going away from his family. He knew only that they all had to leave the mountain.

"Maybe someday," he managed to say.

"Maybe tomorrow or the next day?" Jones asked him.

"I'll wait awhile."

"What you figure you're waiting for?" Jones said, with a glint of play in his eyes.

"Maybe to see what will happen," M.C. said, vaguely.

"You'll be here a long while," Jones said. He laughed.

"Maybe not so long."

"You see something then?"

M.C. sighed. "I try to tell you," he said, "nothing like reading the future."

"Then what's it like?"

Sadly, M.C. searched for the words: "See it when something's to happen. Feel the whole thing in my mind."

"I say, do you feel something? Do you see it?" Jones asked.

"The spoil heap is going to slide."

"There you go again, like a broken record," Jones said.

"You asked me," M.C. said.

"Now if the spoil fell," Jones said, "would it have to hit the house?"

"No," M.C. said slowly, "but it could. It probably would."

"Since it's been there, has any bit of it ever fallen?"

"No," M.C. had to admit.

"You'll be here a long while," Jones said, smiling to himself.

"Maybe not," M.C. said under his breath.

Jones began another tune. At first M.C. thought it was going to be the one with the strange words, but it wasn't.

> There she stands by my side
>   It's a cold and clear evening.
> Don't she look just like my bride
>   On a cold, clear evening?
>
> Hug her and kiss her and call her my own
>   And she just might marry me.
> On a cold. On a cold, cold,
>   On a cold, clear, even-ing.

He sang the verse over and over. M.C. wished he would stop it. He blurted out, "Better get over there, wait on the road for Mama."

M.C.'s mother always did catch a ride over the bridge, on the one road that went in and out of Harenton before it veered west.

"You worry too hard," Jones said. "I haven't forgot your mama yet."

"Did you get your day's pay?" M.C. asked him.

"Now you're worrying about my pay?" Jones said.

"I'll keep it for you. Leave it," M.C. said. There were drinking places in Harenton. Suddenly, he feared Jones would spend the money on something foolish, although he rarely did.

"I could leave it," Jones said, "and you might cut out of these hills tonight with it while I'm gone." At once, he looked as if he regretted the words. "Don't always worry so hard," he said, by way of apology.

"Wouldn't want Mama to have to come all that way home by her lonesome," M.C. said. He fell silent and closed his eyes.

Jones had turned to watch his face, M.C. could tell. And deep within, M.C. could feel darkness like thick trees, and something else that he could not name.

Jones stepped off the porch. "Don't worry so hard," he repeated. "I can't collect my pay until around afternoon tomorrow. Meantime—" He fished around in one of his pockets. His hand appeared again, clutching coins. Jones counted them one by one, whispering over them. "Here's most of the dollar I promised. Owe you seventeen cents."

Dollar-dollar. M.C. could feel his throat seem to thicken.

"Take it," Jones said. He grabbed M.C.'s hand and tried to pour the coins in.

M.C. jerked his hand away. "I'm not going to take your last cent."

"Take it," Jones said. "I get me some pay tomorrow."

"I can't do nothing with it up here anyway," M.C. said. "Take it."

"No!" he yelled, with a desperate anger, and love for his father welling inside him. "We don't have even some milk for the kids!"

"Okay, okay," Jones said quietly. But he stood there a moment, as if searching for proper words to speak. None came to him and he walked away from M.C. without a backward glance.

M.C. sat with his eyes closed. Hugging his legs, he rested his chin on his knees. He listened until he could no longer hear his father moving down through the hot silence that was Sarah's Mountain at this time of day. Thoughts and sights flitted in and out of his mind. He pictured Great-great-grandmother Sarah running swiftly, carrying something. She tripped and fell. Something splattered bloody on the ground.

M.C. shuddered. The vision shifted. He saw the spoil, and Jones trapped in it, with mud oozing into his ears. M.C. shook his head rapidly to dislodge the painful sight. He thought about leaving the mountain, where he would go, what he would do. Still he could not imagine leaving without the whole family with him.

Woven through his thoughts was the sound of Jones singing of courting. M.C. tried humming to himself, but he couldn't get rid of the sound. Nothing, not even his pole, could keep away the sad feeling, the lonesome blues of being grown, the way either his mother or his father could with their singing.

Wistfully he wondered if he'd ever care about someone the way Jones cared about his mother. Jones's song was still in his mind when he conjured a picture of Banina, his mother. It was one of his favorite sights of her coming home from a far hill, late.

It was M.C.'s birthday. They had known she would bring something for a present. They were all there on the side of Sarah's, waiting. There were the kids. And there was Jones, trying to look as if he weren't waiting for her half of his life, but not trying too hard. Because Jones didn't mind waiting for Banina forever if he had to. But it was Macie Pearl who hurt most for her mother, who ached for her through every minute of every day without her.

They all would see Banina at the same moment, coming over the last hill across from Sarah's. They would see her in the last light of evening. The sun had gone down over her left shoulder. Dusk came quickly where the hills shut out the light. There was not even a streak of purple gossamer where the sun had gone down. She had walked all the way from the river road where it left Harenton and turned westward. It had taken her most of an hour walking hard. Even though she went down the sides of hills and along passes, she walked mostly on the upward path.

In the pale light, her yellow dress looked white. She paused at the summit across the way. She had seen M.C. on his pole even when she could not for certain recognize the others. His mother leaned back, cupping her hands around her mouth. A yodel cry like no other filled the air.

For a moment there was no sound other than that voice of hers which seemed to fall from the sky:

"Yad d'looka—M.C.—alodaaah . . ." It started low, with breath enough for a long, hard line:

"O-leay-aMama-home-alo. May-alay, alay-a-Macie-o-alaeu." The voice went up the scale with perfect lightness and control.

"Mama!" Macie Pearl screamed. "I see you! Mama, Mama, alay-alaeu!"

There had been laughter, half-mocking before his mother sang again. She waved. M.C. had let his pole out in its sweeping arc. Lennie Pool and Harper raised their arms. With palms seeming flat against the air, they gave a silent salute. Macie was jumping up and down like a starving creature about to be fed.

Then Banina had begun to sing. Coming home, walking with the strength that was tired now but never left her, she sang them how the day had been for her. She sang so all the hills could hear. As night came creeping, came sweeping over the land, her voice told the hills what they already knew, but in a way that only she could tell it.

"Daddy!" Macie had said, going to her father.

"Shhh! I want to hear it all." It was Harper.

"Daddy!" Macie had said again.

Jones grunted. He had been listening, but he shook himself seemingly awake. With one arm, he lifted Macie Pearl onto his shoulders. She held his neck with skinny arms. Her heels dug into his armpits. Then the two of them went down the side of Sarah's. Jones was trotting so that he would reach Banina before she hit the gully and darkness.

M.C., with Lennie and Harper, had waited for that moment when their mother's laughter would explode in the night, when she ran into Jones and Macie in the dark. It happened.

They had heard her talking in that high, hill way she had that gave no hint of the voice behind it. There was still enough light on the outcropping where they waited for them to see her face clearly.

The air had turned slightly cooler, M.C. remembered. There had been a breeze, warm and damp, with rain coming. And then, where there had been only shadow, she was there. Jones, with Macie riding shoulder-high, materialized next to her.

M.C. had given Banina a pole trick. Although it was his day, the trick was his birthday present to her. He took his feet from the pole pedals. Placing his hands on the pedals instead, he balanced his body in a shaky handstand.

Her laughter had exploded again. The contralto sound of it came as if from an echo chamber as it bounced around the hills.

"M.C., honey," she said, "that's real pretty, but you're going to bust your head wide open, like a sweet melon fall down from a wagon. And break your poor mama's heart, too." Then she giggled.

M.C. remembered smiling. He'd kept his face hidden from her until he had slid down the pole to stand before her. He stood there, seeing that light he loved so out of her eyes. She had skin tanned reddish from the sun. It looked dark, smooth and shining with perspiration. She was nearly

86

as tall as M.C., with a posture straight and proud. She was pretty good as a swimmer. Like M.C. and Jones, too, she loved water. Unlike the land, water was something to play in.

With one hand, she had taken M.C. by the shoulder to peer into his face. It was then he noticed she held a shopping bag in the other hand. With her pocketbook inside and on top, she had carried the bag the long distance home.

"I'm fine," M.C. said, without any prompting. They had so little chance to be together, he had answered her unasked question to save time. At once they were deep in conversation.

"You going to swim with me sometime soon?"

"When can you swim if you be working?" he had asked.

"Early," she said, "by dawn light in the cirque. You think you can make it?"

"I'll even let you beat me."

She had laughed and turned from him to the two boys. She set the shopping bag down and reached in under her pocketbook. Her hands came out of the bag, full of something for each of them.

Shyly, the boys came slowly to stand before her. It wasn't their birthday, but they knew she wouldn't forget them. Not until they were close to her did they discover she held three neat sacks of candy. They took the candy and Harper gave one sack to Macie. Silent, looking up at Banina, they had waited to see if that was all. But no, for she had leaned down over them. Soon she and the boys were whispering and giggling, planning some game or other.

Maybe breakfast would be taken at the foot of M.C.'s pole. Or maybe they would all sleep out tonight within the mystery of the grape arbor.

She took her pocketbook out of the shopping bag. Reaching down again, she had come up with a big, square box. She opened it and handed it to M.C. He caught a whiff of chocolate. Cake, just for him to share with them. Last, she handed him a package tied with ribbon. He knew it was a shirt, or something. Socks. Maybe a pair of dress pants. He had been too happy even to say a word of thanks.

"Fall on your bending," she had said softly, then, "I'm tired, me."

Jones had swung Macie down. M.C., with Macie at his heels and the boys behind her, had led them away from the darkness that had encircled them. With the square box of the cake held carefully in front of him, and with the birthday package on top of it, he had been the strutting leader of the parade. Jones had folded Banina to his side and they had all walked into the house away from night.

5

M.C. felt cool all over. For a long while he sat where Jones had left him, remembering the way his mother had come home to them.

No more birthdays here, he thought.

As if waking, he saw that the sun had slipped away from him down the side of Sarah's, across the gully and to the right toward the cirque and the westward river. With his mind remembering, he had been staring riverward. He'd seen something odd for more than fifteen minutes without its registering on his mind. Up from the river, there was something that glinted and flashed. It vanished and then, in a split second, it glinted and flashed again.

Things always did sparkle and glitter along the river.

But not so far from it, he thought.

He grew tense straining to see. He should have moved

sideways so that whatever was glinting wouldn't shine in his eyes. He knew his family ought to be out there somewhere, waiting on the road or just about to start on their way home. He began to worry now, searching for the thing that would suddenly glint, flash at him and suddenly vanish.

For a time he lost it in the trees stretching for miles above the river. He got up and walked over to the side of Sarah's where he could see more of the steel town and the timber line along the hills. Time passed before M.C. spied a glinting flash on the eastern slope of a foothill. He cupped his hands around his eyes, cutting out from his sight all but that one vision.

Not moving steady, he thought. Is it a walking light? No, the glints are too fast. That's what it is. Running . . . to beat the night. It has far still to go? The sun has caught to something. But what glints like that, on and off?

M.C. thought of rushing down there. It would take him time to reach the steel town. Besides, he wanted to be home when the dude came back.

Maybe it's Mr. Lewis. Or the other one.

He thought of the girl: She still out there wandering?

He wondered why his father had supposed he would have spent time with her. Maybe he should have. Maybe he would next time.

Was there to be another time?

He stood utterly still, waiting to see if his mind could tell him. He felt slightly dizzy, as if he were swaying too hard on his pole. Falling into a reverie, he could no longer see the countryside. Instead, he sensed the girl close to him in the darkness. Although she was invisible, he could feel her slight form change and charge the space around him. But then the vivid impression of her faded. Once again he saw hills, daylight.

So that's who, he thought, searching the land.

To catch her moving along without being heard or seen would take a lot of time.

Clear dark down there by then.

He knew how night could be a trap, once the sun had been blotted out by hills.

Would have to move so fast and quiet once I got near her. Like stalking on a hunt.

With his hands in his pockets, one hand touched rabbit fur. It froze a second, and then he remembered he had carried the knife wrapped in fur the whole afternoon.

I'm too tired. Stalking will take muscle.

Dude would stay close to town. Mama and them on the north side, if they've started home.

Has to be the girl.

M.C. had an idea. He rushed inside the house before he knew for sure what he would do with the idea he had. In the kitchen, he looked around, searching for something. Seeing the stove, he remembered he hadn't prepared anything for supper.

Only leftovers. Mama can do that.

He held his hand over the stove and could barely feel heat rising. So he threw in sticks of kindling and a few pieces of coal. He grabbed a box of matches and pocketed them.

Next to the icebox, he saw the bucket and mop with which he was supposed to clean the kitchen after every meal. M.C. felt the mop.

"Wet!" he said. But then, something dawned on him.

Hurry up, he told himself.

He carried the mop to his mother and father's bedroom. The room was semidark. There was a light with a pink shade clamped to the headboard of the bed. Above it on the wall was a calendar with a brown baby smiling.

He could see well enough without a light. The old and worn catalog was on the floor behind the door. Pages were missing from it. He tore out more pages, as many as he could in the few seconds he would allow himself. When he had a bunch, he rolled them up, moving quickly into the kitchen. Next, he pulled long strands from the mop and tied the rolled papers to the mop handle.

He raced back outside. Undoing his belt, he buckled the mop against his body so that the handle with the papers on one side balanced the mop head on the other. He struggled up his pole; by the time he reached the top, his arms ached from the unnatural climb. He positioned himself on the bicycle seat and searched for the glint of light in the hills

Silence all around. Have I lost it?

Searching the low hills, he saw that they had turned dusky. It was evening-time and the hills were letting light slip from their folds. A good time to see something bright. Sure enough, he caught a glinting and a narrow flash out of the corner of his eye.

M.C. jerked his head around to see. He smiled, taking matches from his shirt pocket. Pulling the mop from his belt, he lit the catalog pages tied to the handle. At the moment the rolled pages caught and flamed, he held the mop like a torch above his head. M.C. leaned forward. His pole trembled and flowed out in its long, easy arc.

In the trees at the top of the hill across from Sarah's, there came a glinting that stopped abruptly before it could flash.

M.C. laughed softly. You see something! Is it the pole or just my flame?

And before he thought, he burst out yelling at the top of his lungs: "Hey-hey, pretty! Hey!" shouting in a regular rhythm that echoed, bursting over the hills in a minor key that was bloodcurdling.

In a moment he stopped. He looked around, embarrassed. He ducked his head, as if to hide himself, swaying, until his flame burned itself out. After a time he flung the smoldering mop to the ground and searched the hills again.

Silent darkness gathered from the river, through Harenton as streetlights came on, and into the trees stretching to Sarah's. The glinting light had disappeared with the sun.

Just a reflection, M.C. said to himself. But what kind? What's she got with that glint to it?

Minutes passed and he saw nothing. He waited until darkness gathered around the house below him and then around his pole, as it slipped black and liquid over Sarah's Mountain.

From the ground, M.C.'s pole might show a dull gleam. But at the top of it, he knew he would be invisible, the same as night. He was safe from anything living.

How far do spirits rise? he wondered, scaring himself.

"M.C."

As though from out of his mind, a voice made him freeze.

"*M.C., it's just only me.*" The voice, now at the foot of his pole, outside the circle of junk.

"Who—Ben?"

"Yea. How you doing?"

"Man! You liked to scare me to death. When'd you come?"

"See you climb up with that mop and burn it, yelling your head off."

"Did you see there's something glinting?"

"Is that what it was?" Ben said. "Too many trees down here. But I hear you call 'pretty.' It's the girl?"

"Think so," M.C. said. "Why'd you hide? We could have played."

"I thought first somebody be still in the house."

"They're all in town," M.C. said.

"Well, I wasn't sure," Ben said. "M.C., you coming down?"

"Not yet."

"You have a rabbit in one trap."

"Yea?"

"Think so," Ben said. "Least, it's something trying to break loose."

"Has to be a rabbit," M.C. said. "No time for it now. I'll get it in the morning." He could almost taste the wild meat they'd have for tomorrow's supper.

"I can get it for you in the morning," Ben said. "Have it all skinned and ready by the time you come."

"Leave it," M.C. said. "Like to skin it myself." He pictured the act of slitting the back fur; with both hands, tear-ing it down and pulling the skin over hind legs. He had a vague kind of premonition. "If I haven't come by sundown, you can skin it," he said.

Moment upon moment passed between them in silence, when out of the hills near the cirque and lake where the children played shone a powerful beam of light. Aimed directly at Sarah's Mountain, no part of it was a glint or even a flash.

In all the darkness, it looked like the distant headbeam of a train. But it was not powerful enough to cover the whole distance. M.C. could see it without himself being seen.

"What in the world is that?" Ben said.

"You see it from down there?" M.C. said.

"Sure, looking like a searchlight."

M.C. slid down the pole fast, forgetting what friction could do to his hands.

"Ouch," he said. There was a searing pain in his right palm, but he didn't slow down.

"Oooh, burned my hand!" Climbing over the junk, he ran to the edge of Sarah's. He licked his palm to cool the burn. Ben came up like night moving to stand beside him.

"That first glinting came from across on the hill," M.C. said. "But this light is halfway between the hill and the lake."

"It's what was glinting?" Ben asked.

"The glinting was a reflection. This is a light of some kind," M.C. said. "It saw me burning the mop. It took a turn back and went over there. Where . . . it thought to hide the pack and whatever else, and it got . . . she got herself a light!"

M.C. smiled to himself. The light beam was moving now, up the side of the hill and then, veering, came down in his direction.

"She got curious," Ben said.

"And she came on back, trying to figure out what she saw," M.C. said.

"What kind of girl is going to walk around at night?"

"One that's not afraid of nothing," M.C. said lightly.

"Or one that won't know she's got something to be afraid of," Ben said.

He and M.C. spoke easily, quietly, watching the light. The beam was moving down toward the bottom of the hill across from Sarah's. There it hung suspended, a single jewel in darkness.

"You stay here," M.C. said.

"I'm going with you—please?" Ben said.

"No!"

"Yes!" Ben's voice, quiet, but pleading now.

M.C. sighed. "But you stay out of it, you hear? Stay behind and clear out of sight. Not a sound."

"Okay," Ben said, holding back his excitement.

Swiftly, soundlessly, M.C. ran through the undergrowth on the path down the side of Sarah's.

"*M.C., is it a hunt?*"

"*I said not a sound!*"

But he pictured a hunt, maybe the last good hunt he'd have before they had to leave the mountain.

Feeling the dark but picturing daylight, M.C. remembered a hunt in the sun when Ben had been behind him on an animal trail. It was possum they hunted then. They had seen possum moving along and followed, creeping on their knees. Possum was so easy to hunt. It heard them coming and climbed a low branch. There it lay still, playacting death. Not even its eye moved; like a dead piece of coal it was. The skill for M.C. was flinging the rock with all of his force and hitting the mark. He had done it. He knocked out the eye, leaving a bloody hole. Still the possum would not move. They came swiftly and crushed its head.

Then take the knife, M.C. thought. Bleed it at the throat with a deep twist.

Possum was as simple as it could be, once you found it. But finding its trail might take a whole day.

Moving to his left now, M.C. reached the gully where it began at the foot of the plateau. He raced through it and over its lip into the trees bordering. He stopped, with Ben coming up to stand close behind him. They spoke not a word, but they saw the light slowly moving, edging down through the trees at the foot of the hill above the gully.

It was M.C.'s plan to get behind the light. Working his way soundlessly forward, he swung to his right. He crossed behind the light now in the trees in front of him. Suddenly the light flicked off.

He stood still, his body slightly bowed, in order to fall quickly into a crouch if she suddenly turned around and shone the light. His arms hung loosely at his sides.

I'll wait for the beam.

He did wait. Darkness was complete around him. Ben was near, close to his back.

M.C. had no idea whether the girl was still in front of him, near the edge of the gully.

97

She in back of us? Turn on that light one more time. Has she heard me coming?

He couldn't stand the waiting. Half against his will, he started forward into the trees. Ben sucked in his breath, a slithering sound, as if to warn M.C. to stand and wait. But M.C. couldn't. She, whoever she was, had come this far.

How you know it's her?

He had lured her, like a deer caught by a delicious scent. Has to be her, he thought. And he had to go meet her. Is it a hunt?

M.C. touched branches, prickly pine boughs, with the fingers of one hand. Blinded by darkness, he walked slowly enough to remove his foot from a dry twig before it could snap. His right hand nested in the fur in his pocket. He felt the keen knife blade, warmed in its fur jacket by his own body heat.

Suddenly he stopped, sensing that darkness was itself a hunter and had turned on him.

Blindly, he looked up until his face pointed skyward. There were stars giving off a soft winking blue and cold white. He lowered his head, and at every stage he could still see the stars. Sarah's Mountain would have blotted out the stars at that angle of his head.

I'm facing the hill across from Sarah's!

But the clue had been in the climbing movement of his feet.

M.C. reached behind him for Ben. He found his forearm and held onto it. He turned them both 180 degrees, carefully, until they were facing the mountain.

Letting go of Ben, he started forward again. His skin

came alive with the chill of premonition. He was going the right way now. His feet were level; his hearing caught the slightest sound. Always when he hunted sure, his senses seemed newborn.

M.C. stepped onto the barren lip of the gully without a sound; and yet he knew it at once by its hard surface.

Wouldn't have crossed, he thought. Leave herself in a trap—hear her every move. She'd wait on the other side. Can't know I'm here to catch her, can she? She won't know about sound and traps—or would she? She won't know anything for sure . . . if she needs a light.

Resignedly, he stood in the open at the gully edge, the trees and Ben behind him.

I forget. Some of them know how to lure you, too.

She not any kind of deer.

A faint clicking sound and M.C. was blinded by white light from the midst of the gully.

He threw up his arm as a shield. And in a crouch, he leaped for the light. It flicked off while he was in motion. M.C. landed on his feet but pitched forward, hitting the ground on his shoulder and hip. He slid crazily on sharp rocks. Pain made him turn over onto his back.

Light shone down on him.

Something began to jingle and rattle, the sound going around him in a slow, eerie rhythm.

She wore bracelets. They jingle, M.C. had time to think.

One hand was in his pocket on his knife for protection. He reached for the light with the other hand. The light flicked off again. But he was rolling over, still reaching, and caught her, part hard shoe and part ankle. The shoe kicked out and connected with his forehead. In a shock of pain, the blow knocked him flat on his back.

His head hurt so, he could have cried. He moaned once and then moaned again. He was thinking fast, the second moan was playacting. He lay still with his head turned slightly away from where he thought the light would be.

The light shone again, coming from behind him. He waited and continued moaning softly. He listened through the painful ache across his forehead. She moved in closer to him. He closed his eyes.

"You had to start it," she said. "Up there on the mountain, with your fire and your shouting." Her voice was anxious and whining.

She came up on his left to stand over him. He lay calm, resting, so that his eyelids would not flutter. He made his breath grow ragged and shallow.

"What is it?" she said.

She kneeled. M.C. heard the light scrape as she placed it on the ground by his shoulder. He wondered if Ben could see them. Sure, he could. The light was still on, shining full on M.C.'s face.

"Hey, are you all right?" she said. Gently, she shook M.C. by the shoulder. But he played possum dead.

"Oh, what have I done!" Her whining voice was above him. She was close to his face. Then her fingers, cool, like soft points of delicate pressure, were outlining the bump that had swelled on his forehead.

Carefully, M.C. began to move his left arm. She must have thought he was coming awake, for she gave a sharp cry of relief. Without touching her, he was able to slip his arm all the way across her back at the waist.

Swiftly, he grabbed her above the left elbow, pinning her arm to her side. She fell hard on his chest. His fingers had her arm in a vise, and something else—a handle.

At once he felt the imprint of a heavy, unsheathed blade between them.

But his mind didn't dwell on it, not even in surprise. He jerked the knife away toward her back, forcing her to move off a little, so he could slide the belt around to which it was attached. He pressed her arm down on the knife now at her side. If she struggled, she'd risk being sliced.

Both his arms were around her tightly.

He discovered he had taken his own knife from his pocket and was clutching it at her back. Feeling her soft, yet solid weight against him, he stared straight into her stricken eyes.

"Hi," he said. Impulsively, he kissed her lightly on the lips, the way he might have kissed a child good-by. At once he knew he shouldn't have. She hadn't felt like a child.

Her eyes filled with terror. She kicked at him, her hard shoes bruising his shin bones.

"Hey," he said, now grinning with the triumph of catching her. Yet his mind remained sharp, wary, a hunter's mind.

She's got a free hand. Scared enough to—

The thought came to him, clean and deadly.

He saw blinding light suspended in darkness above his eyes. His turn to feel terror, and he let her arm loose.

No time to reach the light before she flung it viciously at

his head. But the light hung there for a brief instant, in which he was aware of his hunter's hand holding the knife at her back.

He used it, expertly. He could make a bleeding animal slash with it. But he stopped himself in time. She was no deer. Instead he thrust delicately through her shirt and made a clean check mark into her skin. A cut, but not deep. Just enough to draw blood and hurt.

In that one instant given him, all was sequential, ordered. She stiffened, uttering a sickening whine of fear, and reaching behind to clutch her wound, she dropped the light. M.C. jerked his head away to protect it, and knocked her off him.

The light hit him hard on the shoulder. It was a bruising blow, but it was better than having her fling it to brain him.

M.C. was on his knees, reaching for the light beside him. Out of the darkness, she kicked it away. Next, she had it and was running away.

"Didn't want to hurt you, I had to!" he yelled.

He saw the light swing over the lip of the gully. It caught Ben standing with his arms out from his sides. Rabbit flushed and blinded. The light was beamed back into the gully as though propelled and floated past M.C.

He heard her voice high and hard, with no whine in it: "You bother me ever again and I'll cut your heart out."

"I was only playing!" he called out. "You hear? You, girl? But you would've killed *me!*"

He watched the light fade away in the trees, westward. Knowledge of how easy it was to hurt somebody, or be hurt, sobered him.

I used my head, he thought. But if I hadn't of grabbed her— I was just playing. I was.

He heard sound coming near.

"Ben?" he said.

"They're coming."

"Who is? Hey, Ben?" But there was no answer.

He heard voices and recognized them. They were at the gully edge.

"Daddy," M.C. said.

A pause before his father said, "Who would have killed you? I heard you yell it. Who?"

M.C. couldn't see any one of them. He got to his feet, brushing his pants. His head ached where the girl had kicked him. He wouldn't touch it for fear it was cracked.

"Scared somebody," he managed to say.

"What were you doing off of that mountain, anyway?" Jones asked. He came into the gully with the others following.

"Mama?" M.C. said.

"Right here," Banina said. Just her voice made M.C. glad they were all together.

"I say, what were you doing down here?" Jones asked him.

"Coming to meet you all," M.C. lied. "I ran into some . . . some stranger."

"I don't like the sound of that," Jones said.

"Let me lead," M.C. said suddenly. "There's no light at the house."

"I can lead," Jones said, but he made no move. "Why were you yelling bloody murder?"

M.C. kept his breathing steady in the dark. "It hit me on the head. I guess I scared him. But when it hit me I got mad and yelled. I can lead," he said again and started out of the gully.

Jones said no more. M.C. hoped his silence meant he was satisfied. All of them walked single file on up the path M.C. felt with his feet. His mother, Banina, walked just behind him and to the side, with the children coming on behind her and in front of Jones. M.C. heard a sound like paper crackling and knew his mother must be carrying something.

"You want me to handle that bag?" he said.

"Just some noodles and milk, I can manage," she said. "M.C., do you know who it was?" Talking about the stranger with the light.

"No," M.C. said softly. He was listening and feeling. Someone was stalking them. Off the path a ways, it was Ben who moved when M.C. moved. M.C. could feel him there, keeping pace with the rhythm of his climb. And he felt a little easier inside, where the girl worried him.

"People always do come into these hills," his mother was saying, as though they had been talking the whole day. "For years people wander in and out again. We don't have to do anything. We don't have to call, they just come."

"The dude has come," M.C. told her.

"I heard," she said. She laughed. "Jones says he's come to hear me sing."

"Come to take you out of here to make records. You have to get Daddy to leave," he said.

"M.C., don't you bother him about leaving," Banina said.

"Mama." They were near the outcropping. M.C. had to

make her see before they got home and the dude came to hear her.

"You don't know," Banina was saying. "You don't understand all of it."

"It's not just me saying it," M.C. told her. "The dude, he says it. He says the spoil is coming down right now, an inch at a time. We have to get out of here."

Whispering at him, she said, "Do you think that pole is just for you?" In the sound of her voice was a secret, something only for him to hear: "It's all he has."

"You talking about my pole?"

"There's nothing else."

"What?" M.C. said.

"When Jones and I came back here to stay," she said, "I made him take all the stones away." She spoke so fast, M.C. could hardly distinguish the words. "I told him I wanted a yard just for my child to play in, but he wouldn't leave it alone."

"Mama."

"M.C., you remember, you would always stand and watch. First it was just one piece of junk where a stone had been," she said. "Then, another and another." She whispered urgently, right in his ear. They were on the path in the sweetbrier, almost to the outcropping.

"You're talking about the burying ground," he said. "Well, I know it's there."

"And years go by," she said, "and you decide on that pole yourself. Only, it wasn't just a pole for you."

"M.C." They came out on the outcropping. "Everyone of Sarah's that ever lived here."

"Well, I know that."

M.C. stopped on the ledge. He could see the shape of the house, darker than the night. He saw the faint, ghostly glint of his pole.

"M.C. The pole is the marker for all of the dead."

Brightness flowed into his brain, as if someone had lit up a screen hidden so long in the dark. He remembered childhood, when he was the only one small on the mountain. Watching, sucking his fingers in his mouth. His father, struggling with stones, rounded, man-hewn. Jones, wrenching them from the soil dug away from their base. And looking fearfully at Banina standing over him, as if he hated, despised, what he had to do, but doing it because she said he must. The stones?

He hid them, probably, M.C. thought.

Then Jones had dragged pieces of junk up the mountain, letting them lay where the stones had been.

"You mean, he's taken my pole—he has to stay because the dead . . ."

". . . he can't take them with him," Banina said, "and he won't leave them."

M.C. remembered his father talking about Sarah earlier in the day: "*She climbs eternal.*"

Banina stood beside M.C. The others were coming up from behind them.

"I don't *believe* it!" M.C. whispered. "He's crazy!"

"He's Jones," Banina said simply. "And don't you ever forget it."

M.C. trembled slightly.

My pole. The junk in a circle. A monument.

He sighed. Mechanically he moved through the dark toward the house. He felt utterly tired and beaten. He knew that to make Jones leave, he would have to wrench him from the past.

How? he wondered. How?

Abruptly, he stood still as his senses continued to respond to the night. He tensed at the sound of a scraping noise. A cold chill passed over him and he thought of ghosts around his pole. Something in the darkness was watching from the porch.

When Jones came forward, M.C. got a hold on himself. He began to stalk when Jones stalked. Wide apart, they gauged the distance between one another by the sound of their breathing. They were still father and son in rhythm, surrounded by night.

Banina and the children came on cautiously from behind them. As silent as night creatures, Jones and M.C. eased up to the porch.

6

―――――

"I can't see a thing," a voice said. It was a whisper of fright, but M.C. recognized it. "It's just me," the voice continued fearfully. Feet shuffled back and forth on the porch. Then came a chuckle.

"James K. Lewis. Is that you, M.C. Higgins? I don't expect I'll ever get down off this mountain tonight."

"Couldn't tell who was waiting—you almost had it," M.C. said softly. His own voice sounded strange to him.

The dude laughed wildly in relief. "I found my way back just at darkness," he said, controlling himself. "But there wasn't no one here. I saw light down there, and later I heard some commotion. But I figure I best stay right where I was. I hope it be all right that I come back."

"You come down from the top of Sarah's?" M.C. asked.

"I come from around behind, yes," Lewis said. "Been

back there awhile, looking and asking and talking. It's a revelation, I'll tell you, how folks will wait for ruin before they fight."

The Higginses stiffened slightly. M.C. understood the dude's meaning. But it was Jones who strode up the steps and into the house in swift and violent movement. He turned on the narrow light of the front parlor. He came bursting out again, bullheaded, his shoulders made huge, framed in the light behind him.

Banina and the three children hurried inside. M.C. sat glumly on the step of the porch. The dude crouched beside him. Jones remained standing. Still framed by light, he looked as if he meant to block the door.

"He's my father," M.C. said, as if Jones were a mile away. "We all call him Jones." His voice, vaguely mocking, distant.

The dude jumped up. "Pleased to meet you, Jones," he said. "I mean, Mr. Higgins," too loudly—so that he startled Jones.

Jones had braced himself, ready for anything, before he realized the dude only wanted to shake his hand.

He grunted and nodded there in the half-light of the porch. Finally Jones extended his hand, being always polite with strangers. He gave a glance through the screen door into the house. His Banina was in the kitchen with the children. Jones wasn't going to call her out; he would invite the dude in to meet her. Or M.C. would, or they wouldn't. All this he seemed to say in that one glance through the door and back to the dude.

James Lewis sat down beside M.C., and Jones took up his position again in front of the doorway.

Anxiously, Lewis watched M.C. He kept quiet, no longer attempting to read the signs of their silence.

"Well, it's late," M.C. said after a time. "I reckon she's tired," speaking of his mother. "Should be, after that long walk. But you never can tell. She not like anybody."

"I sure know I feel bad, pestering," the dude said.

"Mama knew you'd be coming. I told her," M.C. said.

"Well, then, I'll just wait. See if she might just feel like a song and come back out."

"Wait all you want," M.C. said. Sitting there, he had so many thoughts—the pole a marker, not just his as he had thought it was. Jones. His mother, who was like nobody else.

She was like nobody else because of Jones. She could start out in one direction, and Jones never would say it was the wrong way or that she couldn't go. He either followed her or he didn't. He would show he didn't approve by not following, but he never would stop her.

Her, leave with the kids. And me. Him, stay with his graves, M.C. thought.

Will the spoil heap get him? (Yes)

Do I care? (Yes) Enough not to leave him here?

M.C. studied brush and trees around the edge of Sarah's. Full of darkness, he wondered briefly if Ben was hidden there. His mind leaped lightly to thoughts of the girl out there in the dark by herself.

Tomorrow. I'll hunt her. Find her and keep my distance.

Abruptly, he got to his feet. "Come on inside," he told the dude. "Meet Mama, anyhow."

James K. Lewis entered the parlor. He bowed his head, as if he were about to pray. The room did have the hush of ceremony about it. It had a crimson wall-to-wall carpet. Banina proudly called it her plush carpet and so it was. It felt like velvet when you walked barefoot on it. She had got it in Washington, D.C. Out of some embassy where she had worked, she had got this remnant of formal carpet when they put a new one in its place. She never minded that M.C. or any of them tracked dirt in on the carpet. But when they did, she would make them spend some time cleaning it. But she never would say they should stay out of the parlor.

M.C. remembered it for most of his life. Banina said the carpet never would wear out. Most of the time, they walked on it without shoes on and it never did wear out.

She came from somewhere in Washington. It was after a war, a time when she had met Jones. But all that was some secret between her and Jones. They could giggle about it clear to silliness. Something about him driving a truck. Maybe it was the dream of once touching the wheel and gas pedal of a working car that had got him off the mountain the first time. But he found Banina and she had given up her job. They had returned to the hills where Jones had always lived.

M.C. called his mother. When she came in, he brought the dude to her.

"This the man you been hearing about," he told her. "Come to hear you sing."

"James K. Lewis," Lewis said. "I mean no offense coming here so late. It's that I heard how fine you can sing, is all."

Suddenly he sneezed. Holding his leather hat in his hands, he raised it to rub the edge of it against his nose. He had scraped most of the mud off his city boots, M.C. noticed. Still, he had tracked in mountain dirt on Banina's carpet.

" 'Scuse me," Lewis said.

Banina gave Mr. James Lewis a long, cool look. M.C. couldn't remember a stranger ever having set foot in the parlor or any other part of their home. But Banina acted as if the dude's coming was neither an event nor an everyday occurrence. She didn't just stare at him, she peered into him, diving deep into him with her wide-set eyes like gold spoons cutting through some shaking jello.

Why folks say she is so beautiful, M.C. thought.

The way she could cut right through you with her eyes. And scoop you out with them, while all the time never once telling something about what she was thinking.

She had about the most pretty face in all of the world, M.C. was sure. And hair, no longer than an inch around her head. Brown, with some red streaks either from the sun or a liquid she sometimes got from the drugstore in Harenton. Her hair fit her like a stocking cap. It set off the straight line of her brows and those high, hard cheekbones.

"Shoot," Banina said to the dude. She was smiling, with just a slight curl to her upper lip. "You come all this way?"

Her mouth was full and soft, just like Macie Pearl's but quicker to laugh. M.C. had the same mouth, but his never laughed much either. Why was it Banina was the only one of them who knew how to laugh so much? But then her mouth could be full of sweet sound while her eyes held back warmth for as long as she wanted.

"You must be tired," she told the dude. "Here. You don't have to stand."

She gave him a seat on the gold couch she had got from somewhere. It was the single large piece of furniture in the room, with a radio on an end table beside it. Floating on a sea of red plush carpet, it was a sun-drenched island of rest. The cushions were filled with an unheard-of softness. Listening to the radio, you lay on them and they would carry you down into dream. Banina said the cushions had goose feathers, but M.C. didn't know whether to believe that.

With hat in hand, the dude sat down on the couch. They all found seats on the floor around the edges of the room, except for Banina. She stood in the center, as easy as when she leaned against a tree, looking at the hills.

M.C. watched as the dude looked around at them, at the room and then at Banina, scanning her from head to foot. M.C. could tell Lewis didn't believe that such a tall, thin woman could hold any kind of voice.

He wished the dude would just set up his tape recorder along the path coming up the side of Sarah's. Just set it on the ground and catch Banina's voice sailing out of the sky at the end of a long day. Then the dude would know. But he wouldn't catch her voice in this room, or any other.

"This sure is a pretty place," James Lewis said politely. With all of them staring at him, he nervously crossed his legs in a way M.C. never had seen a man do. All of the children laughed, even M.C. Then the dude uncrossed his legs and sat the way Jones always did sit with his legs stretched out in front of him toward Banina.

"Mrs. Higgins, I'm just a collector," Lewis said softly. "I

know in my heart I come here not to pry or anything, nor to hurt anybody. I don't want you to ever think I come here to take away."

"No need to apologize," Banina said.

"Well," the dude said. He placed his hat on the couch beside him and eased the tape recorder off his shoulder and out of its case. When he pressed one of the keys, the top of the machine clicked open. Lewis took out one green cassette and replaced it with an unused one from his pocket.

"You children can go on in and eat," Banina told them. "M.C., you drain the noodles. Then you all can come back and listen."

The children kept silent until they were all in the kitchen, M.C. with them. They whispered while gulping down the hot noodles and the cheese sandwiches M.C. prepared for them. He passed out cups of milk.

"Mama's going to sing!" Macie said.

"Knew she would," M.C. told her.

"The dude will take her voice," Macie went on, "and make the records from just her voice?"

"No," M.C. said. "He sells the tapes to somebody . . . and then Mama has to go over Nashville, see, and make the records there."

"But when is she famous?" Harper asked.

M.C. didn't know by what process their mother became a star singer. He knew only that it could happen, her voice being richer and purer than any of the voices he heard on the radio.

"After he takes her voice out," M.C. said finally. "When

114

he sends for her, she goes. When the records are made and you hear them on the radio."

Wide-eyed, the children stared at him. "We'll leave here, too," he said. He didn't mention they would leave their father behind, that they would live without him.

They fell silent, chewing, with thoughts of riches.

Macie Pearl finished and hurried back into the parlor. She gave her mother a warm hug. Then she went over to the couch and the tape recorder, as though Lewis wasn't there. "See, Mama?" she said, "you just sing and it picks it up here." She pointed to holes at the top of the machine. "I talked in one at school once before they locked it up."

Jones went to the kitchen and came back in with jelly glasses and a jug of apple cider. His face looked peaceful—if Banina wanted to sing, it was all right with him. He filled three glasses to the top and handed one to Banina and one to James K. Lewis. Again he sat down on the floor, this time with the jug beside him. He and Banina drank deeply from their glasses while Mr. James Lewis sipped from his.

"Mercy!" Lewis said, "this is some fine homemade!"

"It's a mystery how it comes out so well when the trees of these hills won't be worth a shake anymore," Banina said. Still standing, she held her glass up to the light above her. The light, a smoky glass globe, hung above her head. The cider sparked in her hand.

It's going to be a show, M.C. had time to think.

The dude watched Banina, at the light causing shadows beneath her cheekbones. He pressed a key down on the tape machine and nodded to her. But it was Jones who began it.

"Yay-o," Jones said. He was looking at Banina, his face closed to all of them but her.

"Yay," the children answered. Even M.C.'s lips moved with the age-old response to a call to begin.

"Wine, wine," Banina said, half singing.

"Yay," Jones said. "Drinkin' the apple . . . Drinkin' . . . ." He eased her into the song.

". . . *the wine, wine, wine,*" Banina sang. Her full voice was a shock in the room. M.C. watched the dude's eyes light up. Lewis's face, his whole body came alert to the sound, not just country and odd, but fine and strange, fine and individual.

Macie scooted over to M.C. He let her lean against him, but he didn't take his eyes from his mother.

"*Drinkin' the wine, wine, wine,*" she sang.

> *Down on your bending*
> *Kneebone to the ground.*
> *Ain't nobody goin' n' worry 'bout you dyin'*
> *By you'self*
> *Lord, in a field*
> *Drinkin' the wine oh wine.*

The way her voice could curve a line of melody sent shivers up M.C.'s back. It didn't matter that her singing was a show she had to put on for the dude. She had to sing out what came into her head. Her voice could make it music. It could express all that within her she had kept secret and separate from them.

"Is that what you want?" Banina said to the dude.

James Lewis sat still, as if he wouldn't move again, M.C.

thought. But he answered with a quaver: "You just go on ahead and sing whatever you feel up to."

Looking around at them, she said, "I'm tired, me." For a moment she rested her hand on her shoulder, staring at it. "But I'll go ahead on."

"Hear her come home singing a yodel," M.C. said, but nobody seemed to hear.

His mother began another song. It was a witchy song about an evil called Juba. An old song out of Carolina, she had once told M.C. She let the tiredness she felt drain into it so that the minor cadence became haunted with ghostly melody:

> *Juba walk, I say, Juba walk.*
> *She walk in while you be cookin',*
> *Juba catch you while you not even lookin'.*

Chorus:

> *Standin' at the stove,*
> *Standin' at the stove.*
> *Siftin' in the san',*
> *Siftin' in the san'.*

> *I seen Juba serve the meal*
> *(She give me the husk . . .)*
> *I seen her serve the buttered bread*
> *(She give me the crust . . .)*

> *Never eat the broth from out of her cookin'*
> *For Juba boil you*
> *When you not even lookin'.*

Chorus:

> *Standin' at the stove,*
> *Standin' at the stove.*

> *Siftin' in the san',*
> *Siftin' in the san'.*

Then came a wondrous song of peace and of quiet:

> *Lay me down, down, down*
> *In the low-land shady*
> *Low-land shady*
> *With the sky upon my eyes.*
>
> *Sarah's Mountain to my shoulder*
> *And my feet in the clover,*
> *Feet in the clover*
> *I will dream away the time.*

"Yes. Yes!" the dude said.

"Sing it more," Harper said, and so Banina sang of the "Low-land Shady," never singing it twice the same:

> *Years of restin' on my back,*
> *The Lord, he lost my track*
> *So I'll breathe here forever*
> *In the low and shady land.*
>
> *And the mountain to my shoulder*
> *And my feet in the water,*
> *Feet in the water*
> *I will toil away the time.*

All the while Jones sat with one hand on the jug and the other holding his glass, his face contented and closed. Impenetrable.

Later, with their mother's voice rising and falling, the children fell asleep. Lying there on the plush carpet, one by one they had closed their eyes.

Jones took them one by one to their beds. Banina paused, watching them go. Something went out of her singing after a while, even though she sang on. She let her voice go quiet so as not to waken her children. The dude understood. Still he changed tapes and let them run out.

They talked, James Lewis and Banina, with M.C. listening, looking from one to the other. The dude asked her how long they'd all been in the hills. M.C. waited to see how much she would tell a stranger.

"All the children were born here," Banina told him. "Jones was born here, but he had gone and come back. I come from Washington, but I wasn't born there. Born farther off near Boone, North Carolina. I left it. I met Jones after World War Two. Now that was a time. Talk about some singing." She laughed. "We all did some singing then. But jobs were tough for Jones to find. We came back here."

M.C. sat quietly, interested in how his mother had altered the truth so effortlessly.

"Weren't so tough to find," Jones said, coming back in to sit down again. "It was that we both knew hills better than anything. So we come on back to them."

Know the hills, M.C. thought, you won't listen to what they say.

"*Goin' down a hill feelin' bad,*" Banina sang, smiling at Jones, "*I walk back to home feelin' good.*"

"That's the truth," Jones said.

Not the hills no more. You're seeing a scar, M.C. thought.

But he stayed silent. He glanced at James K. Lewis. Suddenly he realized Lewis hadn't said a word to his mother about going to Nashville.

Lewis was smiling. "I can surely understand how you can love these hills," he said. "Living on a mountain like this.

119

It must make you feel real fine. I never had nothing like it, you see, living in an apartment in the city until I moved out a ways and got me a little house. But I don't own it. Just renting."

"It's good when you own," Banina said softly. "Least the roof is yours, no one can take it."

"Do you ever want to farm it?" the dude asked.

"We're not farmers, to speak of," Banina told him. She glanced at Jones.

"It won't farm," Jones said. "Too steep a grade to keep the topsoil."

"How far up do you own?" Lewis asked him.

"Up to this outcropping," Jones said. "About six acre."

All of the time, M.C. had been trying to puzzle out something until finally he said, "Why come she wanted it—I mean, Great-great grandmother—if it wasn't any good for growing?"

"Well," Jones said, "land changes. Way back when, that gully was flat and pure. It caught the run-off from the mountain and the topsoil. She could farm that gully although she didn't own it. Don't imagine anybody cared, just a single strip of flat land." He stopped, unwilling to say more in front of the dude.

"Who owns on up above you?" the dude asked amiably.

Jones's face closed in on itself again. Banina gathered up glasses and took the jug into the kitchen. She came back to stand just in the doorway.

When no one would answer, M.C. said, "The coal people."

"Now that's the worry," Lewis said seriously. "You know, I got kind of turned around up here this morning," he said to Jones. "I was up there and that spoil heap is really something awful." He looked at Banina, who studied one wrist, probing it with one finger of the other hand. He looked at M.C., who nodded eagerly at him.

"It's sliding about a half-inch, inch at a time," the dude said, "but I'm not telling you nothing you don't already know."

A long time of silence, in which Jones shifted his position, bent and stretched his legs and folded his arms. When he did speak, his voice was matter-of-fact: "I figure it will slide like that until it reaches the yard. There, on the level, it will halt."

"Then what?" M.C. said softly.

"Say?" Jones said.

"Then what will we do with it?" M.C. spoke eagerly.

"Well, then," Jones said, "we chop it up. We wait for the cool days of late fall, winter. We let her harden. Then we take a section at a time, rope it and drag it down into that gully, way off to one side so's we won't have to see it."

"I didn't know that!" M.C. grinned, so pleased to find out that Jones had been thinking about the spoil and planning. "So that's how," he said.

"Yes," Jones said.

James Lewis raced one hand through his crisp, graying hair, as though his scalp itched. He cleared his throat. "I don't believe it will slide all the way," he said cautiously. "The grade of that slope will be too steep." And then,

121

politely: "I'm afraid there will be a momentum and a pressure that will bring it all crashing down." And then he folded his hands, looking worriedly at Jones.

M.C. stared from one to the other. He waited for Jones to tell James K. Lewis he was dead wrong. But Jones merely stayed silent, looked stubborn. An uncontrollable feeling of dread spread within M.C. It cleared away all but the truth. Just a moment ago he had believed the spoil heap would inch its way down because Jones had said it would.

He almost tricked me with it, M.C. thought.

He had believed Jones was thinking and planning.

But he only want to make us stay on the mountain.

After that, M.C. wouldn't look at Jones or anyone.

Tension grew and touched each one of them in the room except Jones. He, alone, seemed untroubled by the awkward stillness, until he got to his feet, saying, not to the dude, not to anyone, "We'll rope it and drag it on out of the way."

Crazy. Liar.

Standing there, Jones forced the dude to stand also. In the act of rising, he had dismissed James Lewis as clearly as if he had said, *"Leave my house."*

Incredulously, the dude peered at Jones. Slowly it dawned on him that Jones meant for him to go.

M.C. watched his mother pull herself up straight in formal leave-taking. He tried sitting for as long as he could, hoping to keep the dude there a while longer.

Get him to talk some more, reason with Daddy.

But he felt himself being dragged to his feet by invisible bonds of formality, learned so long ago he was hardly aware of them.

Lewis pocketed his tapes. He eased the tape machine back into its case and slung it over his shoulder.

"Thank you so much," he said to Banina. "You are truly a performer. I can't tell you how much I appreciate it."

"Was my pleasure," she said, smiling, but oddly detached.

"All the same, I took your time," Lewis said. "Now I have to sort it all out." He indicated his recording machine. "See what will be the best course to take." He laughed nervously. "Mizus Higgins, you have swept me off my feet! I don't know where to go with you, off-hand." He grinned. "But I will sort it all out. And then I'll come on back."

"All the time you need," Banina said quietly.

The dude nodded and spun around. He was not quite able to meet Jones's cool eyes on him. Stiffly, Jones bowed before the dude could extend his hand. Lewis bowed in return.

To M.C., he said, "I surely do thank you, son." A worried expression on his face before it faded in sadness.

"Wasn't nothing," M.C. said, as sharply as he dared. The dude and his father both had pulled him one way and then the other until he no longer knew what was true and what wasn't. But he was sure the dude would find a way to take his mama's voice. He wouldn't dare believe they wouldn't leave the mountain. But an awful thought swept into his mind.

We'll all stay here and die.

"You pay your respects," Banina was saying to him.

"Good night," he said to the dude.

"Good night, son," Lewis said.

Banina let M.C. pass.

He headed through the kitchen and on, not stopping until

123

he was in his cave. Without a light, he undressed in a moment and crawled into bed, tired to his bones. His eyes fluttered closed when his head hit the pillow. Vaguely, he could hear the front door open. His mother's voice, smooth, yet formal; and then the door closing.

Later Banina came in, hovering above him. He knew she tucked the light blanket around him as though he were a child; yet he couldn't respond. He was too deeply gone and dreaming darkness.

I'm running.

One jump ahead of Jones trying to rope him.

7

BANINA woke up M.C. to go swim in the cirque, the way she would do sometimes. It was an hour when the moon was going down. A false dawn of neither night nor day, when gray light seemed to rise from the earth. Birds chirped in clusters of awakening sound, only to fall silent again as false light faded away in dimness and murk of hills.

In M.C.'s cave, it was night in which his mother was an irritating darkness. And if he hadn't gone with her the way he really didn't want to go—he just wanted to sleep on in the coolness—she would have gone swimming by herself. She wouldn't have awakened Jones or any other one of her children. For she made up her mind that a swim at dawn was something she wanted to do only with her oldest son.

Banina was like that. Jones and the kids would join them as soon as they were up.

M.C. had covered his head with his arms, pulling the blanket clear over his face. He had a hollow feeling, a numbness of too much worry left over from the night before. He supposed it would be with him a long time.

"Come on now, M.C.," his mother said, "we'll miss the sunrise!" Whispering, she was darkness bent over him, pulling at the blanket.

"Leave me be." His muffled reply. "What time is it? Is he gone? Leave me alone."

"Is who gone? Mr. Lewis? Poor old dude," she said. "Jones had to lead him most by the hand down the mountain."

"Why didn't he stay 'til morning?" he asked sleepily. But then he remembered.

"Stayed long enough," Banina said. "Come on, M.C. Don't you want a swim in the cool air?"

Desperately he held out for the dark of his cave. "Act just as silly," he scolded her. "How'll they ever grow up when their mama acts like a child."

"The kids? Shoot," she said, in the soft way she had. "Best be a babe for as long as you can. Now come on. I'll go by myself, I'm telling you. Some old bobcat sure to stalk me by myself. You fixing to let him jump Banina Higgins right there in the piney woods?"

So M.C. had to go with her. But not without muttering about it first. Secretly he was pleased she had chosen him, although he never let on. Of all the times he was alone with her, he never got used to how pretty she was. When he was much younger, he had worried that she wasn't his real mother, although he never told anyone.

"How come I don't look like you?" he would say to her.

"You've got my mouth," she had answered. "You look like Jones out of the eyes, but you have my mouth and my walk."

Now the two of them moved swiftly the same, up one hill and down another on their way to the cirque. Banina walked slightly ahead of him. She was barefoot and already suited up in an old but still good one-piece bathing suit. She had her shoes and her work-a-day clothes in a shopping bag which M.C. carried for her. He walked to one side of her. In the murk, he could see her and only a short way in front of her on the path. He didn't much like being in the woods in the heavy shadows before dawn. It was an eerie time in which trees and undergrowth appeared changed and ghostly.

Probably scared old dude. Run all the way. And the other one. Now I bet she's out here somewhere.

Banina stopped on the path. At once M.C. halted, every muscle tense and fearfully ready. He peered ahead and caught sight of the incredible spring of a doe in midair. Always, it seemed a larger animal would see you a split second before you saw it. They had flushed the doe, coming on her blindly. She sprang up amidst the trees like a wind-up toy, swift and magical.

Banina raised her hand as if to touch the deer's fluid shape and hold her wild motion.

The doe was gone. "That was a surprise," Banina said,

walking the path again. "I swear, I thought all the deer had gone. Used to be they'd be all around the house in a morning. You remember that, M.C.?"

"No. Yes, a little. Wish I had me a gun," he said.

"You'd kill that pretty thing?"

"Think of the meat," he said, sounding like a man.

"You couldn't kill anything that big. Not you."

"Why not me?" he said, surprised. "What if it is big? Because I never have? Won't mean I never could."

"Could you?" Banina looked to be half smiling at him.

He thought first to lie. Then he grew uncomfortable, remembering the girl all of a sudden, their knives and how they had fought.

"No," he said finally. "Nothing bigger than a rabbit. And him, only for food."

"I was thinking not," Banina said and fell silent.

The woods changed misty gray, with birds awakening. But the trees were still heavy with night. M.C. felt a quiver down his spine as he heard rustling sounds in the undergrowth. Small animals scurrying. He calmed himself.

"It's so nice out here," Banina said, as they came out of the trees. Now they could walk easily to the foothills. The hills were actually outcroppings of mountains called Grey and Hall. And as they began to climb the foothills, Grey Mountain and Hall Mountain came into view like swollen, smoky giants. Black with trees, they looked rolling cushion soft and belly full.

M.C. and his mother turned sharply and began to climb one hundred feet up the hill slope of Hall Mountain. M.C. kept his eyes on his feet. Grey Mountain was behind him.

Without looking, he could feel it, immense and misty.

Banina pulled herself up the slope by grabbing saplings and branches of trees. Where there was nothing else to hold on to, she leaned forward. Knees bent nearly to a crouch, she dug her feet into the rugged hillside and held on to clumps of weed.

"Mercy!" she whispered, panting.

M.C. gave her a boost. "We're almost there," he told her.

She stopped to rest a moment, letting him lead. He went ahead and out of sight. By the time Banina reached the top of the slope, she had come exactly the way M.C. had, following a natural turn and round of the mountain. She reached M.C. and fell on her back, breathing hard.

Hall Mountain loomed over them somewhat to their right. It was dark, brooding with mist, still half a mile away. M.C. was glad they didn't have to climb it. It seemed to grow as they watched it, as crimson light tinted the sky behind it.

Banina sat up, hugging her knees. She was covered with goose flesh, for the mountain air was still cold. M.C. moved to give her his sweater, she motioned him never mind. She fixed her gaze on Hall Mountain, unwilling to give up a second of it. Her sweaty face settled into peace. Her panting stopped. She, and M.C., too, sat as still as forms carved from mountain wind and icy rain.

She broke their silent watching. "Must be what Sunday people call God Almighty," she said about the mountain. "High enough for heaven and older than anybody ever lived."

"Won't make it God Almighty," M.C. told her.

"It does for me," she said.

"God Almighty can't be moved," he said, "but watch and see if somebody don't come along and move that mountain."

Banina smiled. "Never move that God."

M.C. wasn't smiling. "Witchy folks heal mountains by laying hands on them."

She looked at him hard. "Who told you that?"

"Ben. His daddy put hands on the mining cuts."

Banina shook her head. "Never let your father see you playing with Ben. Stay away from over there, you hear? Living all bunched together. Nobody knowing which is real father to what son, and which mother to daughter. The wives never leaving the plateau. Those people aren't right."

"I know who Ben's daddy is," M.C. said. "They're just like anybody else. They don't have no more power than we do. Do they? Wish they did. Wish they *could* change things —can they, Mama?"

"They have the power," Banina said. She stared at M.C. "There's no denying. I've seen it. They are different."

"Seen it?" he said.

"Seen it, and I haven't been back since."

"Tell," he said.

"Well," she began, "it was farmer in the valley behind the plateau. He was using a sickle on a patch of wheat. You know, it with that hooklike blade fitted into a little handle. Anyway, he was working and not seeing the child creeping up on him to surprise him. He thrust back with the sickle. And sweeping it forward, he caught that child in the curve of the blade. Laid his thigh open the way you slice to bare the bone from a piece of ham."

"Oooh!" M.C. said.

"No doctors, only in Harenton, just like it is now. But there was the Mound. I was over there that day with her. We'd just got back here, Jones and I, and she was my neighbor. I liked her. I'd heard the tales of their power, but I paid no attention. Until farmer come running up all covered with blood. The child, so white and blood so much on his leg, you couldn't see it. And she—"

"Who?" M.C. said.

"Viola Killburn," Banina said. "Why, she simply took the child and arranged him on the ground. He appeared death-still. She didn't touch the wound gushing blood all over. But move her hand over it like searching for something above it in the air. All of a sudden, the hand stop and tremble like over a hump and then move slowly the length of the wound curve.

"Vi had her eyes on that wound in the strangest look I never will ever forget. Only her lips move. Secret prayers of the Bible, they say, but I don't know," Banina said. "I know this. The blood gushing away that child's lifetime clotted all in a minute. The wound ceased to flow. It turn gray and darker. It heal."

"Man!" M.C. whispered.

"Vi ran to pick the ginseng and other weeds I don't know the names of," Banina continued, "and she pack the wound with all this messy weed juice and stuff and leaf and dirt right off the Mound. The child was conscious. He have no pain when his father pick him up to carry him home."

A brilliant gash ripped across the summit of Hall Mountain. Banina sucked in her breath, her eyes running with fear.

"It's sun. It's morning!" M.C. said.

He helped his mother to her feet.

"Mercy!" she said. She pressed her hand against her chest. "That took my breath, the way the sun bit into the mountain the minute I'd finished."

"Nothing witchy about it," M.C. said. "And if Killburns have power to heal, why won't you go there? Why is Daddy so bent against them?"

"Theirs might be power for bad in some way we don't recognize—isn't the Lord suppose to have the power for good?" she said and added: "A man, a child will go over there just for a visit. And will end staying and working for them. He'll become practically a Killburn. Nobody knows who is related to who over there. That's what your father and me wonder about."

"I don't know." M.C. sighed. "Ben and me, we're close. But I'm getting tired of Daddy. Tired as I can be."

"Come on," Banina said. "We'll miss the morning sun." And later: "It's not your daddy you tired of, M.C. It's here. It's this place. The same thing day after day is enemy to a growing boy."

And all the ghosts, M.C. thought. All of the old ones.

They went on. Banina led the way along the slope that opened into a pass at the side of Hall Mountain. The reach of land rose gently as they made their way through a stand of silent pine trees.

Changing the subject, M.C. spoke again. "Dude wants you to make records, only he didn't say it. Did he say it after I went to bed?"

"No, not a word about it."

"I guess when he comes back then," M.C. said.

"Maybe." She smiled at him, waiting to walk with him. "You know, I sing 'cause I'm coming home. I'm seeing my family again. I'm seeing the mountain. Loving it."

"You don't want to make some records?" he said.

"Well, if the dude made it easy," she said. She hesitated. "Don't dream too hard."

"It's no dream that we have to leave," M.C. said.

She commenced to walk more quickly. "You live wide awake," she said, "or you quit living."

"Meaning me?" M.C. asked. "Meaning yourself? Or Daddy?"

"All," she said. "All together. All apart. But all."

"Now hurry, M.C.!" she said, whispering back at him, like she thought the rising sun might hear her and go back down.

They came to the place where the pass ended in a ridge just high enough so that what lay on the other side was always a surprise.

He wasn't sure what his mother had meant by "All together. All apart." But he sensed the words were especially for him; understood that she had gone beyond him to know something he hadn't yet come to.

M.C. let his worry wear itself down. He was beginning to feel himself grow eager inside in anticipation of the ridge.

You can't see a thing beyond it, he thought. That's what's

nice. Anybody hunting along will never guess until he is over it. Then, bam! Right there in front of you.

It happened just that way. They made the ridge in a matter of minutes and they still couldn't see over the top of it. Next, they were over the ridge and there was the lake lying there the way it probably had for thousands of years. And something else they hadn't expected.

Seeing that lake in a dawning, M.C. felt it was his soul spread out on it in sparkles. The view for miles nearly made his head spin. There were four mountains beyond the foothills ringing the lake. They were Hall, which was now behind them, and Grey, in front. In their view to the south was Young's and angled to the north was Sarah's, much farther off. The sun came up over Hall Mountain. It lit the sky and the piney woods. It gave the lake a black sheen under white light.

M.C. felt warm sun on his back. Neither he nor Banina spoke, out of respect for the lake, for the dawn and the sun. At that moment M.C. did things automatically. He peeled off his clothes down to his swimming trunks and carefully rolled his sweater, pants and tennis shoes into a neat bundle. He never took his eyes from the lake running smooth with just a slight sound of lapping at land. He bent silently to lay his roll next to the bag of his mother's work clothes. Banina put her hand on his shoulder, slightly turning him so he could look down the shore on their right.

"Already saw it," he told her. He spoke softly so his voice wouldn't carry over the water.

"You knew it was here? You saw it before," she whispered.

134

"No," M.C. said, "but I expected I'd find her again."

He slipped into the water. He could hear his mother right behind him. He swam straight out, sliding through the rich, incredible cold with a shiver but without a sound. Banina stayed a shoulder-length behind him.

"Her?" she said. "Her?" almost loud, so that M.C. had to dive to stop her.

They dove. There was surprising soft light below the surface. There was warmth that passed over M.C.'s shoulders, waist, feet. He kept going down and down until he was below the light. He broke out of the dive and turned onto his back. He could look up at the light and see the point where it ceased to penetrate.

Banina, still in her dive, couldn't break it before she went beyond him. Almost at once she turned to his level, spinning on her back the way he had come. She passed him by and broke the surface a shoulder-length ahead of him.

They broke the surface far away from shore. She flipped on her back, breathing in short sighs so as not to make too much noise. She rolled over in an easy turn and swam toward the middle of the lake. M.C. followed, holding back his strength. They reached the lake's center and turned simultaneously toward the shore.

Banina whispered, "What are you going to do?"

"Do the same as always," he said. "I pull into shore right where that girl has made her home."

"How you so sure it's a girl?" she asked him.

"Yesterday," M.C. said. He explained that the girl had come in with the dude. Water broke away above his lip and flowed smoothly out on either side of his nostrils. "Saw

135

her on the path," he said. "And last night. She made this knot on my head."

"Oh," Banina said. "I meant to ask you about it. Does it hurt?"

"No, it's fine."

Banina said nothing else. When M.C. shifted his easy stroke, she let him lead the silent paddling to shore. She fell far back, watching the rise and fall of his shoulders.

M.C. felt fine, as though he knew as much as he wanted to know minute by minute. The sun warmed him and its dappled light fell through boughs of towering pines ringing the shoreline. The shore was mud-earth made dry and hard by sand and flat, rounded stones. The surface was not unsmooth, not a bad place to pitch a home.

The tent had been raised on a well-thought-out site. It was far enough away from pine needle beds beneath the boughs so that footsteps couldn't be muffled. It was placed on the shore edge away from the water, where footsteps coming would rattle around on the stones. The girl would never be taken by surprise from the shore. She had piled pine boughs and brush on the tent side nearest the ridge. Down from the shore, a pile of brush was all anybody could see. Only from the ridge could the tent be detected.

Never counted on me coming out of the water. Better be quiet, though, M.C. thought.

He thought no further. Minute by minute, sight and sound were enough for him. He reached the shore and lay on his stomach, half in and half out of the water. He was downshore from the tent opening facing the lake. The girl could have seen him coming in from far out in the lake if she'd been watching. M.C. guessed she was still asleep. No reason for her to have heard him and Banina. She would have to peer out and around the tent if she were to see him now.

Sure not going to walk on the stones. But I will sit.

He pulled himself up onto the shore in a sitting position just as Banina came gliding up. He motioned her to do as he had done. They both sat at the water's edge, dripping wet and shivering, even in the warm sunlight. A long, peaceful time of silence between them. They breathed in the fresh air, closed their eyes and became a part of the stillness.

All at once, a whoop and a holler on the other side of the ridge. Macie Pearl broke over the crest with Lennie and Harper hot on her heels.

All three had no time to stop when they spied the tent and their mother and M.C. sunning themselves. They broke open the silence on those tricky, rattling stones with enough noise to wake the dead. Jones came over the ridge carrying towels and breakfast in a tomato basket.

"Shoot," M.C. said, "now they woke her." Jones and the children had stopped on the shore just below the ridge.

"You could ask her if she'd like to take breakfast with us," Banina said.

"Think she's mad at me." M.C. touched the tender lump on his forehead. "Anyhow, I wanted her to see me first, alone."

"Well, she can see you first," Banina said. "Then bring her on up by the ridge for breakfast."

"You should of gone before she waked," M.C. said. "Wish Daddy and the kids didn't come."

"Oh." Banina glanced out over the lake. With some amount of tiredness, she got to her feet. She stood a moment, not looking at M.C. But then she turned and walked away. Passing the tent opening without a glance inside, she headed for Jones and the children. When she reached them, she took up her shopping bag. Wordlessly, Jones handed her one of the two towels; she disappeared in the undergrowth of bushes to dry herself and to dress.

Macie Pearl came running down the beach, bringing M.C. his roll of clothing and the other towel. She had half of a jelly sandwich for him held out on the palm of her hand like a slice of cake. She dropped the roll and towel on dry land behind him. Next she handed him the sandwich, looking brightly at him for a second before she turned and trotted back. She had passed the tent twice on her run and both times hadn't looked inside out of respect for someone's privacy. They all knew they were not to be bold with strangers.

I was smart with the girl. I fought her, M.C. thought.

In a bewildering rush of shame, he felt foolish at having brazenly kissed her.

He crammed the sandwich in his mouth and wolfed it down. He hadn't thought to thank Macie for bringing it to him. If she had expected thanks, she had given no sign.

Swallowing globs of white bread, he wondered how he would ever face the girl.

I can't leave now.

Moist dough was plastered to his tongue as he finished the sandwich. He cupped wet earth and sand in his hand and was holding it against his forehead before he realized he was feeling his bruise. It was tight with soreness.

Maybe we're even. She got cut and I got hit on the head.

He waded out in the water to wash his hands and drink from the lake. Then he sat down again.

Below the ridge, his family squatted or sat on the shore, dividing food from the basket. Banina sat with her back to the lake. The others fanned out around her, with Jones by himself in the center across from her. M.C. saw them all down there, but he was thinking only of the girl. He could feel her waking most certainly in his mind as she did in her tent. Without seeing her, he knew she hurriedly snatched up clothing and fought to get everything on before someone came looking in on her. She couldn't know they would never do that. They wouldn't spy on her. She was the one wandering around watching everything.

No need to be quiet now.

M.C. dried himself, smacking the towel against his legs. He rubbed it briskly through his hair. Flinging the towel out over the stones, he lay on his back. Feeling strong, he was M.C. inside and in every muscle. He was M.C. by the tent in the sun. Minute by minute, he heard the girl move about.

Banina left to go to work. Jones and the children went in for a leisurely swim. The kids hung onto his neck. Jones let them dive off him. When they tried to dunk him, he shook them loose as if they were rubber dolls. Later he had a time getting them to leave the lake. They wanted to stay with M.C. and wait for the girl. Macie Pearl put up the

139

biggest fuss. "I'm going to swim some more," she yelled. "Y'all can't make me leave!"

But Jones made her leave, and the boys, too. Finally the lake settled back into stillness. Trees, shore, all was burning silence, except for the cooling songs of birds.

Time passed for M.C. in a kind of sleepy haze. Sweat broke out in beads all over him. Drops slid down his temples to his neck. He let the perspiration collect at his throat before wiping it away with the palm of his hand.

Lie here the whole day. Sleep. And wake up a burnt-up crisp. too.

He couldn't keep himself waiting in the heat any longer.

"They're gone." he called to the tent.

By now the girl had to have heard him slapping the towel to dry himself and then stretching out over rattling stones.

"You can come out." He hoped his voice wouldn't scare her. He half expected to see the tent jump up in fear, but it wasn't as skimpy as it looked. It didn't make a move.

"Wouldn't hurt you," he called, as gently as he could. "Last night you just took me by surprise. I don't even have my knife with me."

He could be brave. He knew she had a knife. But he lay calmly on the towel. He wouldn't let himself think too far ahead about her. Like, what was she doing all alone in the hills? Like, how old would a girl have to get before she could have permission to go off by herself into dangerous places?

To get permission, that won't make sense. Who will give a daughter permission to run loose?

She has a car. Maybe they let her just go.

140

Still, M.C. couldn't figure out why the girl was there in the hills and in that bone-colored, odd-shaped tent all by herself instead of in town. Nobody lived alone in the hills.

Without warning, the girl appeared in the tent opening. Casually, she turned and looked at him.

With the lake shimmering and the summer sunlight making room for her, she looked like a figure living in darkness. Some premonition, dream, he hadn't even thought to have. Bright flashes cut into his eyes as he looked at her, distorting his vision. She seemed to be standing in a halo of shadow.

M.C. felt a sudden, reckless excitement. He gave her a low and perfect whistle through his teeth. Comical he was with just his head lifted up to look at her.

"Hi, there," he called over in his deepest voice. Grinning, he lazily gave her a hand wave. "They call me M.C. Higgins, the Great."

8

"WHO?" the girl said. She smirked at him. Her voice was mocking but she remained cautious, all the same. "M.C., what?"

Embarrassed, M.C. wouldn't give his title again. He sat up on one elbow. "I'm M.C. Higgins. That's what they call me."

Something glinted, catching the sun and flashing it in streaks of light. He forgot to ask her her name when he remembered the glinting light coming through the hills as he sat on his pole.

So that's it, he thought.

It was the knife the girl wore attached to her belt by loops of leather thong. It had a long, single-edge blade with no rust on it anywhere.

M.C. waited for her to say something else. But she just stood there with one arm raised slightly higher than the other. He didn't think much about the way she was standing, except that it looked awkward, until he got up and took a step toward her. Her arm shot across her waist closer to the knife. The knife was nearer her left side. She reached toward it with her right hand.

He wondered if he should dare her. Yet more than any dare, he wished she wouldn't be afraid of him. More than anything, he wanted to see her without that blade glinting in his eyeballs.

He reached for his pants in a roll at his feet. Shaking them loose, he turned the pockets out. "See?" he said. "Not a knife or nothing. I didn't come here to bother you. Didn't even know you were here."

He tossed his pants away and took another step toward her. In a second her hand was on the knife handle.

He sighed and sat down again on his towel.

"Ought to can go somewhere without somebody jumping me." Her voice was peeved and whining. "Can't even camp without a bunch of people coming around nosing."

He thought he'd better try to explain, but then she turned slightly and the blade stopped its shine. He could see her clearly. She had a round, expressionless face. And he couldn't make it fit with that nervous energy that ran beneath the high quality of her voice. She looked calm, but underneath he could tell she was afraid.

"Where you come from?" M.C. asked suddenly. "You ever scared being all by yourself?"

"What's to be scared of?" she said. The way she looked at him, he had to lower his eyes.

"I just wondered."

"Well, I go where I want," she said, "and see places I never seen."

"Your folks don't mind?" M.C. asked, keeping his voice polite, coaxing her.

Reluctantly, she began to talk. "It's only my mother," she said. "Since I was fourteen, I work and buy my own things."

"What kind of work?" Her eyes were not so distant now. He stood, but made no move forward.

"Well, from September to the end of May," she said slowly, "I get out of school at two o'clock. I go to this center where they gave me a job in the offices. I work until about six o'clock, but I have to keep up my grades or lose the job."

"Sounds real nice," M.C. said.

"Nice enough to get me my car and the tent," she said proudly.

He already knew she had a car. "Where *is* your car?" he asked.

"On in the town."

"How much did it cost you?" he asked innocently.

She answered in the same vein, "Three hundred dollars."

"You mean, you made that much money?" M.C. asked.

"I made more," she said. "I made almost nine hundred."

M.C. shook his head, stunned at the thought of so much money.

"I haven't spent more of it than ten dollars a week in the

whole time," she said. "I save it. I knew I was going to travel—do you work?" she asked.

M.C. looked off at the lake. "Nothing much to do around here," he said finally.

"Well, it sure is pretty," she said. "I've seen places before, but this is like being lost in a wilderness when you know there's a town close by. I walked all yesterday. I love to walk. Everything's so quiet! I never had so much fun."

M.C. smiled at her, pleased that she liked being alone the way he did. He decided she wasn't bad-looking. "Your mother won't mind you going off all by yourself?" he said.

"She minds," the girl said. "But I call her when I leave one place and go somewhere else. See, I have a letter from her in case I get stopped by the police. They see you're young and they think you're a runaway."

"A runaway?" M.C. said.

He thought she was going to laugh at him, but at the last second she didn't.

"They say a half a million kids a year run away from home. People don't know, but they don't ever find half of them."

Bewildered, M.C. shook his head again. "I sure didn't know that," he said. A vision came to him. He suddenly felt melancholy, and he saw himself running from a huge, gray house. All at once he fell and the earth opened and covered him completely.

"Don't come any closer," she said.

He found himself walking aimlessly toward her along the edge of the lake. "What? Oh." He stood still with his hands at his sides. "I said I wouldn't bother you."

"Well, you just ought to see my back," she said, her voice whining again. "You took a deadly weapon and committed a serious offense."

"You were going to hit me with that light," he managed to say. "What else could I do?"

"What was *I* supposed to do when somebody jumps me out of nowhere?"

M.C. felt remorseful, speaking so casually about the night before. Neither of them mentioned that M.C. had kissed her. But he thought of it. She seemed to think of it almost at the same moment. Simultaneously they looked away from one another.

"We're even, then," M.C. thought to say. "I won't bother you."

"Wherever I go, I try to make friends," she went on, "but some kids just aren't to be trusted. I never know what kind I've run into until it's too late."

"Who you saying is a child?" M.C. said. Angry, he wanted to sound older. Instead, his words came out as though he had asked an innocent question.

"Look, I didn't come here to pick a fight with you all."

M.C. heard something behind him. He turned and down the lakeshore away from the tent came his brothers and Macie Pearl. They must have skirted the lake on the other side, hiding behind trees. They had run off from Jones. Now they came up, not too close to M.C. but close enough to hear every word passing between him and the girl.

Seeing the kids made him so mad, he snatched up his towel. "I'm leaving," he called down the beach. Throwing the towel over his shoulder, he caught a stone in it and thumped himself in the forehead, right on his bump. The stone hurt and he knew he looked foolish. "I'm leaving right now!"

"We just come to swim," Macie called in her sweet voice. "You know we always do swim here." She looked around M.C. at the girl to let her know who it was owned the lake and the shore and all of the pine trees.

Harper laughed and pushed Macie toward the water. She plunged in just to show M.C. she didn't care about him or the girl. The boys waded in behind her.

"They your family?" the girl asked, watching them go far out in the water.

"Yea," M.C. said. "They have to follow me around like a bunch of baby chicks." He stood taller; he didn't have to try to look mean.

"Must be nice though, having someone else around," she said.

"You the only one?"

She nodded. "I don't mind it most of the time. But when I'm traveling, well, it'd be nice to have a sister. There's so many things to see . . . you want to say, 'Hey, look at that!' "

M.C. wondered about being the only child with no one younger to watch out for, but he couldn't quite picture what it would be like. Stealing sidelong glances at the girl, he knew he liked her. It was true, though, she was older than he.

She had nice skin, with a smooth sheen to it. Her hair was black and natural. She had a face not beautiful the way his mother's face was, all deep and distant. Her eyes were the best, being so full of light. They were bright-shining but skittish, shy, like they didn't know where it was safe to look.

He tried not to stare at the rest of her. But he could tell she wasn't any little kid. She wore brown slacks that were creased with country dirt. She had on a blue shirt with long sleeves rolled high. It was none too clean, either. She was lean, healthy-looking. Not tall, M.C. could tell from where he stood. Not even as tall as his shoulder. Still, she had to be older.

He followed her gaze to the children out in the lake. "That's Harper and Lennie and Macie Pearl," he told her, pointing out each one. "I'm Mark," he lied, "but everybody call me M.C." He wouldn't tell her he was Mayo Cornelius for fear she would laugh at the name.

"M.C., the Great?" she said.

"Yea." He grinned.

"Why 'the Great'?" she asked him.

"'Cause I can swim the best and everything."

"Everything, what?"

"You stick around and you'll see," he said easily.

He liked the way they were talking, almost playing. "My mother, Banina, and my daddy were here," he thought to tell her, "but they had to leave early."

"They come to see who was squatting on their land, I bet," the girl said. Her hands rested on her hips. One leg was forward, making her appear lopsided.

"It's not our land. Macie Pearl will just pretend. These kids swim here so much, they think they own the whole thing."

"Who does own it?"

"I don't know," M.C. said. "Everybody just swims here. Nobody I know of ever bothered with owning it."

"Somebody has to own it," she said. "Somebody owns everything. But I'll find out. Anytime I stop somewhere that isn't a campsite, pretty soon somebody comes along and says how I have to move on. Won't even let one person and a little tent sit somewhere."

"They make you move on out?" M.C. asked.

"Sure. Land's the basis of all power, see, and people hold on to their land."

M.C. had to smile. Land was just like anything else you could lose. He thought of Jones.

Power won't be the reason some people hold on to it.

But he said nothing.

"I'd like to have me some land someday," she went on. "Something like this, maybe with some water on it."

She didn't notice he kept on smiling at her. She seemed to have forgotten about her knife and any need for it. She had moved closer to the lake where the dark gleam of it reached her eyes. She watched the kids, whose games caused huge splashes. The lake rippled with ever-widening rings; her eyes widened with the wonder of it.

Very slowly M.C. came nearer. But she was intent on the lake.

"You weren't around here yesterday," he said. "I know, because Macie and the boys were swimming and they would have said so."

Vaguely, she looked at him and then turned back to the lake.

149

"I followed them over here," she said, "and when they left, I moved my stuff up over."

"You know," she said, "animals come up to the water all in the night. They scared me to death, but then I got up my nerve. I crawled right up in the tent opening. Didn't move a muscle and I saw this deer drinking! It was just there and then it was gone and I didn't see it leave, either."

M.C. nodded, remembering the doe he and Banina had flushed from a thicket.

"They'll do that," he said. "Deer will catch a scent of you. He move so fast, you can blink and he's gone."

"I'd love to live right here on the lake," she said. "Without one camper to hang the flag and break out the beer. I'm Pisces. I love water."

"You want to swim?" he asked her, standing on one foot and then the other. "The water is not so cold now."

She frowned. "I like a diving board. Anyhow, I misplaced my bathing suit."

"Just wear some cut-off jeans," he said. "Shorts, if you have them. Nobody's going to mind. You can dive from the rocks down there where the beach ends."

"I have shorts," she said. She stared solemnly at the water. "I have all kinds of things with me for any event. But I'm all out of Band-Aids." She looked at him hard. "I need one for that cut on my back."

"Let me take a look at it," he said, before he thought.

There was an awkward silence until she said, "It's just a little cut."

"I'm sorry," M.C. mumbled. Louder, he said, "The water's fine this morning."

In an instant he had plunged into the lake to begin a perfect breast stroke. In water, all of the awkwardness of a youth standing on land left him. With his knowledge and skill in it, he made no unnecessary move. His powerful arms shot upward, then outward and rearward, as he cut through the lake like some bold sea creature. His back turned gold from the sun glistening on it.

Hemmed in by mountains, surrounded by tall pines, the dark surge of the lake was magical. Fascinated, the girl watched it and the way M.C. cut through it, until she could no longer resist. She backed away, turned and disappeared into her tent. When she came out again, M.C. and the children were down at the far end of the lake.

She wore wrinkled, pink shorts and a faded man's shirt with sleeves cut away. She had tied the shirttails in a knot at her waist. M.C. thought she was about as nice-looking as she could be. But rather than strike out into the water from where she was, she came around the shore.

"Come on in," they shouted to her.

She preferred to walk down to the end of the beach. There she leaned on the rocks and plunged a foot in the water. "That's cold!" she said, looking pleased that they had invited her.

"Not underneath," Macie said. "Just on the top. You get in, and it's real warm."

M.C. said something to his brothers, and then: "Don't let Macie . . . I'm going through."

Head first, he upended himself and vanished beneath the surface. The water grew still again as if he had never been there. Macie rode on Harper's back until he grabbed the rocks and shook her off. Once he had climbed up on them, he gave Macie a hand. Lennie Pool followed.

The girl watched the water but it remained smooth and dark.

"What's your name?" Macie said, curious all of a sudden.

The girl smiled at Macie. But then her eyes flicked back to the lake where M.C. had gone under. She began to walk back and forth, her hands on her hips.

The children watched her.

"What's he doing down there?" she asked them.

They said nothing.

"I don't think he's coming up, you'd better do something."

Macie broke their silence with a giggle. "He's not even down there," she said. "Just over and behind these rocks." She led the way around the edge of the rocks. Harper and Lennie went, too, and cautiously the girl followed.

On the other side lay a surprise. It was an opening in the rocks. No one who didn't know would suspect it was there. The rocks fell back in a small clearing where there was a silent pool with grassy banks.

The children stopped at the edge. Macie turned brightly to the girl and smiled.

M.C. surged up from the center of the pool in a great splash. He sucked in air as though he would never again get enough of it, as the girl covered her mouth to stifle a scream.

The kids laughed at her. "It's a water tunnel," Harper told her in his soft, urgent voice. He told how the tunnel went under the rocks beneath the water at the edge of the lake and ended at the pool.

"Only M.C. can travel it," Macie said. "We ain't allowed. The kids from town don't even know there's a tunnel."

"You wouldn't know it, either, if you hadn't caught me doing it once," M.C. said. "Better keep the sense never to try it, too."

"How do you hold your breath so long?" The girl, talking to M.C. as though he were older, showing respect for him now.

He pulled himself up on the grassy bank and wiped water out of his eyes. He had to smile. She kneeled next to him, her fear of him and the children gone.

Proud he'd done something she never expected he could do. And she had come from somewhere by herself in a car. But he could be by himself, too. He could travel through water like nobody. First he thought of lying, to tell her he could hold his breath longer than anyone. The kids would know.

Finally he said, "It's not so long. I came up before you all ever got here. Hear you coming, and I just went under and waited. Then I splash up like I was out of breath."

She didn't seem to mind he had played a trick. "It's dark in the tunnel?" she asked him. Her face so close, he could see tiny bumps he hadn't noticed before.

Shyly, he looked at his feet hanging in the water. "It's gray light, kind of," he said. "This pool is at the end of the tunnel. Sunlight drifts in and gets faded, I guess. But

153

I see, a little. It's ghosty, though, when fishes slide over your skin."

She cringed with the picture of it. Watching her, Macie shivered with delight.

His eyes on the pool, M.C. sensed the girl watching him. Felt himself reaching out for her, the way he often reached out when he sat next to Jones. His skin itched and came alive with little things he seemed to know about her. She might travel alone, but every minute she was scared being by herself. The impression came to him, swift and certain.

Already he felt attuned to the girl, less self-conscious at having her so near.

He rubbed his arms and neck until the itching went away. Tiredness settled in the knot on his forehead in a dull ache that came and went. He wasn't feeling quite himself this morning. Yet he didn't want to go and leave her.

"What's your name?" he asked.

She shrugged. "No use of saying names."

"I told you our names," he said.

"I could tell you a name and you wouldn't know if it was really mine."

"Where do you come from then?"

"Same thing," she said. "You wouldn't know if I came from where I said."

"Then why not tell?"

She said nothing. She looked at him and quickly away, as if she wanted to speak out, but couldn't. Soon she was looking from the pool to the rocks and back to the pool.

She did this several times before it came to M.C. what was on her mind.

"A water tunnel won't be like a pool," he told her, "or even a lake."

She nodded, staring at the rocks.

"A pool or even a lake is simple. Water will lift you," he said.

She sat still, with just her head turning to look at him and then away.

"But tunnel is a bottleneck. No place to take off the pressure; or maybe pressure's not the trouble. It's just a tight place without a top, and you can get sick to your stomach."

A long silence in which she said nothing.

"How long can you hold your breath?" M.C. asked her.

"What?"

"If you travel that tunnel," he said. "How long can you go with no breathing?"

Wide-eyed, she stared at him. "As long as anybody." All at once she breathed hugely, holding the air in.

Macie and the boys scrambled close to see. Everything was still. The girl's eyes began to pop and tear. She held out while none of them moved, until at last her breath burst through her teeth. She fell back, panting.

"That was long!" Harper said.

"Maybe forty-five seconds," M.C. said. "Not long enough."

The girl sat up again.

"Try it once more," M.C. said.

"You don't think I can do it," she said.

"I'm not thinking a thing. It just has to be longer," he said. "Long enough to reach the pool."

"Well, I don't know," she said, her voice edgy. She searched M.C.'s face.

"If you're worried, don't try it," he said.

Then she was smirking at him. "Sure think you're something, don't you?" she said. "I saw you on that pole. Not just with the fire, but in the daylight. Sitting up there with nothing to do and no place to do it!"

Her anger shot through him. It hurt him and he didn't know what to say. He hadn't meant anything bad by what he said.

"The tunnel is fun," he said quietly, "but you have to have the lungs to hold out."

The girl sucked in her breath again. M.C. kept his eyes on the pool. He didn't want to be watching her if this time she failed. He tried just to feel when the time was long enough. But in spite of himself, he began counting in his head.

When he knew she would have to breathe, he turned to her Still she held out. Tendons and veins stood out on her neck. Her eyes were squeezed shut. Her cheeks and mouth were twisted in an awful face.

She exploded, bursting with air and squirming on the ground, trying to breathe again. Uncomfortably, M.C. turned his face away.

"You did it!" Macie yelled. Lennie Pool grinned and Harper clapped his hands.

"M.C., she did it!" Macie screeched. "Didn't she?"

He nodded at Macie to let all of them know. But he was wondering if he had forgotten something he should have remembered to ask.

Never taken someone through that tunnel, he thought. Maybe I shouldn't.

"Are you going to swim it right now?" Macie asked the girl.

But she couldn't answer. She seemed to be having that cold, sickening feeling that came from holding your breath too long. M.C. knew this. Drying sweat caused his skin to itch again.

"We maybe can swim it later on," he said. "Give you plenty of time . . ."

The girl shot up from the ground. Even though she looked weak, she stood with her hands firmly on her hips. "You think I can't do it." Her eyes snapped at him.

M.C. couldn't get himself loose from those eyes, they were so pretty. Slowly he got to his feet.

There grew a silence between them that separated them from the children. They stood close together, watching each other.

"You have to do just as I say," M.C. told her.

"Why?"

"'Cause I know how to get through."

She thought a moment. "Okay," she said.

They were in a world all their own, where she was older but he was the leader. He knew why she had to try the tunnel.

Not because I've done it. 'Cause I'm the only one.

He turned and led the way over the rocks to the lake. The girl followed close on his heels.

The lake lay as serene and peaceful as when they had left it. Way down at the other end was the ridge. In between

157

the ridge and the rocky end where now he and the girl crouched was the tent, like an intruder in the sun. All around them were pines, undergrowth, greens and browns closing in the magical shimmer of the lake.

He and the girl hung onto rocks just above the waterline. The children were clinging a foot above them.

"The tunnel's right down there," M.C. told her. "About eight to ten feet down. Maybe twelve feet long and that's a couple of body lengths." He paused, looking out over the lake. "Now I lead," he told her. "I lead and we hold together like this." With his right hand, he took hold of her left arm, forcing her to balance herself with her back against the rocks. "Hold on to my arm just above the wrist."

"Like this?" She grabbed his arm with fingers stronger than he'd expected. So close to her, he felt shy but calm.

"We jump here, we get more power," he told her. "We get down faster but it has to be done just right."

"How?" she said.

M.C. didn't know how. He was figuring it all out as he went along, working fast in his head the best way to jump and the quickest way to get through the tunnel.

"Best way is . . . if I jump backward and you jump frontward." He spoke carefully. "See, I hit and go in facing the tunnel. I have your left arm and you are pulled over. You follow in just in back of me. Now. In the tunnel, you have your right arm free and I have my left." They would use their free arms to push them through if they had to, and they could kick with their feet.

"Tunnel sides are moss," he said. "Push off from them when you bump them. It'll feel slimy but it won't hurt."

"Okay," she said.

"Pay no mind to fishes," he went on. "Most times, they're but just a few. They don't do nothing but get out of your way."

She nodded. M.C. could feel her tension through her arm.

"You all ready?" Macie asked from above them.

M.C. looked at the girl. "I'm ready," she said.

"You have to hold out for most of a minute."

"I can do it," she said.

"If you lose air, just stay calm," M.C. said. "I can get us out."

"I said I can do it!"

Her anger cut through him again, making him ashamed, he didn't know why.

"Macie, you count it off," he said grimly.

"She always get to do something," Harper said.

"He told *me,* now shut," Macie said.

"Stay out of the water. Wait for us at the pool. Now," M.C. said.

"Ready!" Macie yelled. "Get yourself set . . . ."

The girl grew rigid.

"You have to stay calm," M.C. told her. He held her arm as tightly as he could without hurting her. Her fingers dug into his wrist.

"Watch your nails!" he warned. They both sucked in air.

"Go, y'all!"

159

They leaped out and plunged. They hit the water at the same time but M.C. went under first because he was heavier. The girl turned facing him before her head went under. That was good, but pulling her after him slowed M.C. It semed to take forever to get down to the tunnel level. Water closed in on them. Sounds became muffled and then no sound at all. They were alone as never before. And there was nothing for M.C. to do but get it over with.

9

M.C. liked nothing better than being in the deep, with sunlight breaking into rays of green and gold. Water was a pressure of delicious weight as he passed through it, down and down. It was as if feeling no longer belonged to him. The water possessed it and touched along every inch of him.

He pulled out of his downward fall at the sight of the gaping tunnel opening. He no longer felt the girl next to him. He knew she was there with him by the impression she made on the deep. And he would remember her presence, her imprint, on this day for weeks.

Bending her wrist forward, he stretched her arm out straight as he kicked hard into the tunnel. Here the water was cooler and cast a gray shimmer that was ghostly. Pressure grew like a ball and chain hanging on his right shoulder. It was the girl like a dead weight.

Kick with your feet!

With a powerful scissoring of his legs, he tried to swim midway between the ceiling and bottom of the tunnel.

Push off with your hand!

Her dead pressure dragged him down. His knees banged hard against the bottom. His back hit the tunnel side as he realized she was struggling to get away. Fractions of seconds were lost as he tried twisting her arm to pull her body into line. Fishes slid over his skin, tickling and sending shivers to his toes. They must have touched the girl. For he had no moment to brace himself as she shot up on her back toward the ceiling.

Won't make it.

Horror, outrage stunned him. He had taken for granted the one thing he should have asked her. For the want of a question, the tunnel would be a grave for both of them.

She kicked futilely against the tunnel side and rose above him, twisting his arm straight up.

Yank, like Macie will pull down on a balloon.

If he could get the girl turned over, they might have a chance. But his breath seemed to be gone.

Not a grave, it's a tunnel.

In his lungs, emptiness was pain. But the will not to fail was there in his burning chest, in his free arm pushing hard against the deep. His legs were still loose and working. Then a sudden surge of strength, like a second wind.

Be M.C. Higgins, the Great.

He yanked the balloon down—he mustn't break the string. At the same time he propelled himself forward, knowing she would follow as she turned over.

An awful pounding in his head snapped his brain open. M.C. shot out of the tunnel like a cork from a jug of cider. And arching his back, he swung mightily with his right arm.

Dark balloon to the light above.

He hadn't the strength to hurl her to the surface. But he was right behind her. Before she could struggle down again, he was there, pulling at her. She opened her mouth in a pitiful attempt to breathe. He pounded her back, hoping to dislodge water. And held her close a split second to calm her. She was rigid.

Girl, don't drown.

Swiftly he caught her ankles and tossed her up over his head. She broke the surface. He was there, feeling sweet air just when he would have to open his mouth or have his lungs collapse.

M.C. fought against dizziness, aware he had his hand on her neck in a bruising clasp to hold her up. He had to let go or break it.

The girl was gagging, trying to breathe. He heard his own breath in a harsh, raw heaving. He was daydreaming a distant cheering. Then he saw the children, feet jumping up and down on the grassy bank. A swirl of rocks before he realized the girl was sinking. He must have let her go. But he had the sense to catch her again around the waist.

Still M.C. Still the leader. He had taken her through the tunnel and they were back in the world together. Still all the blame was his. But he could fix it. Could keep the children from knowing about her.

Moaning cry, coughing, she clung to him.

"No." He knocked her hands away. With just the pressure of his arm and shoulder on her back, he forced her flat out. As though she were dog-paddling, he glided her into the land. The feet jumping on the grassy bank fell back and were still.

Macie stood there on the bank, closest to M.C.'s head.

"She's weak," he said to Macie. "See if you can help pull her some . . . my wind is gone."

Macie clasped the girl's arms. M.C. had her by the waist. Halfway out of the water, she kicked M.C. away. She slithered and kneed her way over the bank. On the grass, she hunched into a ball, and struggling to breathe, closed her eyes.

Dark balloon.

M.C. climbed out and crawled a distance to collapse on his back. He was away from the girl, with the children between them, but he kept his eye on her. They were close together in his mind, where a vision had started. Day after day, they swam the lake. Hour upon hour, they sunned themselves on the shore.

M.C.'s chest wouldn't stop its heave and fall. His mouth watered with stomach bile as the pounding ache spread out across his forehead.

None of them moved. For a long while neither Harper nor Macie asked a single question. Lennie Pool never did say much.

M.C. felt as if every muscle were trying to get out of his

skin. He was sick with exhaustion. But light out of the sky bore into him, warming and relaxing him. It was a healing band on his eyelids. As the ache in his forehead moved off, tunnel and water filled his mind. His eyes shot open, blinding the awful memory.

Seeing that M.C. was awake, Macie came over to him. "You did it!" she said happily. "Were you scared?"

He knew he would vomit if he tried to talk. He swallowed hard.

"You sure took your time. Was it any trouble?" Macie went on.

"Just took it easy," he said finally.

The girl brought up pool water she had swallowed. Half an hour later, she sat up shakily on her knees. In a slow, mechanical sweep, she brushed grass and twigs from her drying clothes.

M.C. raised his head. "You all right?" he asked her.

When she stood, the children stood with her. M.C. was on his feet as well, as though he moved only when she moved.

Slowly she seemed to change. He watched her grow stronger, throwing her head back, thrusting out her chin.

"I went all the way through that tunnel," she said, smiling vaguely. "I could have drowned—I can't even swim a lick."

The children gaped at her. Shocked, they turned to M.C.

"And you took her down?" Macie gasped. "You took her clear through . . . you didn't even know!"

The kids began to giggle, jostling one another, with the girl looking solemnly on.

M.C. felt the heat of shame rising in his neck. Only this one secret between them, but the girl wouldn't have it. She made him stand there with the kids laughing at him. He stared at his hands, at the jagged nails which he bit down to the skin while sitting on his pole.

"I can't stand a lying kid," the girl said.

Worse than a slap in the face, but he said evenly, "I'm not any kid. And I didn't lie."

"You told your sister we took it easy," she said, smirking at him.

"*I* took it easy," he said. "If I hadn't, you wouldn't be here, girl."

The children stared at him soberly now. The girl looked uncertain.

"It's no joke not to tell somebody you can't swim," he said.

"Somebody didn't ask me," she said sullenly.

"Didn't need to ask—you should've told me!"

"I just wanted to see it. I didn't know it was going to be so *long*."

"So you want to see something and we almost drown?" He was shaking now with the memory of the tunnel. "Ever think of somebody but yourself?"

The girl shrank back. Uncomfortably, they watched her. M.C. hadn't meant to make her appear stupid. But she was quick to apologize.

"I'm sorry," she said simply. "You told me you were some M.C., the Great. . . ."

The look she gave him, as if she knew only he could

have saved her, made him feel proud. He had to smile. "You have some good nerve. A lot of real good nerve," he said at last. But then he couldn't think of anything else to say. He stood there, feeling uneasy, until he thought to change the subject.

"You a friend of Mr. James K. Lewis, with the tape recorder?"

"Who told you that?" she said.

"He did. He was around to hear my mother sing."

"I just gave him a ride," she told M.C. "Traveling alone like I am, it's good to pick up somebody going all the way down the road."

Slowly they began to talk. M.C. walked away from the pool, the children and the girl following. He headed over the rocks and presently stood on the lake shore.

"Ride with an old guy and folks think he's your father," the girl went on.

M.C. had just his toes in the lake. The children bunched around him. The girl talked almost freely. She was smiling, speaking about the dude:

"He'd point out some nice clean place to eat. We'd stop and he'd order me some breakfast—man! And then we'd stop for lunch and he'd pay for that, too. I sure didn't mind taking him down the road."

Bewildered, M.C. couldn't picture *the road*. "Which road you talking about? What do they call it?" he asked.

She laughed. Leaning toward him, she studied his face as if reading a map. "I bet you've never been out of these hills."

M.C. brushed his hand over his eyes where his head ached dully. Waves of feeling for her came and went, leaving him speechless.

"I knew it," she said. "You have cities all over the place and you haven't seen a single one. You have Covington and Portsmouth. Louisville." She looked out over the lake. "Aren't you curious?" The air above the water quivered with heat. "But I do know people in Cincinnati," she said, "haven't even been downtown, let alone Cherry Grove. Some of them, born on one street and never even go but two blocks away their whole lives. I don't know how they stand it."

She peered at M.C. again. "But I found out about you all before Mr. Lewis ever did. You find out things from watching the kids of a place. Least, you find out faster."

"Find out what?" he asked.

"Well," she said, "find out what there's to see. What there's to know, just to be knowing."

M.C. was silent. Every word she spoke sank deep into his mind. He remembered first talking to the dude. Blocks of cities mixed with his thoughts of the prairie. He wondered how a traveler figured out which way to go and what road to take.

How would he and his mother and the kids find the way? But, of course, they would have the dude to guide them.

A harsh yodel broke over the lake. It sounded clear, yet coming from a distance. It was M.C.'s father telling him something. Jones was moving, M.C. could tell. He wasn't calling the children home.

M.C. listened. The call would echo loud as it bounced

through the hills. But coming at them, it would fade in midair. Jones was heading toward the river.

"It's my daddy," Macie explained to the girl. She turned brightly to M.C.

M.C. cupped his hands around his mouth. He pitched his yodel as loud as he could in answer. And the pain in his eye sockets broke open and spread. It stopped him for only a second before he let Jones know he had the children with him.

M.C.'s yodel was better than Jones's. It began and ended with the same hard strength and quality as Banina's. It could carry for a half-mile and Jones had to hear. Sure enough, presently he called back a last word to M.C.:

"Yod-a-lay-da, M.C.-a-lun, a-lunch-a-ladieauuuu."

"He'll be back after noon," M.C. said quietly. Jones's yodel had come from around Hall Mountain. "He's going into town."

The children had momentarily forgotten the girl. She said not a word. But M.C. could tell it was her turn to wonder.

For a yodel cry was like no other sound. It was a power of breath and voice. Like the lake, it was a magic belonging only to those of the hills. M.C. had the magic now and Macie would have it one day. So would Lennie Pool and Harper. She might have realized how it held father to mother, children to each parent and to each other, as it passed down the line of living.

They all saw the girl seem to change again. Her shoulders slumped forward. Suddenly she seemed worn out. Shivering slightly in her damp clothing, she looked beaten down.

"I have to go in," she whispered. Turning away, she dragged her feet, kicking up stones as she went to her tent.

"Can we come in a minute?" Macie called to her.

"I don't care," the girl murmured. Falling to her knees, she crawled inside the tent.

"Something wrong with her," Harper said.

M.C. kept his silence as the children went up to the tent in a group. Reluctantly he followed, as though forced against his will by an unseen power. Some nameless feeling for the girl had hold of him. With his brothers and sister close by, he was drawn back into the world with them again. He felt cut off from the girl and out of place in the bright sun.

The children pushed into the tent as if they were still outdoors. Tripping over themselves, they were about to pull the tent down around them. M.C. hurried in to organize them, motioning them not to speak, nor to touch or bump into anything. He showed them how to settle down around a pile of clothing on one side of the tent, so as not to disturb it.

The tent was big enough for one person to live comfortably. Two people could sleep in it, but with any more, it became crowded and stifling, not a pleasant place to be at all.

Now the tent was crowded. There was no room for M.C. So Harper let M.C. have his place while he stretched himself belly-flat on the stones outside, with just his head and shoulders in the tent. M.C., Lennie and Macie Pearl sat in a line on one side. The girl was stretched out on the other side in a green sleeping bag. She lay exhausted, with her hands clenched into fists beneath her chest. M.C. sat farthest away from the tent opening, with his back against the damp coolness of the canvas wall. He could look straight into the girl's eyes, her head was that close to his feet. Her eyes were closed and fluttering as though caught in fitful sleep.

All at once her eyes opened, staring M.C. down. He thought she would say it was too crowded, that he and the kids should get out. But shivering slightly, she simply closed her eyes again.

Next to her against the tent wall was that huge light she had beamed on M.C. the night before. It was all shining metal. Seeing its handle, he remembered how it had felt in his hands. Beside it on the tent floor was a towel and folded washcloth on which lay a number of silver and gold bracelets and one long necklace made out of seashells.

M.C. recalled the rattling and jingling sounds of the night before. He had to smile at the washcloth where now their mystery lay solved.

In his thoughts, he reached across the girl to touch the pretty necklace, motionless and still. He had a vision of her sitting up in the tent and slapping him hard, saying, *"Don't you ever touch a single thing that's mine!"*

It was so real, he was shocked when he realized neither one of them had moved.

Hanging from the tension rods that supported the tent was most of what the girl possessed. There was a large nylon bag with not much in it. Just a blanket, a canteen. There were some socks and some shiny things wrapped with care in plastic.

171

There was hardly any food in the tent and no pot or pan to cook with. Just some apples and some dry cereal. Some crackers and beef jerky.

Climb the hills with that little bit to eat? Not even a can of beans.

M.C. glanced at her to find her staring at him again.

"Too hot in here," he said softly. The air in the tent had grown warmer and smothery. He didn't know what else to say or where to look to avoid the girl's eyes. Seeing her curled tightly in her sleeping bag, he knew he shouldn't have spoken of the heat.

"You all get on outside," he said to the children.

The boys never had to be told twice. They scooted out in a second. Only Macie Pearl looked stricken, as though to leave would break her heart.

"You have to go, too, Macie," M.C. told her. "Get some air in here."

"I'll sit still. I won't talk," she pleaded.

"Macie, do what he says," the girl said. It was the first time she had called any one of them by name. Something in her voice, so weak and tired out, made Macie sigh and leave.

With Harper out of the way of air movement, with all of them gone, M.C. felt he could breathe again.

After a time he asked the girl: "Are you sick?"

"I get chilled some," she said. "All the dew that comes as soon as it's dark. My clothes get all wet—I hate it!"

"You ought to change what you have on from swimming," M.C. said. "You ought to take your bed and everything out in the sun. . . ."

Impatiently she kicked in the sleeping bag, dislodging from the foot of it a shoulder purse made of brightly woven cloth. The pocketbook was pretty, M.C. thought, and it bulged full of things.

"Look," she said abruptly. "I meant to be down in that town by now—always forget to buy some food. But now I'm so weak. I *hate* eating out of cans!"

Again she kicked and turned in the sleeping bag until she had it twisted out of shape.

M.C. couldn't understand her. Right outside was a lake full of food. Bullheads and sunfish for whoever came early enough after first light and before swimming started. Even at noon anyone with a pole and a line and time to spare could catch something. He and his family never did any fishing. For them to resort to it for food was unheard of. Water was the opposite of land, which they possessed and loved. The lake was amusement, relaxation. But for her, he thought of fishing and looked around the tent for a pole and hooks. He found none.

She had the knife hidden somewhere, probably in the sleeping bag with her, just to be safe. A knife could skin a rabbit in ten minutes.

First you must catch it in a trap, M.C. thought. He grinned, remembering Ben had said he had a rabbit.

"I just need some meat for some strength to get on down into town," she said. "I'd love to have just one glass of milk. I can *taste* it." And then: "A hundred and fifty dollars insurance on the car. Sure didn't leave me much for food."

M.C. was halfway out of the tent before he turned and, not quite looking at her, motioned her to follow.

"Look, can you get me some food?" she asked anxiously.

Outside, the kids were waiting for M.C. Hot air hit him, but it was less moist, less stifling than that inside the tent. He stared at the children, seeing them as though they had been carved from sunlight. But he thought only of the girl.

Crazy nerve. She don't know a thing. I know about woods.

He called inside: "Change, and bring that bed and things out here to dry. Come on over to my house. . . ."

The noon mill whistle rose on the air, screaming soft and far and then loud and near. The sound of it wavered on air currents, echoing, bouncing off hills, until it died.

There had been no movement inside the tent. M.C. had to coax her. "We have some food. Throw out the wet stuff. Daddy went to shop some more. I have to get these kids on home."

He saw the girl unwind herself from the sleeping bag before he turned away. When she had changed into the slacks of the early morning, with the knife glistening on her belt, she brought out the sleeping bag and her swimming clothes. She had her cloth pocketbook hanging from her neck like a feedbag.

M.C. spread the sleeping bag and her wet clothes in front of the tent. Then he grabbed his shoes and pants and pulled them on. He flung his towel around his neck and tied his sweater around his waist. Once he looked at the girl. She stood waiting, uneasily, it seemed to M.C.

"We're closer to home than town," he thought to say. "Least, there's cider, if there's no milk."

She looked so bedraggled and uncertain. He felt her tug

hard on his feelings. He started out at once, before she could change her mind. He led the way from the shore over the ridge with her and the children following in a bunch. He was heading back over the same ground he and Banina had come hours before.

They went through the pass at the side of Hall Mountain. At the end of it, M.C. half-slid down the steep hill slope and on through pine trees alive with dappled light and birds. He didn't gaze at the sweep of mountains. In his excitement at having the girl come home with him, he was going too fast. He saw everything around him as if in a fog. Pure outlines of branches, pine boughs, grasses, filled his brain with haze.

All at once he stopped and ran back to the bottom of the hill slope. There was the girl near the top, stepping down in great, comical strides, her arms held straight out from her sides.

Run. It's easier.

But she went on striding faster and faster until the momentum caused her to hurtle forward. She would have fallen if M.C. hadn't been there to catch her by the arms.

She pushed him away. He didn't mind. She was just like him. She didn't like making mistakes either.

"Take you by the hand so you don't break your neck," he said, teasing her.

She half-smiled but kept her eyes on her feet. She was almost past him before he realized she meant to take the lead. He got in front and headed on alone, hurrying too fast as before.

Home was not so far now. Soon they were in the foothills

below Sarah's Mountain. They were descending and his tennis shoes were full of small stones and dirt. They moved in and out among the pines until the trees began to thin out.

Now close to the gully, where in the night he had frightened the girl, he paused, searching the side of Sarah's Mountain looming ahead before he understood what he was looking for.

Up there, his pole flashed silver-bright. It was lone, cold steel without its rider. He had a vague feeling for it, but that was all. The girl filled his head so, he hardly thought about it.

The trees fanned out above the path, making clumps of shadow and shafts of brilliant light. He should have slowed down, for suffocating heat with trees and bush so close nearly took his breath away. He breathed with his mouth open. He could feel the towel wet and icy around his neck as his shoulders seemed to split open the air in front of him.

He concentrated on home and the girl. Once he paused to turn She and the children were coming. He could hear them, but he had left them out of sight.

Something on the path ahead. Where there had been light and shade, there stood a black something blocking M.C.'s way.

Not a deer. A Killburn?

Fear gripped him. But he was moving so fast, he couldn't stop. He would have busted right past whoever it was standing there if he hadn't suddenly been caught under one arm with the strength of a bear. It was a grip like a vise, twisting M.C.'s arm and scaring him out of his wits.

"What's the big hurry in all this heat?"

Jones, coming back with a sack of groceries in the other arm. It took him only a moment to see the state M.C. was in.

"What you so afraid about? Somebody after you?"

"Man!" M.C. said breathlessly. His legs almost buckled. "Didn't look like you standing there. Looking like a witchy." And then, with relief at seeing his father, he confessed all in a rush: "Took that girl through the water tunnel. She can't swim a single lick!"

"You ought to have your head whipped! Where're the kids?"

"Coming with the girl," M.C. said.

Jones jerked his head around. He waited for what seemed forever to M.C. before the children and the girl came into sight far down the path.

"What do you mean by bringing her home?" Jones asked. Before the sound of his own voice had died, he knew why. His eyes softened as he stared at his trembling, wet rabbit of a boy.

"She got this idea in her head to camp but she don't know the first thing," M.C. said. "She don't even have any food."

"So you figure you'll give her a feed off me," Jones said.

M.C. could tell Jones wasn't angry. "And then I'll teach her to hunt," M.C. said eagerly. "How to skin a rabbit."

"First you must catch the rabbit," Jones told him. "Maybe give a woman's touch to baiting your rabbit traps. Leastways, it can't hurt."

M.C. kept silent, reminding himself he had a rabbit already caught. Before long, he would have no need of the traps anyhow.

I'll give her the rabbit, he thought. We take a skillet down by the lake. . . .

Jones turned and with a backhand wave to M.C., headed home.

M.C. let him go. When the children and the girl were close, he led the way down into the gulley and on the path up Sarah's Mountain. At the foot of the path, he waited until they were all there, bunched around him.

"Up there's where you live?" the girl said. Her skin appeared even sleeker, shining with perspiration.

M.C. nodded and pointed to the ledge outcropping.

"I don't see anything," she said.

"The house is there. Come on," M.C. said.

"Sure is a big mountain. You all own it?" she said, as they started to climb.

"Up to the outcropping, we own it," M.C. told her. "Been in the family forever. And someday, it's going to be mine."

The girl was at his elbow and she looked at him with something close to awe. The children moved around them, staring from her to M.C.

"It's always handed down to the oldest son," M.C. told her. "My oldest son will take it from me."

"Can I still stay here, even when it's yours?" Macie asked him.

"Sure," he said, "stay as long as you want."

"Stay until we have to leave," Harper said. "Until dude come back for Mama."

"You all thinking of leaving?" the girl asked.

The children waited for M.C. to tell it. Abruptly he stopped, his head down.

Overcome by the power of two separate thoughts, he had the worst kind of mournful feeling.

Talking about staying forever.

It was as if his head contained two minds. The one knew they would never leave the mountain. The other knew they had to leave. At any time he could think of one and forget the other. Or think of both and be stopped, torn with not knowing what to believe.

Wish it was over, one way or the other, he thought.

He left the girl's question unanswered and went on up the path. She was at his back now. Glancing around, he saw she was climbing like a child learning to walk, sliding and falling and not making any kind of time.

"You can't stand straight," he told her. "See, stoop and lean forward." He showed her and she tried it. But she had little strength in her legs. In a minute she had to sit down on the path. Macie and the boys stepped over her knees and waited off to one side.

"How do you *do* it—all the way from the lake and then up this mountain?" she asked. "Even Macie can do it, it's impossible!"

"Not when you do it every day," M.C. told her, coming back and kneeling next to her. He pulled up long stalks of dying grass burned by the sun. "We learn from since we're babies. You get lost and go on. Least, once I thought I was lost."

He grinned suddenly, engagingly, and the girl couldn't help smiling.

"Daddy," M.C. said, "off in the trees watching me. See it's this game to see if I could find my own way. Knew it

179

was a game, but I still was scared. I still was bawling my head off. Knew he wasn't going to come get me."

"That's cruel," she said.

"Well," M.C. said, "I just had to keep on walking, nothing for it. And I walk a long kind of time. Then, see, I get interested in finding where I am. I remember—I stop crying. I stop remember even Daddy is there. See, the scare is gone out of me. I think and I think and I remember this: Home is higher than the hills. Home is higher—up and up. So see, the highest mountain is right there. I climb and climb and I'm home. Never lose me again."

"So it isn't cruel," she said. "It's teaching."

"Daddy has to teach something so he won't have to learn something." He yanked a clump of grass up by the roots and threw it hard into the weeds.

"You don't like him?" the girl said. "Maybe I shouldn't ask." But she waited.

He thought a moment. Years and years of his father. Walking, hunting with him. At the table. On the porch.

"Nothing to do with liking," he said finally. "Him and me, it's a feeling— But I like the mountains. But we have to leave. Mama's a great singer going to be a star."

The girl looked at him as if he were joking. His face was closed. Stubborn. She stared around at the bedraggled children looking on with their alert, serious faces.

"You believe that?" she said.

"It's the truth," he said. He got up, spun around and headed home. "Come on. These kids have to eat."

He left her to make her way with Macie Pearl and the boys. He was across the yard and on the porch before they had reached the pathway through the briers. He saw his pole and the junk around it. It was gleaming. A marker. Not his alone.

Jones waited inside the door. "You sure took your sweet time," he said.

"Girl can't even climb good!" M.C. said. He came in, holding the ends of the towel around his neck, and collapsed on the couch with seats like cushions of air.

"You want to dirty up the sofa?" Jones asked him.

For a moment M.C. lay there, letting his body sink down and down into the softness. Then he tossed the towel toward the kitchen where it landed smacking against the floor. Sliding down to the plush carpet, he stretched out on his back and closed his eyes.

"Ought to have better sense than to be caught out there at the top of noon," Jones told him. He picked up the towel and came back to watch at the open door.

"Hadn't been for her, would have been back sooner," M.C. said.

"Let the horse out of the barn, then you close the door," Jones said.

"I told you she was hungry."

"Appreciate your sympathy, too," Jones said, "but I still can't figure why you try to drown her and yourself, either."

"I didn't though, did I?" M.C. said.

"No, but I ought to tan your hide anyhow."

"You can maybe try." M.C. opened his eyes. He had his hands clasped behind his head and slowly brought them down to his sides. He could feel himself, pulsing heat, itching for a fight.

Jones turned just his head to look at him. He smiled. "Never fight a little old thirteen-year-old with a crush," he said amiably.

"I don't have a crush!"

"Sure, you do," Jones said. "You don't even know how much a crush you have."

"Have not!"

"Have."

"Well, you don't like *nobody*," M.C. yelled, "least of all strangers. You afraid you might learn something."

Jones laughed. "She going to teach me how to shiver in the cold? Dude going to show me how to lose myself? Shoot." He turned back to the open door, where now he must have seen the children and the girl coming out of the undergrowth of briers.

"But don't you worry," he whispered back at M.C. "I'll be so nice to her, you won't know it's me."

M.C. could hear them. He couldn't see them or the girl, but he could tell that Jones could. They had stopped around his pole. The girl must have studied it in all of its height as Jones studied her.

M.C. could see Jones's eyes flicking up and down, looking at her. He thought he knew when Jones's eyes steadied on her face. For they seemed to soften. And there was a trace of a smile around his mouth, as if he remembered something pleasant.

"It looks higher when you see it from far away," the girl was saying to the kids.

"It's M.C.'s own pole and nobody but him can climb it." Macie, speaking in a voice full of pride.

The girl: "Well, some others must of climbed it before. You see it with flags waving all over the place."

Macie: "Not this pole. Nobody but M.C."

The girl: "Is that a fact?" Her voice, rising up the scale to an indignant whine: "Well, I'll be darn."

Grinning, Jones turned his head to M.C. He whispered, "You know what she thinks she going to do?" But seeing M.C. as tight and taut as a bowstring, seeing the boy's furious eyes on him, Jones let the question go.

He walked past M.C. "I'm fixing the lunch myself," he said. "Be a little while 'cause I'm making my potato soup."

Who cares?

M.C. was hungry as he could be. Starving.

The kids were clomping on the porch now. Macie and Lennie Pool hurtling around, jumping up and down the steps. Macie screamed her way into the house, with the boys rushing in behind her. After the screen door had banged, the girl eased it open again. She stood there, sleek, not tall. Darkening M.C.'s doorway.

10

—————

JONES molded and shaped the lunch from bits and pieces of aging food. He had gathered two pounds of soft potatoes, an onion as large and as damp as his fist and a Mason jar of lard that had been used but once before. He strutted back and forth, pulling the meal together from different parts of the kitchen. From far back in the icebox, he produced a crock of souring milk, some beef broth for stock and a half-shriveled section of green pepper.

Sitting at the kitchen table, they all watched him. That is, the children and the girl watched him while M.C. watched the girl to see what kind of effect Jones was having on her. For it was true, Jones was a sight to see whenever he made a show of preparing his special potato soup.

M.C. had eaten nothing more than half a jelly sandwich

the whole morning. They all were starving. But he ignored his gnawing hunger. Grudgingly, he had to admire the way Jones could stand at the stove with Banina's apron pinned to his shirt just below the chest.

He ought to look simple, M.C. thought.

Jones looked like he was enjoying himself, with his sleeves rolled high and his head cocked to one side. Suddenly he would pull himself up and look proudly at them while he skillet-fried diced potatoes and chopped onion in the lard.

M.C.'s stomach ached from the delicious smell of sizzling onions. They were all laughing at Jones, even the girl. Jones stirred the food just a little too far away from the skillet. The lower half of his body was turned clear to the left, while the top half of him stayed turned to the right. He had to stretch his stirring arm way over while he kept his left hand hooked in his belt. With his chin stuck out, he peered into the skillet, moaning softly with the wonder of sweet-browning potatoes swimming in fat.

Jones poured in some water and a great cloud of steam rose up over the pan.

"Now you're cooking up a *storm!*" he said.

The girl giggled and covered her mouth. Jones glanced at her with what was clearly friendliness, M.C. could tell. True to his word to treat her kindly, Jones had made her some coffee when she first came into the house. And because she was company and maybe not used to patient waiting, he had prepared her a half-slice of toast from the oven. He carefully explained to her that his special potato soup took time to fix. He acted as if she had been with them forever.

And right off the girl's eyes had been shining at Jones just as though he was her own real father, or at least one she wished she had.

Jealously M.C. watched them, his sullen eyes flicking from one to the other. In spite of his anger, they softened whenever he looked at the girl.

Jones had asked her straight out what her name was. And straight out she had told him, when all morning she wouldn't tell M.C.

Thinks I'm a kid. Well, I know things, too.

She told Jones she was Lurhetta Outlaw, just as if she had been telling that strange name to everybody all morning long.

"Lurhetta who?" Macie said.

"Lurhetta—Outlaw?" Harper said.

"Now that's got to be a true name," Jones had said. "Nobody'd want to make up a name like that."

Lurhetta said that was why she never told it. Defiantly, she turned hard eyes on each one of them at the table. For no sooner had she said "Outlaw," she told Jones, people laughed or thought she must be lying.

"Bet they began to look at you sideways, too," Jones said.

"They sure would," she said, "and make me so mad."

"Don't you be shaming ever to tell who you are," Jones told her.

"But it must mean that somewhere, my people were . . ." Anxiously, she looked at Jones. ". . . were busted up with the law."

Touch her face and rub away the sad—

"I'm not asking you nothing about your background,"

Jones was saying, "but it seems to me 'Outlaw' can mean more than a single thing. It can just as soon mean your people got no protection from the law, so they was outside it, so to say. Way back when, how many black folks had any luck with law, anyhow?"

The girl's eyes were round and wide. "Sure, it could mean that," she said. "My mother once knew this teacher from New York Manhattan who said the New York Manhattan telephone book was full of Outlaw names. Said they all lived in Harlem, Manhattan, too."

"That's something!" Jones said. "There has to be a story in *there*."

M.C. had heard of Harlem. Heard somewhere that there were as many black people in Harlem as equaled the whole population of Cincinnati. He didn't know if it was true or not.

Wonder if it is. Wonder if I ever will see it.

"So don't you be ashamed by your name, ever," Jones told Lurhetta Outlaw.

Later now, and they still sat watching Jones perform at the stove. In spite of himself, M.C. warmed to Jones's easy and natural kindness, which he seemed to turn on and off at will. There were times, like right now, when the simple act of his father slicing green pepper into a skillet wasn't just a comical picture M.C. would remember. It reminded M.C. of the *feeling* Jones had talked about yesterday.

Was it only yesterday?

He recognized it now as the same feeling that would rise in his chest and in his throat when sometimes he walked into the kitchen and saw that stove. So that now it seemed that the kitchen was full of the feeling day after day of Jones and him at lunchtime.

We leave, and how much of him will walk away, too?

Sitting there with his hunger curled hard in his stomach, M.C. rested his gaze always on Lurhetta Outlaw.

She leaves, and something of me will walk away with her? Maybe she won't.

He stared at her, with the idea of her staying dawning ever brighter. She stared back blankly, but M.C. took no notice.

Jones poured a pint of beef stock into the skillet and let it simmer until all of the vegetables were tender. The whole time, he pranced back and forth, banging pots and pans and making the kids and Lurhetta laugh. He took a second skillet and filled it with lard to melt on the stove. When the lard was bubbling, he threw in chunks of hard bread, which deep-fried crisp and brown. The whole time, Jones kept up a stream of talking.

"Now! Anytime I want to quit the day labor in steel, I got me some work cut out. Find me a fancy restaurant . . . ."

". . . not too fancy," Lurhetta said.

"Down-home fancy," he told her. And they both said at the same time: "Waaay down-home fancy!"

Jones tossed the cooked bread into a pot to be kept warm at the back of the stove.

"Haven't forgotten a *thing*," he told them.

Next he seasoned the vegetables with salt and pepper. He looked around: "Where'd I put that tin of nutmeg?"

"You spent some money on nutmeg?" M.C. asked him.

"What you have against some nutmeg?" Jones asked.

"Mama never will spend money on it."

Jones made no comment then, no more than to say, "Your mama be home before dark. So she told me this morning."

Lurhetta looked around at them. "I haven't ever seen your mother," she said.

"She works," M.C. said.

"What kind of work does she do?" Lurhetta asked.

"Nobody ask you what *your* mama do," Macie Pearl said.

"Macie," Jones said, in a way that said she had been rude, but she had been right, as well.

Lurhetta stared angrily at Macie until slowly she realized she had crossed over an invisible line of formality.

Jones reached into a cupboard and felt around. He was silent until he found the nutmeg where he had put it.

"Macie means if she tells you something, then maybe you feel forced to tell her something. It's just a way in the hills," Jones said. "Whatever you want to say is fine. Most folks say what they want to say, but ask no questions." He poured milk and the contents of the skillet into a large pot. Once he shot a glance at M.C. It had a hint of challenge in it.

Talking about strangers. He means she will always be one, M.C. thought.

"You asked me my name and where I come—" Lurhetta broke off as her voice was drowned out by a weird, outlandish yelling from the front of the house.

Kindness and light seemed to drain from Jones's face. He grew rigid and slammed the nutmeg tin down on the counter. M.C. felt coldness on his scalp, as though his hair stood straight up as the sound grew louder. The children stared

wildly. Lennie Pool slid off his chair; and pulling Macie
down with him, hid under the table.

> *Ah'm hot an' ah'm a-co-o-old . . .*
> *Ah'm a snowbody, Ah'm a snowbody.*
> *Freeze-a-water!*
> *Hear-ah . . . Ice-a-m-a-a-a-n . . .*

Jones rushed from the kitchen, through the parlor and to
the front porch. M.C. was right behind him.

"Daddy," he said.

"Don't tell *me!*" Jones said through his teeth. He flew out
the door just as the iceman was about to come up the front
steps.

"Back off, damn your hide!" Jones told the man.

"Daddy," M.C. said.

Lurhetta Outlaw spoke from the soft light of the parlor:
"What is it? What's going on?"

M.C. gave her a glance and turned back to the scene out
front. "Witchy folks," he whispered.

"What?" Lurhetta said. She came up next to him.

"Daddy is working most times when they come," M.C.
said. "With the kids off swimming, I'm the only one here, on
my pole."

"Who?" Lurhetta said.

"Well, look at them. Witchy people," M.C. said.

"*Listen and learn it.*" In an instant flash of memory, M.C.
recalled Jones telling him long ago: "*You can be stalking.
Hear a sound. You look to see but there's nothing. Turn
back, and he's there on the path blocking you. Don't try to
pass him by, for he knowing where you be before you
know, and knowing what you will do. He, with skin so fair,*

190

*he is near white. But hair is always thick and tight so you
can tell, and always almost red. Them gray eyes, cold. And
even if he do smile pleasant, they stay cold. Don't you turn
away, but back down the path the way you come. For he is
merino. Or witchy, as folks here always know him. . . ."*

Three of them stood there in front of M.C.'s house. Three
men with an odd, yellow cast to their skin and with reddish
hair. Their faces looked almost alike, with no eyebrows,
with broad, flat noses and with lips too perfectly formed.
Eyes, silver gray.

Each carried a fifty-pound block of ice on his back by
means of an ice tong. And each had tied a burlap sack
around his neck so that it hung like a cape under the ice.

Clutching the tong with one hand just above the shoulder,
the icemen were weighted down in a peculiar crouch. Each
held his left arm straight out for balance. At any moment
one would be racked by shivering. At any time one of them
would seem to be dancing. Legs wide apart, with that one
arm straight out, he would bounce around on his toes.
Would tremble as with the St. Vitus.

The three icemen were fanned out in front of Jones in a
semicircle.

"Don't you touch that step," Jones said softly, "nor no
part of my house, you hear?"

"Daddy," M.C. said, coming out on the porch. He had
dealt with the icemen many times. In spite of his father's
warning, given him so long ago, he looked forward to their
coming when he was alone. They didn't mind M.C. They
never talked to him very much and they never tried to scare
him by laying hands on his pole or the house.

191

The leader iceman was Ben Killburn's father. The other two were Uncle Lee and Uncle Joe, although M.C. didn't see them often enough to have figured out which was which. The leader came slowly forward toward Jones. Around his waist he wore a thick rope belt on which were strung several icepicks and burlap sacks.

"Get back! Get on back!" Jones yelled.

Mr. Killburn grinned. "Afternoon, Mr. Hig-gon," he said, in a voice that was as smooth as oil.

"M.C.!" Jones fell back to the door, holding it open as Lurhetta Outlaw stepped out.

"How much ice do you want, Daddy?" M.C. asked.

Killburn stood still now. He grinned absently as he untied a sack from his belt and spread it on the ground. Easily, his muscles bulging, he heaved the heavy block of ice onto the sack and took up an icepick. In a crouch, he waited. A ripple seemed to eddy over the three men, ending with one of them breaking out in a dance on his toes.

Jones got hold of himself. He closed the door and stood there with his back pressed against it. Lurhetta stared at him, at his fearful eyes. She looked with wonder at the three men with ice. For a long moment she wasn't able to take her eyes off them; until, indignantly, she turned back to Jones. And just as quickly, cast her eyes away from him.

"Daddy, how much ice do you want?" M.C. said again.

"Get me fifteen pound," Jones said, keeping his voice even and below a scream.

"They don't give any fifteen," M.C. told him. "It's twenty-five or fifty pounds, half or all. You know they won't cut fifteen."

M.C. stepped off the porch and made a motion over the ice to show he wanted half.

Mr. Killburn took off his heavy gloves and began to pick a line down the middle of the ice. M.C. had been waiting for one of the men to remove his gloves. Patiently, he always waited for this moment to see those hands. And always he looked at the six fingers as if seeing them for the first time. The same as with Ben's hands, he half expected the sixth finger to wave about wildly and uncontrolled. But now it curled around the pick with the other five, shooting down and then out of the ice again.

Killburn made one powerful stroke with his pick on the line across the ice. The ice broke in half. M.C. heaved half onto the porch.

Instantly, the Killburn men began a calculation in sign language. M.C. watched closely as their flinty eyes flashed in good humor and their fingers flew. He didn't know why the icemen used signs to figure the price but they always did.

Suddenly they huddled together. Talking low, they glanced at Jones. One Killburn guffawed. In a moment they all had turned back to M.C.

Mr. Killburn held up both hands and flashed them at M.C. eight times.

Ninety-six.

Turning down two fingers of one hand, he flashed the remaining four.

One hundred, M.C. thought, amazed.

Next Killburn held up one hand and one finger of the other hand.

Seven.

He lowered his hands. Then he raised the fingers of one hand with the thumb held down.

"Daddy, they're asking a dollar and seventy-five cents for the ice," M.C. said.

Jones exploded. "Throw them back the ice, M.C.! Break it over their heads!"

The icemen laughed loudly at their joke.

"They were just kidding. They only want seventy-five cents," M.C. said.

"Fifty cents is all they'll ever get out of *me*," Jones said.

M.C. shook his head at Mr. Killburn. He held up one hand as a sign, although Ben's father could clearly hear.

Killburn never changed his smile, but his eyes began to pull M.C. in, like going deep in a well. He turned toward Jones and headed for the porch. The front door slammed as Jones retreated inside.

M.C. gently grabbed hold of Killburn's shoulder to stop him. And reluctantly, the Killburn halted. But before M.C. could stop him, he had placed the flat of his own hand over M.C.'s. He had curled his six fingers around M.C.'s hand, pulling it off his shoulder.

Witchy fingers touching his hand were electric. They seemed to snap and sting. M.C. never would forget the feel of them, ice cold, like something dead. He jerked his hand away.

"Here!" Jones shouted. He swung open the door and tossed three quarters from the porch. They landed near Mr. Killburn. Killburn scooped them up. Then he tucked the sack pulled from under the remaining ice, and the pick under his rope belt and heaved the ice on his back. Shivering and dancing, the three icemen left Sarah's Mountain without a backward glance.

M.C. stood there feeling vaguely helpless. The wild and unbelievable imprint they had left behind seemed still suspended on the air. He wondered if Ben was out there and had seen it all, hidden in the trees.

"Don't you go near my ice," Jones warned M.C. "Wash your hands, you let one of them touch you."

Lurhetta Outlaw stared at Jones in disbelief a moment before gazing off after the icemen.

"Daddy," M.C. said.

"I said don't you touch it!" Jones said.

"I won't touch it," M.C. said. He didn't know why Jones had to make such a fuss. Mr. Killburn hadn't tried to hurt M.C.

Did he mark me with his hand? Maybe now I'm all witchy, M.C. thought.

Part of him believed and part disbelieved. Still he couldn't get that cold touch out of his mind.

Jones heaved the ice onto his shoulder and carried it through the parlor into the kitchen. Lurhetta Outlaw stared after him.

"Treat other people like that," she said, "like they were dirt." She looked disgustedly at M.C. as though he had done something to hurt her.

But he knew she was talking about Jones.

Sounding like some stranger.

"You saw them. Not just 'other people,'" M.C. said, defending Jones. He didn't know why he felt he should.

"I saw some men with ice," she said.

"Not just men."

"No, you're right," she said. "No ordinary men could do the job with that ice. But you all acted like they were poison."

"They each have twelve fingers and twelve toes. And that witchy skin and that hair," M.C. said.

Coldly, she stared at him. Looking older. Making him feel small when she said, "People have all kinds of defects. A man is crippled in the legs—do you say he is 'witchy'?"

"No," he mumbled. Feeling her draw away.

"Then why these people? Don't you even wonder about them?"

"Wonder what?" M.C. said. "I know them all my life."

"You mean, you all always treat them—" She broke off, as if suddenly understanding something. . . .

"People here believe the icemen are witchy," M.C. said. "And anyhow, you can't change my daddy's ways, ever."

"Well," she said, "people make up a story and then they believe it."

"I don't believe it."

"Oh, really?" She spoke softly. "Prove it."

Anxiously, M.C. stood there, not sure of what next to say and uncertain of what he felt. Killburns were witchy, that was all there was to it—could he say that without having her say again, "Prove it"?

They went inside. Lurhetta didn't even glance at the parlor as she passed through it. In the kitchen, she sat down at the table without looking at the children around her.

"You wash your hands before you sit," Jones told M.C.

He placed bowls and cups of creamy soup on the table. There was a delicate aroma of onions rising in the steam from the soup.

M.C. did as he was told and then sat down again next to Lurhetta. She kept her eyes on her bowl, carefully eating the delicious soup. When Jones placed a platter of toasted bread on the table, the children grabbed handfuls before M.C. could touch it.

He waited for Lurhetta to take some, but she wouldn't. So he took a handful and sprinkled it over his soup. Smiling grimly, Lurhetta reached out to take the last of it. After that, the children avoided coming close to her, as they did to M.C.

Jones had warned them.

No matter to them that M.C. had washed his hands, his skin had been touched by a witchy.

Prove it.

And he knew that for the rest of the day they wouldn't touch him or go where he went.

"It's a shame." Lurhetta spoke boldly out of the silence.

Jones had placed cups of milk and cider on the table. The children were quick to reach for the milk.

Lurhetta took a sip of cider. "A real shame they have to work so hard carrying all that ice up and down the hills." She glanced at each of them, impartially, as though they were no more or less than trees in the woods. "It wouldn't surprise me if they died young with T.B."

The children stared at her. If she had expected Jones to argue with her, she was mistaken. Jones stood next to the stove, leaning comfortably against a counter. Eating his soup, he didn't so much as look at her or give a sign that he had heard her.

In the kitchen was most of what Jones cared about. So his silence seemed to tell M.C. And when Banina came home, there would be in the house all that he cared about. Nothing some stranger would say could change that.

Lurhetta Outlaw charged the space around M.C.

Make you some poles from saplings and some thin clothesline to tie to them; just some safety pin and a few worm.

He steadily spooned the soup: Line up the poles so you can catch a mess of bullheads by the time the sun slides down the mountain.

And: Super-shovel is twenty houses high. A strip-miner; an earth-mover giant.

The impression Lurhetta made on his mind was swift and deep.

Super-teeth hold two hundred ton of dirt in one bite. Beside it, a bulldozer looking like a toy for Lennie Pool. It can strip eighty foot of mountain in half an hour so the toys can come on in and get at the coal once under the mountain. Say it's a dead witchy woman come back to haunt and they call her Hannah.

Move on, Hannah! But you don't have to see her. Sometimes you can hear her, and Jones has seen her. Jones has seen a lot.

M.C. felt changed. The kitchen had become altered by considerably more than the feeling between him and Jones day upon day. The squat and black cast-iron stove radiated its life-saving heat, as always. Cupboards, icebox, were the same. The children, wide-eyed and willful, as always.

She has seen everything. She, the difference.

He knew he would never be the same.

11

"A barking dog will go mad with heat like today. That's why they call this time of year the dog days," M.C. said, his voice droning. "I don't have a dog," he told Lurhetta, "but if I could, I'd have me a little hound with the little legs and flop ears."

She said nothing. They sat close together on the gold couch in the shadowed parlor. Having eaten his fill of potato soup, M.C. lay back on the pillows, just as comfortable as he could be. His only worry was that Lurhetta might grumble and go away.

She sat on the edge of a cushion, looking as if she wished she was outdoors. It was two and a half hours into the afternoon. The house was hot with all doors and windows shut. Yet it was cooler inside than out where the sun blazed, burning moisture into the silence of Sarah's Mountain.

They were not alone in the house. Jones was there somewhere. So were the children there, staying out of sight. Quiet and inert, Jones and the kids might be straining to hear what M.C. told Lurhetta.

He kept his voice low, speaking to her as though he still talked to himself. He suspected his family was just staying quiet. They were sitting resting, which was the usual way of taking the power and heat of the dog days.

"A hound is the best kind to hunt rabbit with," M.C. went on. "I don't have me one so I have to build a trap."

"I don't much care for hunting," Lurhetta said.

But he had started and had to finish.

"Snow is hard to hunt in on foot because rabbit will hole up or he will hide in the briers. A trap I use is just some wood scraps with just a gate and this trigger stick. You put in some bean or lettuce leaf and rabbit will trap itself. Sometimes. And then you skin him and chop him like a chicken. You fry him. Or you can add greens and make rabbit stew. It's just the best wild taste I know of, rabbit is."

"Don't you kill it first?" she asked, caught up in the gruesome picture he had drawn.

"What?"

"Before you skin . . . skin it, you kill it?"

"Well, you cut his throat however you can," he said eagerly. "Or chop his head. Then you have to slice across his back of fur and then you pull one way with one hand and one way with the other. Fur skin will split and come right off just as easy."

He smiled at her. "You have a good knife there for skinning." And then he remembered, he had a rabbit in one of his traps.

"You want to see what it's like?" he asked.

"See what?"

"See a trapped rabbit," he said.

"I don't think I want to hunt," she said.

"You don't have to hunt. I already have caught it. Over near Kill's Mound where Ben, where all the Killburns live."

"The icemen?" she said, interested now.

"Sure, I have a rabbit already caught. Come on!"

They slipped out of the house. On the porch, heat hit them. Everything, the yard around the house, was too bright with heat. Only the trees on distant hills seemed cool and restful.

"Look at the flies," she said.

Flies blanketed the porch and the steps.

"I've never seen so many flies. There must be thousands!" Lurhetta said.

M.C. slapped at them, stirring them up in whirlwinds.

"Dirty flies. Must be some animal rotting somewhere," he said. "Or else it's going to rain." He checked the sky, but there wasn't a cloud. That didn't mean much. Clouds could mass on the far side of Grey Mountain where you couldn't see. Come evening, they could rise and spill over the mountaintop like dirty soap suds out of a gray tub.

M.C. stepped off the porch and turned to gaze up at Sarah's summit. Lurhetta did the same. Up there, the spoil heap hung suspended; anyone not familiar with it would think it simply part of the mountain. He didn't explain about it to Lurhetta, but he thought about it as though rains had already come.

And then the heap will slide.

"Come on," he said.

Down into the gully and up to the plateau, where M.C. stopped a moment. "You all right?" he asked her.

"Fine, now that we're on the level. I guess I rested enough at the house."

"Or you're getting stronger," he said, smiling at her. They talked easily in the stillness of the woods.

They went ahead on Sarah's High, where presently M.C. became aware of Ben Killburn stalking them off the path.

"Hi you, Ben," M.C. said.

"*Hi you, M.C.*"

Startled, Lurhetta said, "Where—?"

Ben came closer to the path so she could see him. He grinned at her, wide-eyed and friendly. Then he and M.C. held a short, private conversation about the dude.

"*Did he make it?*"

"Yea, he made it—man!" M.C. laughed. Ben had disappeared off the path.

"*Looking just like I tell you?*"

"Yea. He even let me hear some music. He thought Mama was going to be home. But he come on back last night and man!"

"*Did she sing?*"

"And he got it down, too."

"*So when do you start leaving?*"

M.C. ignored the question. He turned and started talking to Lurhetta. He explained a little about Ben, knowing that

Ben could hear every word. He said that he and Ben were friends, but that they couldn't play together. That Ben was like all the other Killburns.

She nodded. Then she shook her head, frowning. "You all are the strangest people," she said. "I never would have thought."

M.C. tried to see himself and Ben the way she must have been seeing them. But next to her, they seemed to him only ordinary.

"You'll get used to everything," he thought to say. Silent, she shook her head again.

By the time they reached the clearing where M.C. had placed his rabbit traps, Ben was nowhere to be seen or heard.

"Look at the daisies! Can I pick some?" Lurhetta asked. She ran over to the edge of the clearing.

"Watch it, you'll fall!" M.C. yelled.

Now she could see the ravine. She gave a gasp and forgot about the wildflowers.

M.C. went over to her and gently pulled her back a step. Ben was down there. He must have raced ahead and now was taking off from the tree. Twisted around a vine, he swung toward them over the stream and through the ground fog.

"What a *place!*" Lurhetta said.

Ben swooshed near and then glided back slowly and expertly to the tree again. He pushed off at once and rode low over the stream, smiling at them.

"Fantastic!" she said, laughing.

"You want to swing on the vines?" M.C. asked her.

"Yes—no."

"You scared?"

"What if I fall?" she said.

"If you do, you can't get hurt."

"Maybe you can't get hurt," she said, and then: "What's over there?"

"Kill's Mound. All the Killburns."

Lurhetta took it all in—the ancient trees, the stream, the mist and Ben, swinging in and out of it. It was then she saw the bridge.

"Hey, where you going?" M.C. said, as she turned and headed along the edge of the ravine.

"Watch it, my traps are in the weeds."

She stopped still when she heard something thumping down in the ginseng weed.

"Quiet," M.C. said, coming up to her. "We don't want to scare him to death." He stamped down the weeds around the middle trap. Inside was the rabbit racing frantically, its hind legs slipping and sliding, going nowhere.

"Hey there," M.C. said, "you're a big one." Opening the trap, he grabbed the rabbit's hindquarters and dragged it out.

"It might be better to scare it to death than to murder it," Lurhetta said. She walked quickly away through the weeds.

Where's she going now?

M.C. sighed and followed, clasping the rabbit by just its ears.

Lurhetta stood by the post of the bridge. She grasped the guide vine as she carefully stepped to the front of the span.

"Will it hold me?"

"It'll hold more than ten people at once," he said. He explained how he had planned it himself.

"Really?" she said.

"Sure. These old vines are stronger than anything."

Holding tight to the side of the bridge, she inched along until she was halfway across. The bridge began to swing ever so gently. M.C. planted his feet wide apart to make it move more, until it was going with nearly a sweeping motion. Thirty feet below was the bottom of the ravine with its sink holes and muddy riverbed. Moisture dripped steadily from the trees, with the sound and touch of magic. M.C. could feel a damp breeze as the bridge swept through the air.

"Don't!" Lurhetta said. "Please!"

"What's the matter? It's fun."

"I said stop!"

So he stood there, not moving till the swaying stopped. He watched her and felt the rabbit twitch in his hand. Ben came up from the ravine at the other end of the bridge. He waited for them there, alert and smiling, his arms wrapped around a bridge post.

The rabbit suddenly started a frantic running, its hindquarters working against M.C.'s leg, but to no avail. M.C held it expertly.

Softly, Lurhetta said, "Let it go."

"Hey, come on, this rabbit's for food," M.C. said.

"You're hurting it," she said.

Oh, man. "Hey, you know, I don't have my knife with me," he said. He had forgotten it in his rush out of the house.

"I have mine," she said.

He reached out and automatically, she took her knife and handed it over before she thought.

Casually, M.C. made a swift motion with the knife. It all happened so fast. There was no sound, no movement from the rabbit for a second before it seemed to arch its back and let its hind legs hang farther down. M.C. had dug deep and slit its throat. Thick, dark blood swelled out and overflowed from the furry neck.

He held the rabbit out over the side of the bridge. Only a few red drops had fallen on the lattice-weave of vines. He let the rabbit bleed there until its life had drained away.

"You had to go use my knife—that's awful," Lurhetta said. Still, she couldn't help watching.

"What'd you think I was going to do with it?" M.C. said. He glanced at her. "It's just rabbit for food, like chicken is for food—you going to be sick? Then I'd better not gut it and skin it because that really is messy."

"One minute, it's alive and the next . . . you got my knife all bloody," she said.

M.C. looked at the knife where blood streaks clung to the steel. He glanced over at Ben, who watched his every move. He took the knife blade between his finger and thumb and called softly to Ben, "Coming at you."

Ben had time to duck away as the knife whizzed through

the air and hit the post. It struck and trembled on its point a moment before it fell from the wood. Ben scrambled for the knife, found it and headed for the stream to clean it.

"You could have hit him!" she said, shocked at the force and speed with which M.C. had flung the knife.

"Ben knows what I'm doing almost as soon as I do," M.C. said. "He knows how to move on a pinhead, just like I do." He spoke as quietly as he could. And keeping his eye on the far end of the bridge, he made certain no Killburn materialized there.

"We're close to the Mound," he told Lurhetta. "Talk low."

"Up there," she said.

He nodded.

"Are you scared?" she asked.

"No," M.C. said.

"Then prove it." Very carefully, she walked along the bridge to the post where Ben had been.

"Come on back!" M.C. called softly. But she wouldn't. He laid the rabbit out on the bridge. Ben came up the ravine.

"It's all clean," Ben told Lurhetta, handing the knife to her.

"Thanks," she said, putting the knife through the loops on her belt. "You're Ben. I'm Lurhetta. We never even said hello back there."

"Hi," Ben said shyly, looking from her to M.C., who was coming on reluctantly.

"Please to meet you, Ben," she said, smiling at him. Ben broke into a grin, clearly pleased to be there with her and

M.C. Happily, he looked from one to the other—if M.C. wanted the girl with them, it was fine with him.

"Hot," she said. "I sure am thirsty." Glancing up toward the Mound. They watched her as she wiped her palm over her face. "You think I could have some water?" she said to Ben.

A caution of silence in which the three of them seemed frozen separately. M.C. examined the fingers of one hand, pulling the knuckles and cracking them. Anxiously, Ben watched M.C.

"Drink from the stream," M.C. said finally. "It's fresh and cold as anything."

"No sir," she said, "I'm not going down there in all that quicksand."

"There's no quicksand down there," M.C. said. "Just some wet and some fog."

"You never know," she said lightly. "I might go down there and be lost forever." She winked at Ben. But so used to taking his cue from M.C., he didn't know what to do.

"Can I please get a drink?" she asked. Ben's pale face turned red. Hopelessly trapped, he could do nothing more than hang his head and wait for M.C.

M.C. sighed. What could you do with a girl like her, who didn't know enough to even be afraid?

At last he said, "Let her have the water. But bring her right back—is your father at home?"

"He's at home," Ben said, "working in the fields."

Oh, man. "Well, you all come right back, you hear?" M.C. told them.

"Aren't you coming, too?" Lurhetta said. She smirked at him. He knew the look.

Prove it.

"M.C., the Great," she said.

Swaying back and forth, holding on to the side of the bridge. A pretty thing. Just as slim.

"Come on, M.C. I've been to your house. Now I want to go over to your *friend's* house."

A threat. A forcing. M.C. understood the kind of nerve she had. And without another word, he began walking up toward the Mound.

Little Ben seemed to be everywhere at once. All around them. "You really coming over, M.C.?"

"Act like I never want to come over," M.C. murmured. "Mostly, I don't have a minute to spare. But today I've got the time." Not allowing himself to think or to fear, he almost believed what he was saying.

Ben led the way, with Lurhetta behind him and in front of M.C. They were at the foot of the Mound on a stepped path cut out of rock. The strata of rock were worn smooth from years of barefoot climbing and descending, of running children, of sitting and playing. Wind and rain, sun, had given the path a patina neither man-hewn nor natural. Shiny smooth, it existed in neither the past or the present. So that walking on it now, they were neither here nor there, but perhaps heading toward some unknown future.

Something about tall white pine trees forming an entrance grove, a semicircle of evergreens on each side of the path. Entering the Mound, the three of them became aware of their place in the mood around them. They were made less self-conscious among trees whose height alone caused them to reach out and upward, away from themselves. It didn't seem odd that Ben reached out to pat a pale pine trunk, sliding his six fingers along its rough bark. Lurhetta patted the tree, not to imitate Ben, but because it seemed natural to do so. Without hesitation, M.C. did the same and with the same result. He felt he'd introduced himself to a being he hadn't the sense to greet before.

They were on the Mound. It was a place unexpected and out of tune with the hills. Lower than the plateau but higher than the ravine, it was a valley reach of land unmarred by a single curve, jagged boulder or coal seam. It was a fifteen-acre Midwestern plain perhaps transported by Killburn magic to the top of the Mound. An unbeatable square saved from being a burning, dull landscape by the straight thread of a wide stream that dissected it, fed it from underground springs and in the past had made its soil rich and black. To come upon such flatland without a single tree on it in the midst of the hills was a surprise in itself. But ahead of them was the weirdest sight. M.C. had seen it a few times in his life, he couldn't recall where or when. But it was familiar. He turned to Ben. Ben raised his hand, those witchy fingers, motioning M.C. to stay still. Lurhetta was completely absorbed. M.C. knew she'd never seen anything like it before.

A snake rolling away from them down a runner bean row. They must have scared it coming off the path. It had taken its tail in its mouth and run off like a hoop. Grinning, Ben sidled up to it, careful not to step on any runners. He stuck his arm through the circle the snake made and lifted it, a dark wheel, still turning. He held the hoop up for them to see. Then he swirled it around and around his wrist. He let it fly; in midair, it snapped open and straightened like a stick.

Was it a stick by magic?

Falling, hitting the ground, it hooped again and rolled and rolled until it felt safe and hid.

"What in the world—!" Lurhetta said.

"Just a hoop snake," Ben said, coming back to where they stood. "We have hoop snakes and milk snakes, garter snakes, green-grass snakes and some copperheads. Only the copperheads will kill you. Daddy don't mind the copperheads but he's been hating the green-grass snakes for longer than a month. The milk snake will steal the cow's milk, but we don't have a cow."

"You mean your father likes them?" Lurhetta said.

"He feeds them," Ben said. "He sets out milk for the milk snakes just to see them slither. He lets the garters sun and have their babies on the cement of the icehouse step and feed off the gardens. He don't mind any kind of snake, can handle them like they were puppies. Copperheads, he talks to and if they don't listen right, he grinds their heads into the ground."

Uneasily, M.C. laughed. "How come he fell out with the green-grass snakes?" he asked.

"They did something wrong, most likely," Ben said. "Probably made up with them now, though."

"Whew!" M.C. said.

"Anyhow, from here," Ben said, "we have to climb up

and over. Nobody's supposed to walk in the gardens unless they mean to work or to go inside."

The houses of the Mound were grouped together to one side, a short distance away. Surrounded by outbuildings, every inch of space between the buildings was planted with crops. No yards, no dried, caked earth swept clean as were the yards of many hill houses. Up to the porches and foundations of piled stones, every foot of ground was taken up by tomatoes or potatoes. Runner beans, beets, lettuce and peas. Even in the hot darkness under the houses grew ghostly spreads of mushrooms. The trouble was, none of the vegetables looked healthy. Some had a blight of rust eating at the leaves. And others were being attacked by a black and white mold similar to mildew.

"Follow close," Ben told Lurhetta. "Keep careful lookout for creatures if you not used to slithery things."

At the thought of snakes, Lurhetta nearly walked on his heels.

"If I see one, I'm going to crush it," she said.

"Better not," M.C. told her. "Might be one of Mr. Killburn's friends."

They skirted the fields to a point very near the banks of the stream. Here there was an unplanted space along the bank where they could walk inland toward the houses. They went slowly. Ben had cut his pace as if knowing Lurhetta and M.C., also, would need time to take in the view.

For the Killburn houses, sheds and barns were grouped to form an enclosure. This compound was in no way extraordinary to look at, at first sight. The sheds and barns were weathered silver, sagging and almost shapeless. The houses were not the unpainted crate construction of most hill houses, but on the order of rambling, frame farmhouses. They had been added onto at the rear each time a child was born; and they had been painted once, all the same color. A dark, deep brown trimmed in blue. There was still a thin covering of paint on the houses, although they hadn't been retouched in years.

So that what happened right before M.C.'s eyes was that the enclosure of chocolate and silver sheds and barns took on the appearance of a fairyland. Carved out of dark soil and bold, blue sky, it looked unearthly all of a sudden, and slightly sinister.

There were men and women scattered over the land, working at hoeing and picking, and dropping vegetables into bushel baskets. At least four were bent to the task within the enclosure where row upon row of plants took the place of what would have been one large common yard. Every so often a figure would appear at the side of one of the houses, walk into the fields or disappear inside a house. M.C. found it hard to tell which figures were men and which were women, for all wore overalls of the bib kind with straps at the shoulders. But it wasn't long before he discovered that those wearing bright blue overalls with dazzling white stitching were men. And that those wearing faded overalls were women, having obtained their outfits second-hand from the men. He had a vague memory that this arrangement was thought practical and had always been so. Many of the figures wore coverings on their heads against the fierce sun, but the men wore oddly shaped hats of a kind he'd not seen before.

The three of them came up to the enclosure from the rear of a shed. They stepped around tomato plants that were too small and yellowish this late in the growing season. Ben led the way to a rope ladder hanging down from the top of the shed.

"We climb from here," he told them.

Neither Lurhetta nor M.C. said a word, such was the strange feeling they had so near Killburn life.

"You climb like this," Ben said to Lurhetta. He climbed easily as the ladder changed shape, sagging under his weight.

"I don't know. . . . Where does it lead to?" Lurhetta said.

"Just up and over," Ben told her. "Now just do the way I do. We take it a step at a time. Try just to look up as far as my heels. Because at the top, we have to turn the corner —you can't see where, but it's just one step and around."

"What is? I don't know," Lurhetta said, "can't we just walk it?" But at Ben's gentle urging, she followed him up the ladder. All of her natural grace came into play, helping her manage the awkward climb.

Wish we hadn't come, M.C. thought. Wish she'd just learn the hills with me.

He waited, peering around the side of the shed. Up ahead was the stream, which moved sluggishly and was a sickly shade of yellow. Behind it was the first house of the compound. A woman standing still on the small front porch. She faced the common yard of vegetables and just her head was turned toward the shed and M.C. Apparently, she had witnessed their coming and she stood poised, waiting. She was the only one of the women M.C. had seen who wore anything resembling a dress. It was more in the shape of a tent. Homemade, belted, with just a neck hole and armholes, of a faded, neat flower pattern. A tiny child stood holding on to her at the knee. No other children could be seen from below. They were all up above, M.C. guessed, remembering. But he kept his eye on the woman who was watching him. And slowly he sifted her features out from the general look all of the Killburns had. He recognized her as she seemed to recognize him. Ben's mother, Viola Killburn. A big woman, not fat, but strong and lanky, with gentle movements and an easy smile. She was smiling at M.C. right now. Smiling and nodding.

He felt glad, a relief at seeing her after so long a time. How long had it been? He couldn't remember when he'd seen Mrs. Killburn. But he felt good about finding her again. Leaning there at the side of the shed, he would have liked to skip over the rows of vegetables to sit at her side.

Sit on one side, his memory told him, with Ben on her other side.

The both of them leaning against her, without either one of them saying a word. Never a war between her and them and whatever they wanted given. If she had ever wanted anything, they would have given it. But she never wanted.

"Come on, M.C." Ben and Lurhetta at the top of the shed, peering around the corner. Lurhetta looked down at M.C., her face full of surprise.

"You can see everything!" she called down. "There's lots of kids!"

At these words, M.C. noticed the chatter from above. All around from above. He must have been hearing it all the while. But he had been remembering things. Feeling regretful, sad, talking to himself in his head. The girl, Lurhetta, all mixed up with past and future, with vegetables and witchy folks. So that the chatter had been like an internal clock ticking off loneliness of his dreaming, or the staccato of a time bomb set to go off.

The sound of chatter spilled over him and through him. And he remembered with sadness, with regret, that the Mound had been the happiest place he'd ever known.

No mountain to worry. No past. No ghosts.

"M.C., come on."

He could just stay here forever.

"I'm coming," he said, and started his climb.

12

"IT'S the biggest cobweb I
ever saw in my life," Lurhetta said. "See? That's just
what it looks like."

"I know," M.C. said, "I remember now." He eased himself up on the web next to her and Ben.

The same idea as the swinging bridge, but an earlier ver-
sion using rope as well as vine. It was like a half-forgotten
dream awakened into life. M.C. must have been very little
when he'd last seen it. And no wonder Ben's father had
made the swinging bridge so quickly after M.C. had told
Ben the idea. Because Mr. Killburn had had the idea first
here on the Mound. He had used it differently, maybe
better. Unwittingly, M.C. had taken Mr. Killburn's idea,
changed it a little and given it back to him.

What it was the three of them were looking at: Guidelines of thick rope and vine twisted so as to combine. These connected the houses in the area of the common ground. The lines were held to each house just under the roof edge with iron stakes, around which the rope and vine were knotted.

The three of them sat near the top and in between two guidelines where began a loose weave of rope weathered to a softness not unlike old cornshucks. There were at least eight guidelines and in between each was that soft weave. Nearer the ground, the lines came closer together. Their weave grew tighter at dead center of the common, some five to six feet over the ground. Here began a hub connected to the weave. It was some twenty feet across and just as long, made of twisted vines and rope loosely tied into six-inch square shapes.

The effect from guidelines to hub was one of an enormous web or net, or even a green and tan sunburst. In the hub were many children of various sizes and ages. Most had the light, sickly complexion of Killburn people. With a color range from orange to reddish-brown hair, they looked like a fresh bunch of bright flowers jumbled and tossed by breezes, their stems dangling through the square shapes of the hub.

"How many kids?" Lurhetta asked, breathlessly.

"Not too many," Ben said. "Maybe seventeen up here. Twenty-three all together, if you count me."

"It looks like more," M.C. thought to say and then fell silent, watching

At any time, some of the older children would crawl out of the hub onto the weave. There they would flip over under the weave and swing hand over hand to the hub again. Grabbing the nearest stem, the closest leg of a brother or sister or cousin, they would hang on, clinging from leg to leg. Until they had made their way directly above a potato row or a cabbage row, where they would fall lightly down and commence to pull up weeds. At any moment, three or four Killburn children would be hard at work, often filling bushel baskets to the brim with vegetables in seconds. Or they would dance through the rows over to Mrs. Killburn's house. They always seemed to go to that house in particular, dancing on up the steps. A table on the porch held pitchers of lemonade and single-server clay dishes of custard. Women and young men and girls in overalls came out of the house with drinking glasses and returned with empty dishes or pitchers. All of it done in a pleasant, amiable fashion.

The children chattered. The women and young men and girls continued their conversations with one another as they worked. Furthermore, they kept an eye on the babies who were too young for the hub and who spilled out of the door onto the porch like sweet cinnamon lumps.

Lurhetta sighed in awe. M.C. watched her, feeling a growing jealousy, he didn't know why.

"Better be going back," he said once. But she merely frowned an instant before her face cleared and she was delighted.

Lurhetta gazed all around, at men and women far off in the fields and close by in the common. Her eyes roved over the children.

"You must have enough food here to feed an army," she said to Ben.

"Looks like a lot," he said, "but everybody eats only vegetables. Soups and things or just plain-cooked. Sometimes we get too much rain, too fast; or not enough and too late. That water of the stream is changing color. And so when a good year comes with the right kind of weather, we store a lot. Still the vegetables is smaller than they once was."

"I see," Lurhetta said. "And you buy—"

"—we buy milk, coffee, flour, clothes and cloth, just a few things like that," he said.

"And you live—"

"—we live okay. Now that daddy has the icehouse and a new generator, we live fine," he said.

"But you are all one family?"

"We are all relatives," Ben told her. "Just a few, maybe not so related. Sometimes a friend with nothing and no one."

"How long have you all been here?"

"Been here?" Ben repeated. He gazed at the children down in the hub. Some were in groups, playing games. Others stared peacefully down through the squares to the plants below. A few were even sleeping serenely on their backs. "My grandmother is ninety-six."

"Where did she come from?"

"She say she don't know, she was always here," Ben said. "She say those vegetables all around is fields of tobacco. See, she so old, most times she only talk to herself."

221

Ben grinned. "She can be a young girl and she can talk to the pictures on the walls. Talks like they were talking back to her." He laughed softly. "But when my mother bring her tree bark and moth wing, she will mash them up. She will get out her bottles and she know everything. Everything."

They were together, Ben and Lurhetta. They were close, with M.C. looking on, separated from them. He didn't have anything to tell. Nothing with which to break in on their conversation.

He wrung his hands. "We going to sit up here forever?" he said anxiously.

Ben stared at him with the slightest sign of irritation.

Witchy eyes. Witchy fingers, M.C. thought meanly.

Lurhetta suddenly clutched Ben by the hand, as if his six fingers meant nothing to her. She started down into the hub, supporting herself on Ben's arm.

They left M.C. behind. He was forced to follow if he wanted to keep up with Lurhetta.

In the midst of the children, the hub bounced like a trampoline. Laughing, Lurhetta nearly fell. But there were children rising to help her.

"And who are you?" she said to one of them. "And you . . . and you!" Names were spoken. None of them seemed surprised by her. They were not shy or bashful. And none asked her name. Where all were the same, names had no great importance.

The children bounced the net just to hear her laughter. All of the time she held tightly to Ben. And her pretty

222

face, her smile, had captured him and made him her prisoner.

Snare him in the net.

They were on the hub for no more than ten minutes. To M.C., it seemed forever. He disliked so many Killburn children crowding him. The way they always seemed to be copying one another, as if watching a mirror image. Momentarily a child would clutch his shoulder or his arm, like he was planted there for them to hang on to. They leaned into him and yet they seemed not to notice him.

M.C. thrust his hands deep in his pockets and balanced precariously. Once his foot slipped through one of the squares. He was down, not hurt, but feeling foolish, with the children pulling at him. There was no way to get back up with the hub rising and falling, without asking for their help.

"Let me loose," M.C. muttered, once he was on his feet again. Witchy hands, all over him. He didn't dare look at all the fingers. "Ben? I want *down!*"

"What's a-wrong? Too high for you?" Ben said, teasing M.C.

"He's getting seasick," Lurhetta said. "I know I am."

So they got off the hub. They jumped down one by one, careful of the vegetables at their feet. With Ben leading, they headed for the porch. Ben strutted, happy to have friends come over. M.C. lagged behind, seeing all there was around him—the hub to his back now, the porch before him. There were three more houses. The one farthest away faced Mrs. Killburn's house. The other two were

223

situated on each side of her house, facing each other across the common. And surrounding everything, even the chatter of the children, was an enormous stillness which the chatter could not penetrate. No sounds of the town of Harenton, no river boat sounds. But a silence that swept over the land in every direction, as did the sunlight.

Peaceful, the way Sarah's would be only in the early hours of morning.

Mrs. Killburn came out on the porch carrying a pie in each hand. She placed them on the table. Plates were brought out by a teenage boy wearing an apron. He had a fine dust of flour all over him; and obviously he had been baking. Sweet odors of hot baking bread drifted out. Mrs. Killburn cut a pie and put pieces on the plates. As they came up on the porch, she handed each of them a plate.

"Sweet potato pie," Ben said.

"Is it?" Lurhetta tasted it. "Umm, delicious!"

M.C. held his plate just under his nose. He would have liked to say, "No, thank you!" But the pie was too much for him. Its sweet-smelling heat brought to mind the cold weather of winter. Slowly he ate it, trying not to gobble it up in three swift bites.

Lurhetta and Mrs. Killburn were talking. Now and then Viola Killburn had a word or two for M.C.

"Haven't seen you in so long, M.C., where you been? Got just as tall." Her voice gentle and soft-spoken.

"Yessum, I been all around," M.C. said. "I seen Ben about every day."

"Well—" Mrs. Killburn saying the word the way hill

women did generally. A rising inflection so that it came out with sympathy, comforting.

"Banina feeling good?"

"Yessum, she's fine. She's singing and a tape recorder man come along and recording her voice." Instantly M.C. wished he hadn't said that. But it was so easy to tell Viola Killburn things, it had just slipped out.

"Well—"

M.C. sighed and ate his pie.

He realized there was a weight on his foot. A baby, sitting on his toes, like a soft pressure hardly noticeable. It was just a little thing, sucking on a crust of pie which had on it a thin icing of sweet potato. The child had gummed and wetted the crust into the softness of oiled dough.

All at once he laughed at finding the baby there. Watching him, they all did. And gently he pulled his foot away. He bent down beside it to feed it some sweet potato. Seeing the food, the baby opened its mouth. Big, trusting eyes on him. Face full of freckles the exact color of its orange hair. It slurped sweet potato off the fork, making a perfect, tiny O with its mouth. M.C. laughed again. They all did.

Smiling, Mrs. Killburn swept the baby up and under her arm. She held the child around its middle, the way she might rest a sack of sugar on her hip. Neither the position of the child nor the weight of it seemed to bother either one of them in the least. Viola Killburn went on talking to Lurhetta in her calm, pleasant fashion, as the child continued sucking on the crust.

225

"I've never seen anything like this place. You all must never want to leave it, it's so beautiful." Lurhetta's voice, full of excitement and curiosity, laughing shyly. "How do you keep track of all the children? And the food! Where do you keep it?" Her breathless voice a punctuation for the tone of Mrs. Killburn's quiet replies. Nowhere in her manner toward the Killburns were the fear and caution she had shown on meeting M.C. and his brothers and sister.

But I had scared her in the dark, thought M.C. They are witchy and she can't even see it.

It was a fact, none of the Killburns had acted strangely. Viola gave no hint of her healing power.

She'd fool anybody. Lurhetta better watch herself.

M.C. felt slightly ashamed of himself for thinking that.

Sitting on his knees with his back to the common and its hub, its sunburst of children, he finished the pie and set the plate down next to him. He'd been watching Ben watch Mrs. Killburn and Lurhetta. Ben, looking as happy as he could be.

Forgot I'm even here.

Now and then M.C. stared idly at the plump baby Mrs. Killburn held. The child commenced squealing and grinning. Looking out beyond M.C., it squirmed and held its arms out. M.C. glanced around. Two men standing at his back just in front of the porch. He felt his skin crawl. He didn't know how long they'd been there, he hadn't heard them come, but they had been listening. One was Ben's father, so close to M.C. that he could see sweat trickle down Mr. Killburn's throat.

M.C. felt prickles of fear all over him. It took all his

strength not to leap away, as he forced himself to remain motionless. Simultaneously, two women in faded work clothes walked out of the house and on through the common into the fields.

M.C. didn't know the second man. He was younger than Ben's father. Younger than his Uncle Lee and Uncle Joe. But he looked like a Killburn, all the same. And he reached out to take up the baby Mrs. Killburn handed over to him.

The brand-new, starched overalls Mr. Killburn wore had not completely wilted from his labor under the sun. The other man wore the same outfit. And the brilliant stitching of pockets and straps was like a cloth sketch of the prosperous farmer. The strange headgear they wore had once been identical old felt hats. But they had cut triangle holes in the felt to let air circulate. The hat brims they had cut away to an inch of their former shape, the shortened brims then cut deep in a jagged design. What was left of the hats was an improvement over the originals, M.C. was sure. Dashing, kingly crowns.

He sure wished he had one.

"Mister M.C. Hig-gon," Mr. Killburn said. Not looking at M.C., but toward his wife and Lurhetta, who smiled uncertainly at him. He spoke M.C.'s name as a greeting, low and harsh, yet slightly respectful. So that M.C. felt obliged to stand. Awkward and uneasy, M.C. lowered his eyes. This last by way of apology for Jones making such a fuss earlier in the day.

"She's camping over by the lake, Daddy," Ben said to his father.

"Pleased. Sure," Mr. Killburn said. Not exactly watching

227

Lurhetta, but listening at her, his head cocked to one side and his squinting, metal eyes, just to the right of her face. He glanced, listening at M.C.; then, over to Ben and back to Lurhetta.

"Miss Lurhetta—" Mr. Killburn said.

"Lurhetta Outlaw," she said softly.

A moment of silence in which Mr. Killburn carefully looped his thumbs in the straps of his brand-new bib overalls.

"Now if that don't cut the cane!" Killburn said. "Outlaw? Sure now!" He laughed uproariously. "You sure come to the right place."

Lurhetta broke into a grin. There was an instant sympathy between her and Ben's father and between her and the rest of the Killburns, as if they had suddenly opened a magic window to let her through.

"I love it here," she said simply, as though that explained her name.

"Better than a mountain?" Killburn said, and then laughed harshly, still not looking at M.C.

"The best place of all," she said.

M.C. hung his head. No one noticed him. He felt just as if he had blundered into a space too tight for him.

There was movement, a kind of change in the air as Mrs. Killburn went away and came back with a pitcher of water. Both Mr. Killburn and the other man each drank three glasses of water. Lurhetta had a glass of water, too. All talked to her, as though they'd always known her. No one was particularly kind or polite and no part of them was witchy.

Lurhetta was saying how different it was to see houses without any yards of grass, but gardens, instead.

"Grass can't grow nohow with kids tramping," Mr. Killburn told her. "But even the babies can 'preciate some vegetables. They understand that vegetables is part of the human form." He looked around to make sure everyone was listening. "Piece of the body you pull up by the root. Or piece that you cut away when it get the blight. Or heal it, depending on how bad it is." He nodded to himself. Others nodded back. "Or eat it, it's still body," he said, letting loose a strap and raising the hand for emphasis.

Witchy hand.

The six fingers were perfectly formed, perfectly natural. "Just like soil is body. Stream. Mountain is body." Killburn paused significantly. "We don't own nothing of it. We just caretakers, here to be of service."

"Nothing?" Lurhetta gazed at him. "Own nothing?"

"Well, you surely don't think the sun sets and rises, do you?"

She had to laugh. Killburns laughed with her. "It's just a way of speaking," she said.

"Of course," he said. "And the truth is, we are a body just wiggling and jiggling in and out of the light."

"You mean, the earth is," she said.

"I mean earth and everything on it," Killburn said.

Deeply interested, Lurhetta nodded, saying, "But I don't think about it every day."

"Sure now, that's it, then," Killburn said. "If you could think about it every day, you never could own a piece of it. Wouldn't want to. And if you *don't* think about it every day, you get to believing you have a right to own it. You become a sore growing on the body." His eyes, a vivid, mackerel shade: "A scab on the sore, getting bigger, hurting, causing pain."

Suddenly Killburn grinned. He raised his hands and applauded himself in a slow, steady beat that resounded in the quiet. He threw back his head and laughed completely. Other Killburns joined in. So did Lurhetta.

"Daddy," Ben said, "can we show her where we keep everything?"

"Sure now, come on then." Mr. Killburn had turned and walked away before his voice died. Lurhetta and Ben were right behind him. And she was talking over his shoulder as they headed down a bean row, all talk of "the body" forgotten.

"I thought we weren't supposed to walk here," she was saying. M.C. followed reluctantly, not knowing what else to do.

"Best not to trample around too much is true," Mr. Killburn said, "but quite all right if you going someplace."

"I sure like the way that thing up there looks like a spider web," she said, as they passed under guidelines.

"No, sir," Killburn said. "Looks like a eye."

"Really? It looks like an eye to you?"

"Is a eye," Killburn said. "Better than any old eye. Bigger. *A eye* of Gawd." He laughed, as if joking again.

They entered an area behind the farthest house, where there was a fenced space for chickens. Beyond the fence was a barn and an open side door into a small, dark room where the chickens roosted. As they came around to the front, M.C. could tell that the whole of the large barn had been whitewashed once, long ago. But now it was faded silver like all of the other outbuildings. It was then he noticed that every object on the Mound could appear suddenly to shimmer. Houses, barns, hard outlines wavered at any moment.

Because sunlight can't soften, he thought. No trees. No shade at all.

There was just burning light beating down on everything and going through everything in shimmering waves of heat.

They entered through identical barn doors, one of which was open to air and light. Inside, the barn was a massive, two-story shell. Walls and roof and one great oak crossbeam spanning the height. Hanging from the beam was an abundance of drying things, thick as fur. Not vegetables, but thousands of herb weeds and dried mushrooms. On the walls from top to bottom hung gourds, their range of colors so bright, they looked painted. There were vertical rows of field corn on lengths of heavy twine hanging down the walls. M.C. did recall seeing corn rows far off at the other end of the Mound. As the corn aged, it changed colors from yellow to orange, red and some black.

The floor of the barn was dark, packed earth. It had an odor of pungent coolness. Its full width and length had been dug out into pits some five feet across. Each pit was lined with chicken wire and shaped like hollow pyramids standing on end. Some pits were full of vegetables and covered with a net of vine. Some were empty or only partially full, with their nets rolled back. Bushel baskets of produce lined one side of the floor, their contents ready to be sorted and put into the pits.

"For goodness sakes!" Lurhetta said, and abruptly was still. There was room between the pits to walk around them. There was cool light in the barn from the open door and from cracks in the walls and roof. M.C. noticed one small, closed door to their right as they entered; behind it, the muffled sound of chickens clucking.

In the midst of the stillness—the muted stripes of light, the yawning pits—sat an ancient, shriveled woman on a green folding chair. She took cabbages from a bushel basket and rolled them like rubber balls into a pit, whispering furiously at the heads all the while. She did not cease her slow, rhythmic work as they came near. But she grinned quite pleasantly at a cabbage head.

"Hi you, Grandymama," Ben said. "It's my grandmother," he told Lurhetta. Skirting the pits, he went up to the old woman and placed his hands lightly on her shoulders.

Ugly, old witchy.

"This is Lurhetta—see, Grandy?" Ben said.

Lurhetta came near. She leaned around Ben to see the woman dressed in a length of gray flannel. A long nightgown.

"Hello there, Grandy," Lurhetta said. Uncertainly, she held out her hand.

Grandymama tore off a cabbage leaf. Swiftly she rolled it tight in trembly hands and smiling, gave it to Lurhetta.

"Now she don't want that thing," Ben said.

"It's all right." Lurhetta took the leaf. "Should she be in here all by herself?"

"It's her place to be," Ben said.

Silently then, Lurhetta made her way down the length of the barn. They followed, fanning out behind her, hearing at their backs the cabbages in their rhythmic roll and plop into the pits.

So much. Enough food for everybody, M.C. thought.

He couldn't remember ever being in such a place. Couldn't remember the grandmother at all. He fell back a ways to follow Ben and his father.

Too many Killburns under one roof. He wasn't so much afraid as watchful.

Grandymama cackled suddenly, sending a chill up his spine. "Who's parading?" she said. "I see you. Blow the trumpet!"

They glanced around. "No Gabriel here, Grandy," Ben said kindly.

M.C. wouldn't have wanted the old woman to sneak up on him. But she was still sitting, still watching the cabbages. Beyond her stood a figure in the entrance.

"Uncle Joe," Ben said, in greeting to the figure. M.C. never would figure out how Ben knew it was Uncle Joe. For just the bulk of his shape was visible, with an eerie halo of reddish hair, as finely tangled as minute veins. A ray of sunlight touched his shoulder. In the glow like the flare of a match, the buckle of his shoulder strap was caught gleaming upon new blue cloth.

Watching. Not saying a word. Not moving.

"I have to be going," M.C. said. He imagined himself trapped here forever.

Mr. Killburn gave him a look. "Stay as long as you like," he said.

"You want a tomato?" Ben asked Lurhetta.

"Sure!"

"Then here."

"Thank you!"

"It's clean, you can just eat it plain. We clean the tomatoes in the evening, with cloths to make them shine."

"It feels cold," Lurhetta said, "like it's been in a refrigerator."

"Earth of the pits does that," Mr. Killburn told her. "Keeps them fresh very long. Fresh and cold."

Didn't ask me if I wanted one. "I have to skin that rabbit," M.C. said. He shifted his weight and wrung his hands. They felt clammy. "Lurhetta, you want to watch?"

"Oooh, no!" she said.

"Don't you just hate the way rabbit looks when it lay all still and dead?" Ben spoke eagerly, sympathizing with her.

"You're the one told me it was in the trap," M.C. said. His voice quavered, as anger at Ben shook him.

"Well, just because it was trapped," Ben said. "Things trapped get so wild."

"You offered to skin it for me," M.C. said.

"Don't think I would have, though," Ben said, not meeting M.C.'s eyes.

"None of my children ever kill an animal, let alone skin it," Mr. Killburn said.

"You kill snakes," M.C. said softly, unwilling to say too loudly that Killburn killed the same as he did.

"When necessary, but I don't eat them," Killburn said.

They all laughed at M.C. Again the grandmother cackled behind his back.

Witchy eyes, everywhere.

"I have to go." But no one seemed to hear M.C. And he stood there, reluctant to stay and almost afraid to leave.

"How are you for snakes?" Mr. Killburn asked Lurhetta.

"Oh, I'm not too friendly with them," she said.

Killburn laughed. "Well, here," he said. He went over to a bushel basket, one that M.C. hadn't noticed had a plank lid with a heavy stone on it. Killburn removed the stone and lid and reached into a mass of quivering shadows.

"Oh, no!" Lurhetta said.

"It's just the green-grass," Ben said.

"I had to punish them," Mr. Killburn said. "But here, give a look-see."

Carefully, he covered the basket again and came back over to them. He lifted his hand in a fist, from which a small, green head peeked.

Lurhetta stepped back.

"Don't be afraid. He is harmless," Killburn told her. "Look, see how graceful he is. Don't be scared, look at him close."

They all came close to see, even M.C. The snake was the palest green. Each tiny scale was pale and green, except for the scales around the snake's mouth. They were red and caused the snake to look as though it had just feasted on something bloody.

"Now. Touch his head," Killburn ordered. He was speaking softly and with good humor.

Cautiously, Lurhetta lifted a finger and gently petted the snake until its tongue darted out and she jerked her hand away.

"He won't hurt," Killburn said. "His tongue is a feeler, just like insects have feelers. That's the way he finds out and tells me whether you are friend or foe." Killburn laughed.

Lurhetta stared at him and gently touched the snake again. "Why do you punish them?" she asked.

"Oh, well. Now this one," Killburn said, "I call him March Noon because that was the time I first caught him—he gave me several nightmares. You see, the green-grass is pure pleasure to people. Put him on your pillow when you're feeling sick, and he will lick away the fever. He will bring you the prettiest dreams."

"Really?" Lurhetta said, smiling.

"Oh, sure now," Killburn said. "Be near your last breath and he will guard you. And Death come near, he will curl himself into a bracelet. For Death can't stand a bracelet of green-grass around his neck."

"I have to go," M.C. said faintly.

"See you, M.C.," Ben said, his witchy hand smoothing along the back of the snake Killburn now let slither up his arm.

"M.C., I'll see you later," Lurhetta said. Sucking at the tomato, she still touched the snake with the other hand.

"Come for supper. Meet my mother," M.C. said.

"You going to eat that rabbit for supper?" Ben asked

him. Something of their friendship of a few hours ago passed between them. Ben, innocent, and learning from M.C. But on the Mound, somehow that friendship was changing.

"Making a rabbit stew," M.C. thought to say.

"I've never tasted rabbit, but I do like meat," Lurhetta said.

"Well, we won't hold it against you," Mr. Killburn said. And then: "What part of the state you come from?" Soon they were deep in conversation again. Killburn returned the green-grass to his punishment and stood amiably, with his thumbs again hooked around the bib straps of his overalls.

"I come from Alliance," she told him, "but I've been practically everywhere else. I love to travel."

"See you later," M.C. said. Shyly, he waved and momentarily caught Lurhetta's attention. Absently, she nodded but went on talking.

M.C. skirted the pits and the old grandmother, not looking at her. But she reached out for him.

"Here!" she said, cackling. She pulled him around to face her and thrust a cabbage head hard in his belly. "Someone to talk to," she said.

"I don't want it."

"Here!"

He took the cabbage and blundered on. Uncle Joe Killburn in the doorway fell back just enough to let him by.

"Luck with the cabbage head," Uncle Joe said, his voice like a cat's purr.

Witchy, kill you. Burn you at the stake.

Uncle Joe grinned. Gray eyes the color of a sparrow's rain-soaked underbelly. "Now you put that in with the rabbit," he said, "and when hit's done, you throw away the rabbit and you got yourself something."

M.C. walked away as fast as he could without appearing a coward.

He went through the pine trees off the Mound in a dead run, taking the steps of the rock path two, three at a time. He didn't slow down until he reached the swinging bridge. There he glanced around to make certain no witchy was following him. With a powerful heave, he threw the head of cabbage far into the ravine.

M.C. was breathing hard, as if he had run farther than he actually had. Again he scanned the pines above him at the edge of the Mound, but there was no one.

Well, that's that. Nobody with me, not even Ben.

He would have liked to stay awhile up there, where all seemed fresh with growing and sun.

Except for the witchies. Were they witchies?

What he had seen of them made him ponder a moment. Mrs. Killburn, just as nice. Even Mr. Killburn, not so bad if you didn't look at his hands or watch his eyes as he handled the green-grass. What he had just seen and what he had known for so long about Killburns mixed in disorder in his mind. He sighed.

Well. Lurhetta probably stay there the rest of the day. But she'll be over for supper. She said she would.

M.C. started across the swinging bridge. His rabbit lay there where he had left it. It looked different, somehow. He crept closer.

The rabbit had been turned clear the other way, with its head away from the Mound.

Who's been fooling around?

The quiet seemed to close in. Branches of gnarled trees in the ravine dripped moisture and answered nothing.

Bending to pick up the animal, M.C. sprang back in mid-motion.

In death, the rabbit looked to be peacefully resting on its side, gazing down at the stream below. Except that each of its four feet had been sliced cleanly away. A rosy stain of blood covered each stump.

I killed it clean. Not like that.

He searched the Mound.

Dirty devils! What kind of power, if they need rabbit's feet for luck? Be glad to get away from here.

He bent down again and tenderly cradled the rabbit. He carried it that way all the way home.

Make a stew out of you like she never tasted.

Slipping through trees on Sarah's High, M.C. made no sound. No Ben to stalk him. Only a dead animal for company.

M.C., alone.

13

A time just before twilight. The ball of red sun balanced at the summit of Grey Mountain before beginning its slide down the westward face.

The dude was back. He had come the right way this time, through the gully and up the side of Sarah's Mountain belonging to Jones.

"What do you think he wants now?" Jones said, absently scratching a mosquito bite on his arm. He and M.C. and the children sat on the porch steps waiting for evening.

James K. Lewis had arrived seconds before Banina Higgins came into view on the low hill across from Sarah's. And emerging from the briers, Lewis was about to call a greeting to M.C. and Jones when Banina's yodel split open the sky. He stood rooted to the spot, as though someone had struck him a blow between his shoulder blades. Surprise of recognition and then disappointment spread over his face.

"Hurry, get out your tape machine. It's Mama coming home," M.C. called to him.

The dude came slowly to the porch. Jones and the children were on their feet and looking off toward the sound of Banina's voice.

"How-do, Mr. Jones . . . Higgins," the dude said. "How-do, children."

Macie Pearl gave him her sweet smile. Jones grunted and nodded in his direction. All of them, except for M.C., glided off the porch to the edge of Sarah's.

"That's her real voice you're hearing," M.C. said.

"You didn't tell me she could yodel," Lewis said.

"She can sing, can't she? Ought to know she could yodel," M.C. said.

He felt slightly irritated at the dude for no reason; and at the same time he felt fluttery and excited. Lurhetta Outlaw would be coming over to eat with them. The dude would probably tell them what he intended to do with Banina's voice.

"It's a low-down shame," the dude was saying. "I'm clean out of tapes."

"Oh, no," M.C. said.

Banina's pure yodel broke off suddenly.

"*Howdy-howdy, child!*" her singing voice rang out.

"Howdy-howdy, ma'am!" the children called back, their voices young and tender on the air.

241

"A hang-down day, a long, long way—howdy howdy-howdy!" Banina's voice echoed and re-echoed.

"Howdy howdy-howdy!" the children called. The howdys bounced like huge laughter around the hills.

It was a ring-song their mama was calling. M.C. knew it well.

Wouldn't you know dude wouldn't have not one single tape to catch it? M.C. thought.

He looked slyly at James Lewis. If the dude stayed long enough, he'd run right into Lurhetta Outlaw. He sure would be surprised to see how M.C. and her had become friends.

M.C. smiled. He'd get Banina to sing the ring-song all the way through. That should take at least an hour.

M.C. leaned back comfortably to wait. The dude stood there with the voices of the children and Banina's surrounding him. He stared off toward her sound, looking sick to his soul as it escaped him. Finally he eased the tape machine off his shoulder. M.C. took it from him and placed it on the porch. Lewis fished around in his pockets. Dressed in the jacket and suede hat, he looked rumpled and tired. After a moment he found a tape cassette already labeled and used, which he stood holding absently in one hand.

Soon they could hear Banina toiling up the mountainside. Breathing hard through snatches of song, she laughed at herself. The laughter was relief to be home again, about to witness the respect they showed her by being there when she arrived.

The dude stood straighter as she came into the yard. He

waved a cautious greeting, but she hadn't seen him yet. M.C. got to his feet. He wasn't on his pole, he realized at the last minute. He hadn't been near the pole the whole afternoon. After coming home from Kill's Mound, he'd taken care of the rabbit. But he thought little about that now.

Banina was dressed in blue this evening. She grabbed Lennie Pool and swung him once around in a circle.

Just this morning, M.C. thought. She and I, swimming. Seems like days ago.

"Mercy!" Banina said, putting Lennie down. "That took my last strength, I swear." A frown, a tired despair passed over her face before it vanished.

Macie hopped and jumped until her mother caught her around the neck. Banina grabbed Harper and stood holding the two of them close. She stared at Jones.

Different from Killburns, M.C. thought. Closer somehow.

Jones wore a frayed but starched white shirt open at the throat, and pale blue trousers. He nodded at Banina, but did not smile.

Almost shy. Like it's the first time he ever did see her.

M.C. thought again of Lurhetta Outlaw. Where is she, anyhow?

"We have the supper just about all ready," Jones told Banina.

"Now that's a homecoming," Banina said.

"Good old rabbit stew," Harper said.

"M.C., you caught a rabbit?" Banina called over to him.

"Caught him good. A big one," M.C. said.

Jones said, "I put some potatoes left over from lunch in with him. And some carrot and onion and some jowl bacon. And then with a little molasses for some thickening. M.C. says that makes the best of gravy."

"Sounds mighty good," Banina said.

"And some lemonade," Macie said. "Not no cider this day."

"You're not on your pole!" Banina called to M.C. in mock surprise, and spied the dude behind him. "Oh." She pulled back, somewhat cautious.

"How-do, ma'am," Lewis said. "Begging your pardon."

Banina came to the porch with the children hovering close. Jones walked at her side. Far off, yodel cries could be heard. The sun was sinking, soon to bring twilight and other hill children to home. Banina took M.C. lightly by the hand a moment. The children watched wide-eyed, since M.C. had been touched by Mr. Killburn. But then they seemed to settle back, reckoning that Banina's touch could dissolve the witchy one.

"I know it's the suppertime," the dude said. "I just come for a minute, to give you something. Here."

He handed her the cassette in his hand. Banina released the children. She took the tape with a frown.

"It's your voice," Lewis explained. "I thought you might want to have it. I have others."

Banina stared at the tape. There was something final about the way she smoothed her hand over it once and then palmed it at her side.

"Got a line on some singing people on across-river," the dude said. "Ever hear of some Halleys over there?"

They shook their heads.

"Well, I'd better get on," the dude said.

"Mighty thoughtful of you to come way back here and give me it," Banina said.

"Oh, it wasn't anything," Lewis said. "I was getting to like that two-mile hike anyway."

"You're welcome to stay for supper," Banina said.

What's he doing? What's going on? M.C. wondered.

"No, no thank you," the dude was saying. "I'll be on my way before it gets dark. M.C., I'll be seeing you. Be seeing all of you the next time around." He smiled at each one of them and then looked away. He was already traveling in his mind, as his eyes caught onto M.C.'s pole.

"Now that's a beat-all pole!" he said, with huge sincerity. "Where in the world did you get it?" Before M.C. had time to answer, the dude went on talking: "I saw some like it, though, but way off in Florida."

"I know, you told me," M.C. said. "Mr. Lewis—"

"—Set bleacher seats up clear across the beach so folks could sit with their backs to the water," the dude went on. "And way off down the beach was three men with poles just like yours. They were acrobats, though, the men on the poles were." He chuckled. "They'd pretend to fall in death, only to be caught up at the last minute by the other fellow on another pole. The folks sitting would scream wild with fear, to see those fellows dare the devil. Well. Remind me to tell you all about it the next time I come."

"Mr. Lewis," M.C. began, "I'll walk you down."

Their eyes met. Just a fleeting look through which terrible doubt met a knowing sadness. The dude nodded.

"Well, then, I'll get going," he said, as he took up his tape machine from the porch. He would have formally shaken hands, but he seemed to realize that his coming and going made not the slightest difference to Banina and Jones. He hurried off across the yard with M.C. Twice he glanced back before he called, "So long, folks!"

And they called back, quietly, as he and M.C. went down the side of Sarah's:

"'Bye."

They made their way slowly, side by side, down the path. M.C. waited anxiously for the dude to tell him something and soon Lewis began. His easy laughter was altogether pleasant as he squinted off at hills. "Son, you know, my father never told me this type of work could be such a long haul. No sir, he just told the pretty parts. Like, he'd say, after months of looking, he'd come upon some shack one time. Way back in the hills in a stand of dogwood or some kind, way beyond trains and bus lines—but he never did tell me about the hours of sudden rain and the sore feet.

"No roads," the dude went on, "something like this area, he'd come upon a wood-offering with people in it. Hardly worth the rain dripping on the floorboards."

"And it happens with you the same?" M.C. asked him.

"Yes," the dude said. "Like, it's evening time. Just before night. Folks are sitting and I'm still far off, but I can hear that first strum of a guitar. The first voice welcoming the night, just as wispy on the air as a firefly. Or it's like a scent." Lewis smiled. "A scent I have to follow because it's

246

got me like a mystery I have to solve. That voice makes a quiver down in my gut and I follow. And when I can hear it plain, I know it's a find. And when I get there, that voice pulls me in to where these folks have dug a hold in the dirt of some hill."

"That's the way it was when you hear my mother the first time?"

"Even better," Lewis said. "Your mother is about the best there is. What we like to call a natural." He stopped on the path. He didn't look at M.C., but down in front of him. "M.C., I can't sell your mother's voice. I never sell nothing much."

Everything seemed to sink and perish inside of M.C. "Then why are you here?" he managed to say. He sat down on the path and pulled weeds up by the root. "You come so far and you won't even try," he muttered. Tears stung his eyes but he wouldn't cry.

"I come so far," Lewis said gently, "because I suspected that voice had to be out here." He bent down on one knee next to M.C. "No. I knew it was here, like these hills were here unspoiled and beautiful in my father's time. See, so I come back to save her voice before it goes, the way these hills are going. But M.C., I never meant to hurt you or anyone, that's the God's truth. And I guess I have."

"I thought sure she'd go on the stage," M.C. said, almost in a whisper.

Lewis shook his head. "Son, she wouldn't fit on a stage."

"How do you mean, she wouldn't fit?"

"Well, they'd change her, is what I mean," the dude said.

"They'd tell her she had to move a little, she had to smile. And they'd show her how to move and how to smile. They'd teach her how to *project* herself and how to look *chick*.

"No," the dude said, "it'd never be the voice, the woman, singing like this evening, walking home from far."

"Coming here, getting folks all excited," M.C. mumbled. The tears stung him again. He wiped them away.

"And I'm sorry, too," the dude said. "A boy with imagination like you—I knew what you were thinking. It was natural for you to think strong. But M.C., I just meant to tape the voice, is all, to have a record, I don't really know why. Just that I must, like my father before me."

"Now we'll never get out from under the spoil."

"You have to," Lewis told him. "M.C., you must impress on your father how dangerous it is hanging up there. Stubbornness. Ignorance," he added. "Like seeds sprouting from generation to generation."

"Who are you saying is ignorant?" M.C. got to his feet and backed off. Pride made him stand straight and still.

"Son . . ."

"Daddy knows things you never heard of!"

"Son, I know that."

"He's been here for . . . for . . . generations! And you been here but two days."

"I'm real sorry for all the trouble—"

M.C. turned his back on the dude. "We won't be looking for you to come back. Ever," he said.

"Son, won't you wait just a minute, talk awhile—"

M.C. climbed up the mountain. His stomach felt heavy and cold, as if full of clinkers from the cook-stove. He didn't

248

look back once but he held himself tall and forced the dude out of his mind. It took him forever to get back up to the outcropping. His mind was moving swiftly while his feet dragged.

No way at all. Except maybe one. Just for me.

Go where she lives. Maybe get a job like she has. Nine hundred dollars! How would I live? Well, you quit school and work all the time. Talk to her when she comes.

Lurhetta.

He felt a little better now.

I'll send for them. But will there be time? Don't think about it. Don't think.

His whole family was sitting on the porch as he came onto the ledge. M.C. walked near and he could see that Banina looked tired but happy.

"You get back what you give," Jones was telling her, teasing. And taking the tape cassette she still had in her hand, he held it up in front of him.

Banina laughed. "Think of it. There I am, just wound up around and around."

"I want to see," Macie said.

Jones handed her the tape. "Be careful, you. You don't want to spill your mama out."

"I won't spill her," Macie said. "See if I can look at her voice."

"You can't see a voice," Harper said.

"Sure you can," M.C. said, standing there. "See her voice coming down the hill every evening." Talking seemed to ease the heavy cold inside him.

"You seeing Mama," Harper told him.

"That's it," M.C. said. "Mama a singing electric tape."

Banina laughed like a girl.

M.C. thought again of Lurhetta. Where was she, anyway?

Twilight, with sky streaked where the sun had disappeared. Soon would be dusk.

Better hurry, if she wants to get here before dark.

Macie picked at the cassette, trying to catch hold of the shiny tape inside. She held it close to her eyes. "M.C., when will Mr. Lewis make the records?"

"Soon time," M.C. said easily. "He'll be back to get Mama, too."

"Honest?" Harper asked. "He say that?"

"Sure," M.C. said. "Be back before you know it." He lied without any trouble, without a qualm.

"Well, somehow, I don't think so," Jones said. "No sir, I don't think we'll see the likes of him again."

They were all quiet then. Macie tired of fooling with the tape and let it slip out of her hands. It soon lay forgotten beside her on the step.

Jones wasn't ignorant. He was smart all the time.

Glad the dude is gone, M.C. thought. Glad he couldn't catch Mama's real-life voice, too.

"Banina, honey," M.C. said lightly.

The children giggled.

"Calling me by my name!" Banina said, not with anger.

"Sing out that ring-song you were singing home," M.C. said.

She protested.

"Come on, Mama." Lennie, who never said much, slow with words.

Banina smiled at him. "Since it's you asking," she said.

"You have the time," Jones told her. "I'll go in and get the plates ready."

"Everybody make a circle," Banina said.

Jones went inside. She and the children sat in a ring on the porch.

"You, too, M.C."

"No, not me."

"I'm not here to show for you," she said. "Come on, M.C."

But M.C. wouldn't. He stayed standing, with one foot on the step listening to them start out. He felt the song deeply and it cleansed the coldness within him.

He watched for movement on the hills, for a sign, but there was none. Flies raced around him in low circles. There were clouds in the dusk over Grey Mountain, where a moment before there had been none.

Hurry, or she'll get wet.

"*Howdy-howdy, child,*" Banina sang, "*Ring-a-ling, ring-a-ling.*"

"*Howdy-howdy, ma'am, Ring-a-ling, ring-a-ling,*" the children answered.

> "*An' how they call you, child?*
> *Ring-a-ling, ring-a-ling.*"

> "*They call me Macie, ma'am.*
> *Macie Pearlie, ma'am,*
> *Ring-a-ling, a-ling-a-ling.*"

251

> *"Then, howdy Macie-child,*
> *Macie Pearlie-child,*
> *Ring-a-ling, ring-a-ling."*

Banina called to the next child. He was Lennie. They all sat clapping in time with the words which were half-sung faster and faster:

> *"Howdy-howdy, child?*
> [Plaintive and from a long distance away]
> *Ring-a-ling, ring-a-ling."*

> *"Howdy-howdy, ma'am*
> [Again as from a great distance],
> *Ring-a-ling, ring-a-ling."*

> *"An' how they call you, child?*
> *Ring-a-ling, ring-a-ling."*

> *"They call me Lennie, ma'am,*
> *Lennie Poolie, ma'am,*
> *Ring-a-ling, a-ling-a-ling."*

They laughed loudly at "Poolie."

> *"An' then, howdy Lennie-child,*
> *Lennie Poolie-child . . ."*

Banina giggled so, she never did get the "ring-a-lings" in rhythm. But they continued the song on through Harper's name (Harper Higgins, since he had no middle name) and through the ages of all the children:

> *"How much time you been here, child?*
> *Ring-a-ling, ring-a-ling."*

> *"I got eight, I got eight years here!"*

> *"Oh, my-my, child!*
> *Ring-a-ling, ring-a-ling."*

252

"I got nine, I got nine years here!"

"Oh, mercy-my, child!
  Ring-a-ling, ring-a-ling."

"I got ten, I say ten, I got ten years here!"

"Well, my-my, my-my, oh, child!
  Ring-a-ling, a-ling-a-ling-ah!"

Next, they did M.C.'s name with the children singing M.C.'s part. By the time they came to "Mayo Cornelius," they were going so fast, they got his name all mixed up

"Mercy!" Banina said.

"Mercy-mercy, ma'am," the children sang out. Banina fell back and they all broke down, laughing.

"You just as simple," M.C. told them. But the song had moved him. It had flowed in and out of him again, taking with it some amount of his sorrow.

Jones came outside. "Time to eat," he told them.

"I'm sure glad," Banina said. "I was getting just as silly."

"I think I'll go down and meet Lurhetta," M.C. said. He avoided looking at them.

"Lurhetta—who?" Banina said.

"That's the girl at the lake this morning," M.C. said. "Seems like days ago."

"Lurhetta Outlaw is her name," Jones said.

"Outlaw!"

"We gave her something to eat. Half-starved," Jones said.

"I'll go down and lead her up here," M.C. said. Thunder was sounding, distant, but quite clear.

"No such thing. It's suppertime," Banina told him.

"Supposing she gets lost?" M.C. said.

"Supposing she doesn't. You come on to supper," Banina said.

She went inside, following Jones, with the children behind her. Jones told her things, hurrying-quiet, so M.C. wouldn't hear. Macie, who never learned how to whisper, told about the water tunnel and how Lurhetta couldn't swim.

Macie would have to open her mouth. I don't care. Lurhetta gets here, Mama will see for herself.

He gave one last look to the hills. Night had come swiftly.

Save her some rabbit for when she gets here.

But Lurhetta Outlaw never came in time for supper.

Inside, they all sat down at the table. They all exclaimed over M.C.'s stew, at the tender meat, with steam rising from it. Rabbit had a salty, wild taste all its own. They ate it with relish and mostly in silence.

It was M.C. who first felt the house go utterly still. He had just about finished a second helping of everything when he stopped chewing and stared up at the ceiling. Flies covered the ceiling, making a spotted carpet. At once Banina and Jones caught on to his mood. M.C. gazed at the window. It was pitchblack outside.

They were suspended and made fearful on the side of the mountain.

Which way to run, if it's danger? M.C. wondered. Up or down, or around the side?

A sound hit, like a ton of pebbles thrown at the house. The spoil!

No.

The rain.

M.C. stared at the window full of dark. The window stayed dry. Rain came straight down. Next the wind came, hitting the other side of the house in one swoop. The house seemed to shudder, then braced against the wind.

"Good," M.C. said. They all ate again, for wind had come and would take the storm on before it could soak deeply into Sarah's.

But what if rain came without wind to pull it away? How long can Sarah's stand one hard rain after another?

You mean the spoil heap. Yes.

Do like Jones. Don't think on it. Eat the rabbit. Drink the ade.

They finished with supper. Lurhetta hadn't made it. M.C. hurried outside. Dark misty night and light rain. The air had freshened, but it was still warm. He couldn't see the hills, but there were lights from Harenton. More lights along the river. Nowhere was there one single beam of light cutting through the dark.

Stay in her tent. I would, if I was out there.

Inside again, M.C. couldn't avoid Jones in the parlor.

"Are you worried about that girl?" Jones asked him.

"She said she'd be back," M.C. said.

"She can probably take care of herself better than you could in her predicament."

"But she don't know a thing about storms out here," M.C. said.

"But she has only herself to think on," Jones said. "That makes it easier. And if she can't learn from near drowning this morning and near soaking tonight—"

M.C. walked quickly through the house, passing through the kitchen, where Banina and the children paused to see him go. He didn't look at them.

"I'll be in my room. Macie, you call me when Lurhetta comes."

In the cave, he fell on the bed. Without a light, he just lay there on his stomach with his hands covering his head. He shook with minute tremors—anger at Jones, at the dude and at Lurhetta for not coming on time. It came to him that he still had on his clothes of the morning with swimming trunks underneath.

If she's not here by midnight, I'll change and go down there to see if she's all right.

Relaxed now and with a plan, he let his arms fall to his sides. He waited out the hours, imagining he ran the path to the lake. Once he ran too fast. He tripped and fell, knocking himself out. When he came to, Lurhetta Outlaw was there to help him.

He ran the path with a large dog at his side. The dog was the wrong kind, but his name was Great Anger and he carried a rabbit in his mouth. M.C. had a new gun and had shot the rabbit through the heart. Lurhetta was waiting for them by the lake with a good fire going.

Admit it.

I like you, girl.

Much later Banina came, standing in his doorway.

"M.C.," she called softly. He pretended sleep and finally she went away.

Close out the house again. Listening to Sarah's, he would know if Lurhetta came up on the porch. He wasn't sleepy,

256

but he felt tired. Listening to the soft rain, he wouldn't mind running through it. For a long while he thought he was awake and waiting.

The house went dark. Banina and Jones went to sleep. The children had gone off long before. M.C. dreamed he was thinking and waiting.

14

"PUT on these clean things I pressed for you," Banina said. "You've been in those clothes forever."

"I have to hurry," M.C. told her, but he made no move to leave. He had rushed out of bed as if he had been running in his dreams.

"You do as I tell you or you stay in this house," Banina said.

M.C. had awakened to find it was hours past midnight. Shocked, with his hands trembling, he had straightened the clothes he had slept in and rushed out to the privie on that side of Sarah's away from the path. Later he had run back through the parlor and into the kitchen, where he found Banina. Wet weeds had soaked his pant legs and now they felt uncomfortably cold around his bare ankles.

"You ought to see it outside," he said. "It looks like on the moon."

"You'll be on the moon, if you don't keep your voice down," Banina said.

Hoping to please her, he went to the sink and let warm water flow over his head and neck. Banina was fussing-tired, leaning over the ironing board.

"Mama, come take just one look outside."

"M.C., you know I have to hurry." She handed him a towel.

"Just one look and then I'll leave you alone."

"Well, what is it?" She sighed and set the iron on end.

He led her out onto the porch. They looked over Sarah's and beyond.

"Now have you ever seen anything like it?" he asked.

"I don't know. I don't think so," she said.

The mountain was closed in by the thickest fog M.C. had ever seen. It made separate, pale corridors through the trees. The trees were black against it, like huge cut-out shapes pasted on white paper.

"I bet there hasn't been fog like this since the time Sarah ran," he said. "Just like this, and the reason she didn't see this mountain for two days."

"Maybe so," Banina said. "I know I've never seen it like this. Hope it clears before I have to leave."

M.C. stepped off the porch. Looking up, he couldn't see the top of the mountain. Couldn't see the spoil. Just swirls of whiteness, thick and unnatural.

He backed away.

"M.C."

"I have to go," he said.

"You change your clothes. Looking like a ragamuffin!"

"I don't have the time," he said. He inched away, until fog touched him and curled over his arms in cotton strands.

"You take the time. Eat something hot before you leave."

"Now why did I have to wake up now?" M.C. spoke to the fog. "Should have waited until Banina-honey had gone. Then I could do what I please."

"That's the worry with you. You're used to doing too much of what you please."

"Have I ever done wrong?"

"Come back here."

"Have I ever, ever done wrong?" His voice, coming out of fog where his shape was dark and ghosty.

"That's not the trouble," Banina said. She leaned out from the porch, whispering, so as not to wake the others.

"Don't I always keep an eye on the kids? Don't I clean up the kitchen and watch the house?" He should have been gone by now. He knew he should.

"The worry is, you just go through the motions," Banina said. "You had no business taking *anyone* through that water tunnel."

"That was nothing," he said under his breath. "Should of seen where we went yesterday afternoon." He glanced all around. Were the witchies waiting to make him vanish before Banina's eyes? Like the mountain had vanished in front of Sarah.

"Taking a girl through and she can't even swim," Banina went on. "I just lay awake all night thinking about what could have happened to you both. I kept seeing it over and over. You keep on and you're in for real unhappiness."

"It's just pretend unhappiness I've been having lately," he whispered.

At the edge of the yard, the fog covered him completely. He made his way noiselessly to his right, until he knew he was near the porch again. He leaped out and scared Banina to death.

"M.C.! Oh!"

He laughed softly. "I'm going down there and help her cook her breakfast," M.C. said.

"You stay out of the tunnel."

"You think I'm going to swim in this fog?"

"No telling what you might do."

"Now she's going to worry some more," M.C. said, as if Banina wasn't there. "I just thought I'd maybe bare-hand fish and help her out."

"Help her all you want," Banina said, "but don't count on her."

"Mama, I'm going." With a gentle smile at her, he vanished again in the fog. His disembodied voice came, like a mystery: "I'll see you by darkness, Banina-honey."

"Don't get your heart set. M.C.?"

He was gone.

I'm running.

Only he couldn't run because of the fog. He had to pick his way down the mountainside. If it had been night, he wouldn't have had any trouble. He knew night paths through the hills as well as he knew them by light. But M.C. was unaccustomed to fog. And when he was through the gully and on the hill path, he had to worry about direction. He lost his bearings when he went faster than a walk. So he held his hands out in front of him, touching branches, bushes. One moment he would be terrified his hands might touch a face; the next, he was certain Great Anger of his imagination followed him.

Wish I did have a dog. Or a gun. *Something* out here with me.

Ben? No. Catch him later on Sarah's High. How does he know when I'm coming?

All M.C. had was his keen senses and his knowledge of the paths. Points of undergrowth were visible and they seemed to crowd him. His feet wouldn't move smoothly.

Wish I had on my tennis shoes.

His pants were muddy and his shirt was wet from hitting branches. The fog wasn't going to clear and no sun would come to dry up the night rains. But the thickness of mist would get thinner and thinner, until it had the look of metal with no shine.

My pole.

He'd forgot even to glance at it.

By the time he reached the pass of Hall Mountain, his pants were muddy to the knee. He wondered at the quiet, and whether his being there somehow changed the natural and huge stillness.

M.C. stopped. Bending down, he kneeled on the ground. Feeling the ancient height of mountains looming over him, he ran his hands down among weeds to the dark earth. No reason for him to pause there. And yet doing so gave him an odd inkling of something to come.

What is it?

Cool on the surface, the earth was still warm underneath where he dug with his hands. But coolness was on its way down into the earth. By feeling the ground, he had gauged the time for the change of seasons.

Soon time for school. Maybe not for me.

He got to his feet. He knew he had reached the end of the pass when, abruptly, the ground seemed to rise. The fog irritated him, taking from him all angles of depth and height.

How will she find her way to town? Thinking of his mother.

How did she find her way this far north? Thinking of Sarah.

She'd never find her way out of this without me. Lurhetta. What if she's . . . .

He dragged his feet. Seeing the base of the ridge, he had an urge to turn and head home. But the fog had risen enough for him to see his way onward.

It billowed out at the top of the ridge like a pillow against a headboard.

Wish I'd stayed asleep.

But he went on, climbing the ridge where he could see nothing until he was over the crest. Tricky stones clattered; then he was below the fog. The lake was milk-white with a white fog blanket hanging about twenty feet above it. Fog rolled in the trees like smoke.

M.C. smoothed his hands over his arms. From head to foot, he was soaking wet. His hair was white from beads of moisture clinging to it.

Down the shore, he could see the pile of brush she had

arranged to hide her tent on its far side. He walked nearer through the rolling silence, around the pile. There, he suddenly bent over. He stooped, sliding his hands on the stones, as if entering through the tent opening. Pebbles, hard and damp under his knees. He searched the ground.

Not a word.

His insides churned. There was no tent.

Not a good-by.

Lurhetta Outlaw had disappeared without a trace.

She didn't have to go like that.

Almost without a trace. For in the center of that space where the tent should have been was a black handle, flush with the ground. M.C. stared at it. He grabbed it, but it was attached to something. He had to twist and pull it out.

Her knife came out clean. Smooth and sharp, as always, it was a knife fit for a hunter.

For me. Or did she forget it?

Not stuck in the ground like that, if she forgot it. She left it.

He held the knife on the flat of his palms with the hilt and tip in the crook of his thumbs. Carrying it that way, he walked stiffly back towards the ridge. He should have rested. His legs felt weak and rubbery.

All the time M.C. carried the knife, he had visions about it. The way he would hunt with it. How he could easily thrust it into his own heart. He walked the whole way as if he carried something heavy and dead.

Finally at the gully, he skirted the mountain. At the plateau, he stopped still, hearing his brothers and sister come down, excited in the lifting fog, in a hurry to get to the lake to see M.C. and Lurhetta. Then he went on up to Sarah's high, where he walked heavily and turkey-gobbled to the knife.

Now he asked the knife, "Why did she do it?"

And the knife said in the voice of Lurhetta: "Follow me."

But which way? How do I know how to get to you?

The knife would say no more.

Near the ravine but still on the path, he picked out Ben among trees a foot away. Ben glided up to him without a sound. M.C. held the knife up for him to see. He peered around Ben for Lurhetta, but there was no one.

Ben shook his head.

M.C. nodded. Once again he carried the knife as if it were dead. He turned to go.

"M.C., you have a skunk caught this time. Can't you smell it on me?" Ben said.

Instantly waves of skunk odor swirled in the air, gagging M.C.

"I had to knock that trap into the ravine and into the stream."

M.C. nodded and walked away.

"M.C."

He headed home. Soon he plunged through the gully and strained up Sarah's side, carrying the knife out in front of him.

All was quiet on the outcropping when he got there. Banina was gone. Jones must have gone somewhere, for the front door of the house was locked. With the children gone, he knew the back door would be shut tight. Staring at the house, he hated Lurhetta. The clapboards of his home were soiled and discolored from mountain dirt and wind. The porch was cracked everywhere, with the steps breaking away into chunks. Streaked with soot, the roof sagged.

Burn it down. Nothing but an outlaw shack.

Through his blurring anger, he glimpsed his pole in the listless light. Its metal sheen was smooth and sleek and he felt no hate for it as he did for the shack and the girl.

Haven't seen you in forever.

He headed for the pole with a feel for it coming back to him.

Let's go for a ride.

Gingerly, he climbed over car parts with the knife between his teeth. He remembered how to grasp the pole hand over hand and how to twist his legs. He climbed with his legs tight around and muscles pushing. Up and up and faster he went, as the knowledge of how to climb smooth metal seeped back into his mind.

The marker of the dead. But I'm alive.

M.C. had to grasp the bicycle seat and pull up on it with hands and arms working, in order to get his feet on the pedals. He had to almost get his stomach on the seat. Here, he could fall. He could bust open, hitting the ground. But his balance was fine and he didn't fall. He pulled himself up and sat, taking the knife in one hand.

Why did you leave the knife?

Well, out of kindness. I had to leave.

Didn't you like me?

M.C. pressed the knife a moment against his chest, just to get the feel of it.

Never to show her how to swim or to know the hills.

The hurt of her going pressed in on him, like the thinning fog. High up in the air, he swung his pole in its sweeping arc. He thrust the knife at forming clouds. The fog was lifting far off on the Ohio. So M.C. stabbed the river and cut it in two. He sliced off chimneys of the steel mill, barely visible. And he cried out once as his pole swayed and swooped, chopping up the mist-shrouded town of Harenton.

Never to show me which road to take—why did you leave the knife?

Because I don't live on a mountain.

Thank you for giving it to me.

He could see hills before him fading and returning, not solid or steady at all.

He gouged a hole in the side of one, but he had no anger strong enough for murdering hills. He could feel their rhythm like the pulse beat of his own blood rushing. If they faded never to return, would his pulse stop its beat as well?

You need it living on the mountain.

Thank you for it. But not for leaving.

His pole shuddered along its length and was still. He clamped the knife between his teeth again and slid down the pole. Stumbling over car parts, M.C. scraped his leg on a jagged piece of metal. He never felt the pain or the blood flowing. But at that very instant, he saw the single sunflower his mother loved. Next to the pump, its head drooped. Without sun, it looked about to die.

Trancelike, he stumbled over to Sarah's Mountain where it rose behind the house, as if he meant to walk right through it. But he stopped and kneeled suddenly, with both hands clamped tightly around the knife handle, plunging the blade into the soil. Shaking, raging with ever more forceful jabs, he stabbed the earth.

Clumps of rock and earth loosened and fell around M.C.'s knees. They felt cool, smelled faintly rancid. He stared at the clumps, the knife poised in front of him. For a long moment, he waited; a perfect idea formed in his mind.

He jabbed again. Earth had been softened by rain for an inch or more. Twisting the knife handle, he was able to get the dirt and rock up in bigger lumps. Soon he had a small pile, and he leaned back a moment to look at his work. Then gazing far up Sarah's, he saw the dark underside of the spoil heap where it spilled over the highway cut.

The car wrecks around his pole. He went over there, the knife handle held between his teeth, and pulled at a fender. It scraped with an ugly sound, but it came loose.

Lurhetta, thanks.

What for? I only left you the knife. I like to travel, but I'm not a camper. And it's better not to carry a knife, when traveling.

"What I Did This Summer," by Lurhetta Outlaw.

Sounds like the kind of thing they made me write when I was a kid. They'll want a better heading at the top.

How's this? "Of hills and mountains and tunnels," by Lurhetta Outlaw.

They make you capitalize the first word and every noun after it. But it's still too long.

Okay. I have it now. "M.C. Higgins, the Great," by Lurhetta Outlaw.

268

You dig a trench for the fender and then you pile the dirt and rock around.

I said, "M.C. Higgins, the Great."

I heard you, too. I like that one the best.

Or you lean the fender against the pile and make another pile of dirt on behind it. Pack the dirt in tight and when the fender is standing straight, you add more dirt until it's covered. That will take awhile.

Do you think you will ever come back?

Silence in his mind. He was busy piling dirt around the fender and packing it in tight when Macie Pearl came up behind him. Panting hard, she stood there a moment, catching her breath.

Finally she said, "M.C., what you doing? Daddy's gone for lawn work."

"He hates lawn work," M.C. said.

"He went anyhow," Macie said. "M.C., look at your leg. It's all bloody."

M.C. looked at his leg above the ankle, surprised to see he had scraped it. He pressed some dirt into the torn flesh.

"What are you doing, M.C.?" Macie asked.

"Making a wall," he told her.

"What kind of a wall?"

"You'll see when I'm finished."

Harper and Lennie Pool came up. With Macie, they sat near to where M.C. struggled with the knife.

"Making a wall," Macie explained to them.

They didn't ask her what kind of wall, or even why a wall. For they had been to the lake, all three of them, where they discovered that the tent and the girl were gone. Now they watched M.C. closely. They wondered, but they said not a word.

Soon the boys were leaning over and playing with the dirt M.C. had loosened from the mountain. When he didn't object, they scooted closer and began packing more dirt on the mound around the fender.

Macie Pearl crawled over to help with the wall. She watched M.C.'s arm stab in and out of the dirt. Studying his hand and the side of his face.

"Where'd you get that knife?" she asked.

It took M.C. a moment to answer, so hard was he concentrating. But after a time he leaned back on his knees and wiped perspiration from his face. "She left it for me, in the sand," he said.

"Lurhetta Outlaw?"

"Well, who else?" M.C. said.

"Is she gone away?"

"Yes."

"Will she ever come back, you think?"

"I think she's gone and never will come back," M.C. said.

"Oh."

This summer, I travel in my car to mountains. I met a lot of strange people with different ways from us. They had a spider web you could sit on. I learned how to go through a water tunnel and how to trap a rabbit and kill it. I met M.C., the Great, with a tall pole.

The children had another fender, a motor and part of a crankshaft dragged over to the growing mound by the time Jones came up the side of Sarah's about noon. He spied them working at something as the mill whistle blew for lunch. The whistle was a dull scream on the heavy air. The children and M.C. hardly noticed it; they didn't hear Jones coming at all.

Jones came closer to them to watch. He looked from the mound of dirt to M.C.'s stabbing arm. He stared hard at the knife every time M.C. raised up his arm. He glanced around looking for Lurhetta; and then he looked from the metal pieces at the mound to the car parts around the pole. When it came to him what M.C. was trying to do, he gazed up at the top of Sarah's. He could see the dark and giant heap rising out of mist like a festering boil. He looked down at the bent, straining backs of the children, astonishment creeping into his eyes. He shook his head at them, but he continued to stand there, silently watching M.C.'s arm and the bit of dirt and rock loosened with each downward stab.

Jones stood there a long while before he turned and went to the front porch. He kneeled at the side of the porch and crawled halfway under on his belly. His legs stretched and strained; and when he came out again, he was dragging a piece of shovel. It was rusted, old, with only a stump of a wood handle. Jones got up and turned the shovel over and back, poking it into the ground. He lifted it up to examine it, where rust fell away in flakes. Finally he carried it over to M.C. and leaned it on the mound where M.C. was working.

M.C. didn't notice the shovel at first. He saw Jones, and his temper flared suddenly, causing his eyes to go dark and his face to tighten. He then saw the shovel, but he wouldn't give up his knife for it. Jones took up the shovel, holding its broken shaft between his hands and pushing his foot down on one side of the broad blade.

"You can bring up more dirt in one time," he said. He forced down on the shaft and the blade came up full of rocky earth.

Jones dug until he had a good pile. He stopped, but still M.C. would not have the shovel. Jones walked away to the side of Sarah's where he found some broken branches and some brush, and brought all of it over to M.C.

"You can put anything in a wall—trees, anything. You can make it thick and more hard. At the last," he told M.C., "you can make it higher, wider. It will never crumble and fall."

"I make it the way I want," M.C. said. "It's *my* idea."

"Use the shovel," Jones told him.

"I use what I want!" M.C. stood, clutching the knife. "Telling me what to do all the time; what to think—and next summer, the kids watch themselves . . . because I'll be working. And if Mr. Killburn can't pay me, I'll take his vegetables for pay."

"Killburn!" Jones said. "You sound like a fool."

"Who's the fool?" M.C. said, his voice quiet but tense. "I could've been working for them all this time."

"I wouldn't take a milkweed from those kind," Jones said.

"Then you're the fool."

"Watch what you say to me," Jones said. "That girl went off and left, is that it?"

"She left, but that's not it."

"Well then, what is it?" Jones asked.

272

M.C. heaved and sighed. He looked up at the gray sky. "I finally got something through my head," he said.

"Something what?" Jones said.

Not just living on the mountain. But me, living on the mountain.

Living . . . anywhere. You, living.

"I play with anybody I want," M.C. said. "This is my home. I live here, too." Backing away from Jones toward the front of the house: "Ben? Hey you, Ben?"

He kept his eyes on Jones, who came slowly toward him. At the edge of Sarah's, still watching his father, he gave off a minor cadence yodel. He broke it off at its height of sound and turned it into an ear-splitting turkey gobble. The hills took up the noise, flattening it and rolling it over the land in gobbling echoes.

M.C. disappeared in the undergrowth of briers, screaming Ben's name at the top of his lungs. A minute after he had gone, he returned, jumping out at them so suddenly, that Jones staggered back. M.C. didn't stop, but hurried to the wall he was building. He was on his knees again when Ben appeared in the exact spot where M.C. had stood calling him.

"Come on here, Ben," M.C. said, not turning around, nor changing the rhythm of his arm movement. "See, I'm building a wall."

Ben walked all the way around the far side of M.C.'s pole, but no farther. He never took his eyes off Jones. "What kind of wall?" he said faintly.

"Well," M.C. said. "Since I have to live here, I want something big between me and that spoil."

"Have to be awful big," Ben said.

"I'm smelling me a smell," Jones said, staring at Ben.

"Yessir," Ben said softly. "M.C. caught him a skunk and I had to get it out of there. I went home and washed and changed." Gray eyes on Jones. Frightened, innocent.

M.C. watched, his hand tight on the knife. If Ben had to outrun Jones, M.C. knew he would throw the knife to wound. Ever so carefully, he shifted the knife and held the blade point between thumb and finger.

But he's your father.

Not if he runs off Ben.

Absently, Jones scratched at the mosquito bite on his arm. It had become infected and swollen. He squinted at Ben and a ripple of movement seemed to pass over him from head to foot. A shudder of revulsion that he could no more help than he could help picking at the mosquito bite. A moment hung over all of them in silence as Jones, in one great effort, seemed to pull himself together. He cupped his hand over the mosquito bite—it must have been hot with fever. He did not scratch it again.

"Should of let M.C. take care of it. Skunk is worse than anything to handle," Jones said evenly.

"Yessir," Ben said. "I take care of the traps for M.C. when he's busy."

"For M.C.—and you didn't mind the smell a-tall," Jones spoke solemnly.

"No sir, I didn't mind it."

Jones ran his hand over his face once. He smoothed the toe of his shoe over the bare earth, wiping the packed dust clean. Without another word, he went inside the house.

M.C. grinned at Ben. Ben grinned back.

"Want to help?" M.C. said. Ben squatted next to him.

"You're going to break that knife—she give it to you?"

"Left it for me before she went, I guess," M.C. said.

They studied the knife. The edge was not so sharp now.

"I'm going to dull it good," M.C. said.

"We can fix it," Ben told him. "Daddy has a grinding wheel at home, but better not use it anymore."

M.C. stood. His back was stiff, but he had no thought of quitting. He held the knife close to his eyes for a moment. Then he wiped it clean, leaving dirt streaks across the front of his shirt.

"She didn't say good-by to me either," Ben said.

The children were watching him. They had shied away in a close bunch as soon as he had come near.

"Do I smell real bad?" Ben asked M.C., looking over at the children.

"Not near as bad as this morning," M.C. said. "Anyway, skunk is most like anything else in the woods. I never minded it."

"Me neither," Ben said. They grinned again.

M.C. took his shirttail and tenderly wrapped the knife. Carefully, he twisted it up until it stayed.

Jones came out the back door, calling the children for lunch. They were glad to go. Each walked away, looking back at Ben and M.C. as they went.

"I'll eat later," M.C. called to Jones. Jones said nothing, but held the door for the children.

"They don't much like having me around," Ben said.

"They'll get use to you. Now," M.C. said. He looked at

the shovel and bent down to touch the blade. He tested out the shovel, pushing it down into the earth with his foot the way Jones had. He brought up a good-sized pile of stone and soil and heaped it on the mound. Ben moved quickly to shape it.

"Might as well put in the branches and stuff Daddy brought," M.C. said. Heaving the shovel again, he dug and Ben molded and they built.

The lonesome talking inside M.C. quieted down. He no longer had to listen to it every minute, as the memory of Lurhetta's voice became less clear. Her knife was not forgotten. Safe next to his skin, it still had an edge that could cut deep; but it was not as keen as it once had been.

The children soon joined M.C. and Ben again. Never ones to shy away for long, they came closer and closer. Soon Ben's red hair and his pale, freckled skin seemed not so strange. Even his hands looked almost ordinary. They thought to help by dragging car parts from the wrecks around the pole. And where they struggled, Jones came later to stand a moment before going off on his search for work.

Jones shifted his weight from one foot to the other, as though he wished to be on his way, but he couldn't yet leave for some reason. That look of closed stubbornness seemed to melt from his face as he glanced over where M.C.'s back was bent to his task. For an instant his eyes were full of pride. Then he stood utterly still; that mask of closed aloneness fell into place again.

Jones went over and crawled under the porch. The children stopped their work to stare.

"Daddy, what are you doing?" Macie asked.

No reply. The question and the silence that followed caused M.C. to turn. He paused to watch. He could see only Jones's ankles. After some time Jones slid out again, dragging something. His hair was full of dust. On his knees, he brushed dust from his trousers and from his face. On his feet again, he strained under the weight of the thing he carried, lurching over to M.C. And there he lay it on the mound of dirt.

"Just one," Jones said, breathing hard. "That's all I can give you today." He turned and walked through the children, around the pole and on down the side of Sarah's.

The children came near. No one spoke as M.C. ran his hand over the stone slab. It had markings on it.

"A gravestone?" Ben asked.

"Yes. He didn't have to do that," M.C. said, in the faintest voice, "but I'm glad he did."

"Let me see it," Harper said.

"See it," M.C. said. "It's Great-grandmother Sarah's." The markings were worn but the name was still readable.

"Why did your father bring it?" Ben wanted to know.

"Because," M.C. said. He thought a long moment, smoothing his hand over the stone. Finally he smiled. "To make the wall strong."

They all went back to work when M.C. started digging a place for the stone. He made a rectangle large enough and Ben fitted the stone in. M.C. shoveled dirt over it and all of them helped Ben pack it in.

Sarah, good-by.

All of this time, the day stayed gray. Sarah's was gray.

But as the afternoon wore on, the mist rose into gathering clouds from mountain to river. They hung low, crowding above the high steel of M.C.'s pole.

M.C. never looked up, but he sensed the clouds massing. He knew his work was urgent.

Lurhetta, good-by.

Good-by, M.C., the Great.

There began to take shape a long, firm kind of mound. The children fed it. M.C. shoveled and Ben packed it. In the immense quiet of Sarah's Mountain late in the day, they formed a wall. And it was rising.